A TAPPING ON THE DOOR

The light tap on her bedroom door did not surprise Sophrina. She had half expected it ever since she had said her goodnights in the drawing room downstairs. A tremor shook her. She clutched her robe closer about her. In the next breath she cast hesitation aside and in a clear but low voice said, "Come in."

As she knew it would be, it was Penhurst. But her eyes widened at his garb. He had changed from evening clothes into a robe of dark claret brocade.

Sophrina had had only one man in her bedroom before —her faithless husband. And that memory flooded through her as she wondered: *Had she opened the door to disaster again?*

MELINDA McRAE holds a master's degree in European history and takes great delight in researching obscure details of the Regency period. She lives in Seattle, Washington, with her husband and daughter.

AN UNLIKELY ATTRACTION

Melinda McRae

A SIGNET BOOK

SIGNET
Published by the Penguin Group
Penguin Books USA Inc., 375 Hudson Street,
New York, New York, 10014, U.S.A.
Penguin Books Ltd, 27 Wrights Lane, London W8 5TZ, England
Penguin Books Australia Ltd, Ringwood, Victoria, Australia
Penguin Books Canada Ltd, 10 Alcorn Avenue, Toronto, Ontario, Canada M4V 3B2
Penguin Books (N.Z.) Ltd, 182-190 Wairau Road,
Auckland 10, New Zealand

Penguin Books Ltd, Registered Offices:
Harmondsworth, Middlesex, England

First published by Signet, an imprint of New American Library,
a division of Penguin Books USA Inc.

First Printing, September, 1991

10 9 8 7 6 5 4 3 2 1

 REGISTERED TRADEMARK—MARCA REGISTRADA

PRINTED IN THE UNITED STATES OF AMERICA

PUBLISHER'S NOTE
This is a work of fiction. Names, characters, places, and incidents either are the product of the author's imagination or are used fictitiously, and any resemblance to actual persons, living or dead, events, or locales is entirely coincidental.

BOOKS ARE AVAILABLE AT QUANTITY DISCOUNTS WHEN USED TO PROMOTE PRODUCTS OR SERVICES. FOR INFORMATION PLEASE WRITE TO PREMIUM MARKETING DIVISION, PENGUIN BOOKS USA INC., 375 HUDSON STREET, NEW YORK, NEW YORK 10014.

To Mary Jo:
For her advice, encouragement,
and a certain phone conversation.

And to the real Kate.

Prologue

August 1815

The slender, elegantly tapered fingers clutching the thick, cream-colored paper shook ever so slightly. Sophrina Charlton, Viscountess Teel, could not say whether the flurry of sensations sweeping over her stemmed from relief or despair. What was the proper sentiment to feel when your husband eloped with his lover?

At least William had left a note, sparing her the embarrassment of learning the news from one of the society gossips. Sophrina gave a disdainful shake of her head, tumbling her undressed curls. Nothing delighted those women more than a tale laden with scandal, and this one would certainly be the *on-dit* on the Season. To the best of her knowledge, no other lord had run off with the wife of an earl this summer. The gossips would have a heyday with the news. Her eyes narrowed. Sophrina destested those odious ladies for their delight in surprising their victims with tales embellished to shock and titillate, taking a nasty pleasure in the distress they caused. She could now dismiss them as bearers of old tidings.

Ideally Sophrina could avoid them entirely. It would not take long to pack a few bandboxes, and those would get her comfortably to Charlton. The servants could follow later with the rest of her possessions. It was craven to run, but she would rather have people label her a coward than face the curious glances, whispered remarks, and solicitous concern that would surround her.

Not that the news would come as a shock to many people. William's affair with their country neighbor, the Countess of Penhurst, had been an open secret for months in the fashionable circles of London.

Sophrina pulled her lacy dressing gown closer, as if to ward off an unwelcome draft. How naive she had been at nineteen, to think that the young, handsome, and dashing Viscount Teel would interest himself in an unsophisticated girl fresh from the country. He had swept her off her feet at their first meeting at Almack's, and it was not until a year into their marriage that she realized another woman held his heart.

Taking a sip of her morning chocolate, Sophrina looked dispassionately around her cheerfully appointed boudoir. The bright, floral-print wallpaper mocked her with its gaiety. She had been trying for the effect of a rose garden, painting the woodwork in soft hues of green, while choosing a darker shade for the hangings. Perhaps she had achieved her aim too well, for it was far too easy to imagine herself in the orangery at Charlton when she sat in this room.

It did not take any effort at all to conjure up the memory of that hateful afternoon last October, when she had learned the damning truth. The mingled odors of damp earth and mold, and the steamy heat of the glass-enclosed room flooded into her memory, while the devastating words echoed in her ears . . .

Even now, almost a year later, the nausea still gripped her as it had when she discovered her husband making love to her closest friend. Why, of all places, had they chosen the orangery for their tryst that day? It had been her haven, her peaceful retreat, until the peace had been shattered by the act of betrayal.

William and Lea. How ridiculously oblivious Sophrina had been. Had she been of a suspicious nature, innumerable clues would have pointed her to the distressing evidence. But having been married only a year and a half, infidelity was far from her mind.

Sophrina had actually felt sorry for Lea, left at home while Penhurst traipsed about Europe for the Foreign Office. How Lea and William must have laughed together. Sweet, innocent Sophrina, too naive to realize the woman who shared her tea, conversation, and confidences also shared her husband.

She felt such a dismal failure as a wife. Her first pregnancy had ended in miscarriage, and she knew William's disappointment had driven him into Lea's arms. That, and his young wife's lack of town polish compared to that of the vivacious Lady Penhurst.

Sophrina shook her head to free her mind of the unpleasant memories. She no longer needed to pretend her marriage was anything but the hell it had become. William and Lea were in France now, putting an end once and for all to the lies and hypocrisy. Crumpling her husband's note into a ball, Sophrina tossed it into the wastebasket and rang for her maid. If she was going to leave for Charlton tomorrow, there was much to do.

Taking a last look at the marble-tiled entry hall in the London town house, Sophrina motioned to the footman to put the last box into the carriage. She set her feather-trimmed bonnet firmly atop her head and tied the ribbons in a jaunty bow. Let no one say she left London with her head hanging! Soon she would be at peace at Charlton again. The thought buoyed her as no other had during the two days since William's abrupt departure. She could not put the dusty streets of London behind her fast enough.

As the carriage rattled over the cobbled square, she let herself relax fractionally against the thick, padded cushions. The traveling coach was packed to the sky, for in a flurry of organization, Sophrina and her maid, Jenny, had managed to transform an entire wardrobe into a mountain of luggage.

Fortunately most of the *ton* had fled the city after celebrating the great victory at Waterloo, retreating to their country estates or dashing across the Channel to Paris. Her humiliation would not become common news until she was free of town. It was a relief to know she did not have to face the inquisitive stares of sympathetic murmurings of friends. It would be difficult for her to maintain the proper sense of outrage that people expected from the scorned wife.

She knew returning to Charlton was only a temporary measure. William had made no mention of how long he planned to be away, or if he ever intended to return. For the time being, he and Lea were social outcasts. William, as a man, could return and resume his place in society, but Lea's situation would be more difficult. Much depended upon what her husband would do.

Sophrina had heard the Earl of Penhurst was back in England now that Napoleon was safely tucked away for the second, and hopefully final, time. Penhurst's anticipated arrival had probably precipitated the lovers' flight. Would he divorce Lea? Sophrina found that idea vaguely unsettling. As long as Lea was still married to the earl, Sophrina's position as Viscountess Teel did not pose an obstacle for her husband. But if Lea were free to marry William . . .

The only way he could be rid of Sophrina was to charge her with adultery. Her lips curved into a smile of smug satisfaction; he would never be able to hold *that* against her. She felt a twinge of righteous pleasure in knowing William would never be able to have Lea as his legal wife. She might have William in her bed, but Sophrina would forever retain the title of Viscountess Teel.

Chapter 1

July 1817

Sophrina perched indecorously atop the stile, breathing deeply of sun-warmed air and damp earth. The previous day's rain had washed away the dulling film of dust from the landscape, and all looked clean and new again. How she loved high summer! Carefully gathering the billowing skirts of her outmoded walking gown, she jumped to the ground.

Carrying a sketchbook in the crook of her arm, with a basket of paints and luncheon dangling from her fingers, Sophrina skirted the line of trees that marked the edge of Charlton's lower fields. A deep, woodsy scent wafted from the cool interior of the copse and for a moment she was tempted to investigate its leafy trails. Then discipline reasserted itself. Not today. She must finish her watercolors for the dowager Viscountess Teel's birthday.

Her mother-in-law had stood with her during the worst of the scandal, dampening the wild gossip that swirled in the trail of the most celebrated elopement since that of Lord Uxbridge. But gradually, as the pain and hurt dwindled into first disappointment and then indifference, Sophrina found her need for support lessened. Out of respect for her awkward situation, the neighbors did not press her to adopt an active social life, and Sophrina reveled in self-imposed solitude.

Then the dirty, smudged, and long-delayed letter arrived early last year from Italy, telling of the English lord and lady who had perished in the capsizing of their small boat off some obscure Adriatic village. Sophrina ached for the dowager, who still loved her firstborn, despite his faults. Sophrina herself only felt an enormous relief at the news of William's death. One chapter of her life was ended, and whatever came next would be of her own making.

Her first act had been to remove from Charlton, as much as that decision pained her. William's brother Bertram was the viscount now, and he and his wife, Mary, did not need an extra relative in addition to their growing brood of children. The dowager insisted Sophrina remove to the Dower House, but she politely declined that offer as well. She had enjoyed the freedom of being sole mistress of Charlton and wanted to maintain her independence. She had gone from her father's house to William's in such innocence. She had not perhaps enjoyed the process of growing up, but she was grown-up now. So waving aside their protests, she took a comfortable cottage on a small parcel of land near Charlton. She was close enough to walk to either the main house or the Dower holdings, and usually did so daily; but when her visiting was done, she welcomed the return to her own small abode.

Long shadows had stretched out from the brushy hedge when Sophrina at last returned to the stile, the day's paintings clutched protectively under her arm. Climbing over with an unladylike display of petticoats and ankles, Sophrina bent her steps down the circuitous path that led toward home.

Sophrina caught the brief flash of blue out of the corner of her eye as she walked along the meandering stream that bordered the estate. Turning carefully, she saw no one on the path. But a bush alongside rustled suspiciously and she noted an unnaturally blue background to the leaves.

"I did see you, you know, so you may as well come out and say hello." It must be a child who hid there, for the bush was not very large.

The bush rustled again but no one emerged.

"This is a trifle awkward. I could go on my way and pretend I never did see such a thing as a bush with blue leaves. Yet it is quite an unusual sight, and I would like very much to investigate." Sophrina stepped closer.

"Go away," a small voice whispered.

"This grows more mysterious! A bush that can talk. Perhaps I should run to the village and bring people to see this wondrous sight."

The bush rustled in earnest now.

Sophrina reached into her basket and drew out a napkin-wrapped package. Finding herself a dry clump of grass, she sat on the ground and carefully unwrapped some cheese.

"I did not finish all of my lunch," she began. "So I think I shall eat the rest now. I am frightfully hungry all of a sudden." She sensed the hidden eyes watching her. Sophrina made a grand production of eating the small bit of cheese she broke off, smacking her lips and rolling her eyes in an exaggerated display of enjoyment.

She looked at the bush. "Would you like some? There is quite enough for two."

She sensed the hider hesitating, as if weighing the advantages of seclusion over food. Food won out, for after a loud rustle and crackling, a small child crawled from under the bush.

Sophrina nodded her head in greeting, making no mention of this odd manner of appearing. "Do have a seat and I shall share my cheese with you."

The girl, clad in a dress that had once been the color of the sky but was now encrusted with bits of brown leaves and streaked with dirt, eyed Sophrina with a wary look. Sophrina remained very still, and finally the girl sat down next to her.

Breaking off another piece of cheese, Sophrina placed it in the child's small, grubby hand.

There was a vague familiarity about the girl. The tangled flaxen hair was distinctive, but Sophrina could not say where she might have seen her before. She racked her brain to think what neighboring family had a child of this age—judging her to be about four or five—but no name came to mind. Whoever she was, she was far too young to be wandering about by herself. Underneath all the dirt, the blue dress was of a fine quality; this was no farmer's child.

"My name is Sophrina," she said, companionably, but received no reply. From the way the poor thing gobbled her cheese, she must be terribly hungry.

"It is polite," Sophrina prompted, "to introduce yourself after another person has done so. Particularly when you are eating that person's cheese.

"My name is Kate," the girl admitted with a slight reluctance.

"I am glad to meet you, Kate. It is a lovely day today, isn't it? I have been sketching." Sophrina went through the motions of looking behind Kate and searching the ground next to her. "I thought you might have been out drawing as well, but I do not see your sketch pad. Don't tell me you have lost it?"

Kate giggled. "I don't have a sketch pad, silly. I am too little."

"Oh," said Sophrina, with a disappointed tone. "How old are you, then, if you are too little?"

"Four." Her clear blue eyes clearly implored Sophrina for more cheese.

"Well, Miss Kate of four years, what are you about this afternoon? Were you perhaps driving your pigs to market on this fine sunny day?"

"No." Giggling, Kate vigorously shook her head.

"I know! You are a famous scientist and you were trying to capture the most fabulous butterfly of them all, but your net got tangled in a tree!"

This suggestion also drove Kate to giggles.

"Or have you been chasing fairies about all day? I saw some earlier, you know, and they said they were looking for a little girl to play with. Did they find you?"

Kate looked at her wide-eyed. "Did you really see a fairy?"

"Well," said Sophrina, wrinkling her brow. "I cannot say that I exactly *saw* one. Fairies are dreadfully difficult to see, you know. But I thought I saw a flash of something that might have been one and I heard something that sounded like fairy voices. They did not find you then?"

Kate shook her head sadly.

Sophrina instantly regretted her teasing, for the poor thing looked as if she were about to cry.

"Goodness, look how long the shadows are getting. It is time to head for home or I shall miss my dinner." Sophrina wrapped the remaining bit of cheese, restored it to her basket, and rose to her feet, dusting off her skirt. She reached out her hand to Kate. "Would you like me to walk with you a piece toward your home?"

Kate's mouth puckered. "I don't want to go home."

Oh dear, a runaway. Sophrina remembered the time that Bertram's youngest had taken to the road, at about this same age. His parents had been frantic with worry for hours. Kate's would be, too.

"It has been such a lovely day, I can hardly bear to go home, either," Sophrina said. "But I have people there who are expecting me and they would be in a bit of a pucker if I did not arrive on time. Don't you suppose there is someone expecting you as well?"

Kate's lower lip trembled ominously.

"I would think someone's mama might be rather upset if a certain person missed her dinner."

"My mama's dead," Kate whispered.

Sophrina's heart nearly broke. She reached out and gave Kate a quick hug. "I am sorry about your mama, Kate. Is your papa at home?"

At the mention of the word "papa," Kate burst into tears. "I hate my papa!" she cried. "He's mean and I don't like him and I am not going to live with him ever again."

"Goodness, it sounds as though you have a bit of a problem." Sophrina adopted a look of interested concern. "What does your papa do that is so awful?"

"He sent nurse away," Kate sniffled. "And he brought me

to a new house and I always get lost in it and he won't ever let me talk about my mama." A fresh bout of tears started.

Sophrina gathered Kate into her arms. It sounded like a typical domestic squabble.

"Do you think perhaps your papa had reasons for what he did?" she asked. "A big girl of four is almost too old for a nurse, you know. Perhaps he thought it was time to find you a grown-up girl's governess."

Kate scuffed her shoe in the dirt of the lane.

"I remember how terribly unnerving it is moving into a new house. We used to move several times a year between the country and London and it would take ages before I found where things were. I was always ending up in the library when I wanted to be in the dining room. It was most aggravating when I was hungry!"

She looked down, and Kate forced a woebegone smile.

"I think your papa is very worried about you, Kate. I imagine you have been gone from home for a long time, haven't you?" At the girl's nod, Sophrina continued, "Would you like me to walk you home? We could talk to your papa and perhaps he could take you about the house until you don't get lost anymore."

"I want to go home with you."

"That is very nice of you to say so, Kate, but I do not think that would be a good idea tonight. When we get to your house, I shall ask your papa if you may come visit me. Would you like that?"

Kate nodded.

"Well then, let us get started. Where do you live?"

"In a big house."

Sophrina felt a twinge of dismay.

"Do you remember the name of the house?"

Kate shook her head.

"How long have you lived at this house?"

Shrugging, Kate mumbled, "I don't know. Not very long."

"Do you remember what it looks like on the outside?"

Kate frowned as she concentrated, then her face brightened. "There is a pretty garden in back."

"How pleasant," Sophrina murmured. "Is it a house of

brick? You know, red stones? Or is it pinkish, or grayish?"

"I don't remember!" Kate wailed and looked as if she would succumb to tears again.

"Never mind," Sophrina said, taking Kate's chubby hand in hers. "I think I shall take you home with me after all, and then we can attempt to learn where you live."

Kate nodded happily at that plan and skipped along as Sophrina set their steps toward her cottage.

Sophrina's mind raced. What was the best way to find Kate's home? Of course, the vicar. He would be a logical place to start, for he was very punctual in his duty calls and had probably already visited Kate's father. Neither the dowager nor Mary would be of any help, for had they known of any new family in the area, Sophrina would have heard. She should ask Squire Drake's wife, who was always well apprised of the neighborhood gossip.

Sophrina and her small companion had only crossed the halfway point in the meadow when the clear thundering of hoofbeats reached Sophrina's ears. Turning, she saw a monstrously large black horse bearing down on them at a rapid pace. Could this be Kate's papa?

"Unhand that child at once!"

Kate cowered behind Sophrina's skirts, clutching her legs tightly at the man's angered command.

The man who leaped from the saddle of the lathered mount bore little resemblance to the flaxen-haired child who held so trustingly to Sophrina's hand. His hair was dark, nearly black, and his flashing eyes were of almost the same hue. With his face contorted with anger, worry, and something else she could not quite define, he was not a pleasant sight, but Sophrina did not think he would be precisely handsome even in an amiable mood. His face was all harsh lines and angles, not rounded smoothness, while his hair swept back from an imperiously high forehead.

"I can explain—"

"Oh no, there is no need for an explanation," he sneered. Elliston St. Clair's relief at finding the child at last was tempered by outrage at finding her in tow of this bedraggled woman. The chestnut hair and light complexion ruled out gypsy ancestry, but her unfashionable, dirt-splotched gown, sun-pinkened cheeks, and battered basket gave her a vagabond appearance. He flung himself out of the saddle. Thank God he had found the girl in time.

"Thought you would walk off with her, did you? Then hold her for ransom, or sell her off to the cotton mills?"

"I would never!" Sophrina protested.

"That's right, you will never, for I shall have you up before the magistrates tomorrow and you shall be in the hold of a transport ship so fast it will make your head spin. Give me that child!"

Kate let out a long wail of terror and Sophrina's temper rose.

"It is no wonder the poor child ran away from you if this is an example of how you go on!" she yelled with a vehemence that startled her. "I had thought she exaggerated, but it is quite clear she was right. You are an odious bully! What right do you have to scare the girl to death? I think I shall have you up before the magistrate myself for cruelty!"

"Why you . . ." He took a step closer and reached toward her menacingly.

Sophrina stood her ground, and perhaps it was that show of defiance that halted his movement. She saw him struggling mightily to rein in his boiling anger.

"If you will allow me to explain," she continued icily. "I made your daughter's acquaintance—she is your daughter, by the way?"

He nodded stonily.

"Very well. Kate and I met this afternoon when I needed someone to share my last bite of lunch." She felt the clutching hands on her legs relax fractionally. "She was obviously lost and I planned to take her home and dispatch messages around the county until I discovered her parent."

He ran a hand through his tousled locks. His damnable temper had got the best of him again.

"I am sorry," he said abruptly. "She ran off early this morning, and those fool people at the house did not see fit to inform me of her disappearance until this afternoon. I only brought her here last week, and feared she was lost . . ."

"I quite understand your concern," Sophrina soothed, seeking to calm his still ruffled composure. "My nephew pulled the same trick a few years ago and I recall how frantic his parents were."

"Nevertheless, that does not excuse my abominable behavior," he said, with a sheepish look. "Will you allow me to begin again? As if I had never insulted you?"

Sophrina nodded. Eyeing him critically, she realized she had been right, he was not devastatingly handsome when out of high dudgeon, but he at least did not have as fearsome an appearance. His eyes had lightened to a rich, dark brown and the contrite expression on his face gave him the appearance of an errant schoolboy.

He swept her a courtly bow. "I am Lord Penhurst."

Sophrina knew her mouth dropped open in a most embarrassing gape. She glanced down at the white-blond tresses of the girl, who was now inching around her side. The same color as Lea's hair. And William's. Sophrina looked up again and met Penhurst's quizzing gaze.

"I am Sophrina, Viscountess Teel."

She had the satisfaction of seeing him nearly as stunned as herself. And she did not miss his involuntary look at Kate.

"You see how well she resembles her father," he said at last, in a voice tinged with sarcasm.

"She is William's?" Sophrina could barely keep her voice from trembling with her whispered question.

Penhurst nodded, scowling.

"When is her birthday?" The intense pounding of her heart thundered in Sophrina's ears. Her marriage to Teel had been celebrated in May, four years ago.

"Katherine was four in April."

April. The month preceding her marriage. Sophrina could barely believe the implication of that date. William and Lea had been lovers *before* the marriage. The thought stunned her.

"Are you certain about—"

"Oh, I assure you, I am quite certain of her parentage." Penhurst's voice was harsh.

Sophrina's heart, already leaning, tumbled firmly into Kate's grasp. The poor girl was obviously bearing the brunt of Penhurst's anger at his unfaithful wife.

"We cannot blame the innocent for the sins of their elders, my lord."

He returned a piercing stare, then dropped his eyes to the girl again, as if dismissing Sophrina's criticism. "Katherine, it is time to go home."

"No!"

Sophrina knelt down beside her, brushing the last of the dried leaves from Kate's skirt. "You shall miss your dinner if you do not go now, and I know you are still hungry. That cheese was not nearly enough, was it? I promise you, I shall invite you to my house soon. Do you like macaroons?"

Kate nodded solemnly.

"They are my very favorite," Sophrina confided. "But you must promise me to go home with your papa now, and not try to run away again, or no macaroons."

"I promise," Kate whispered.

Giving her a quick hug, Sophrina rose to her feet. "I trust you will not object if Kate visits me?"

Penhurst looked doubtful. "You need not trouble yourself further over the child, Lady Teel. I am sure you must find her presence disturbing."

Sophrina was aghast to hear him speak so of such a sweet girl, particularly in Kate's hearing. "I assure you, Lord Penhurst, I find Kate a very pleasing companion." She could not keep the scorn from her voice. "I am more than happy to welcome her to my home at any time."

He shrugged. "As you wish. I do thank you, Lady Teel, for finding her."

Sophrina winced at his use of her title. It had been such a long time since anyone called her that.

"I truly enjoyed meeting her, my lord. She is a lovely child."

He did not miss the slightly quavering note in her voice. What a shock the revelation must be to her. And what a wretched way to discover the truth. He, of all people, could have presented it in a more diplomatic manner. But the shock of meeting Teel's wife had driven all diplomatic skills from his head.

Sophrina held tight to Kate's hand while Penhurst mounted

his horse. Then, with a quick kiss on her dirty cheek, she handed Kate up to her father. "Good day, Lady Kate."

"Good-bye, 'Rina." After Penhurst whispered in her ear, she added, "Lady Teel."

"I much prefer 'Rina,' Kate. As my special friend, you may call me that."

Sophrina resisted every impulse to turn and watch as the two rode back toward Talcott, Penhurst's estate. William's daughter. William and *Lea's* daughter. Born before William had made her his wife. Conceived, in fact, long before she had even met William that fateful spring.

All those months spent agonizing over her failings as a wife, all the bitter self-recriminations she had heaped on her head had been pointless. William had lied to her from the start. She had not driven him into another woman's arms. It was the most glorious news. Far from casting her into gloom, Kate's existence sent Sophrina into transport of joy. *It had not been her fault.*

Chapter 2

Shifting slightly in his chair, Penhurst took another long swig of his brandy as the approaching evening cast the study into shadow. Lord, what a shock to find Sophrina Charlton still in the neighborhood. And how deucedly awkward for her to have met Katherine in such a way. He was certain the revelation had been a stunner to her. As much as it had been to him when he first learned of his wife's pregnancy—coming as it did after he had been out of the country for months. All the white-hot anger that he had felt over his wife's infidelity rose within him again.

He wondered, for the hundredth time, why Lea had turned to Teel. Convenience, perhaps. It was certainly advantageous to have one's lover living at the nearest estate. Penhurst could only envision the opportunities that proximity had encouraged. Had Lea brought Teel here? For an instant, another flash of anger consumed him, but it subsided as quickly at it came. Lea was not a possession to be stolen away from him. Had he wanted to possess her, the whole mess might have been avoided. But he had not.

Indeed, after the first flush of excitement about his marriage had passed, he began to wonder just why he had chosen to wed in such a hurry. He had never been more than passing fond of his wife, and as his absences increased and the distance between them grew, even that sentiment faded to something akin to indifference. The only strong emotion he had ever felt about Lea came the night he confronted her about the pregnancy, and she admitted the child was not his. Rage and loathing had filled him at first.

Yet it had not taken long for the old indifference to creep back. Could their marriage have been salvaged, even at that late date? Lea swore at the time she had broken with Teel; he was planning to marry another. If Penhurst had taken her back with open arms, courted her, wooed her, would she have become the amiable companion he thought he wanted? Or had their marriage been dead from the start?

Reaching for the decanter, he poured himself another brandy. Teel's wife intrigued him. It was probably a perverse streak within him, which sought to constantly reanalyze and review his failed marriage. Sophrina Charlton was only another piece to the puzzle. A piece that did not seem to fit neatly into place.

Penhurst had known Teel left a wife behind when he and Lea fled to the Continent. Rumor held her to be an innocent miss, no competition for Lea's sophisticated charms. Penhurst had anticipated a pale, drab thing within a flicker of spirit, the type of woman who would meekly accept a philandering husband. But the woman who raged at him in the field that afternoon was anything but unspirited. His anger toward her had been inexcusable, but she returned his anger full measure. Hardly a complaisant lady.

With Katherine's safety utmost in his mind, he had not paid more than cursory attention to Lady Teel. She certainly had not been a picture of elegance, else he would not have mistaken her for a wandering child stealer. Admittedly no sensible woman would wear drawing-room clothes to tramp about the country-side. Recalling her chestnut-colored hair, he realized she had not been wearing the bonnet that was de rigueur with all ladies of fashion, explaining her sun-reddened cheeks. Her eyes were hazel, of that he was certain, for if looks could kill, he would lie mortally wounded.

Penhurst sighed. These morose self-analyses had grown more frequent of late, due no doubt to his unaccustomed lack of activity. Perhaps he should look into things at the Foreign Office when he went up to London again. In peacetime, the diplomatic life was not nearly so enthralling as it had been during war, but it would occupy his time and keep his mind clear. Once Katherine was settled in her new home, there was nothing to keep him in the country.

The grass was still wet with dew when Sophrina arrived at the Dower House the following morning, her skirt hem decidedly damp. But the dowager was never one for lying abed, and Sophrina was very eager to acquaint her with the news of Penhurst's presence in the neighborhood—and the incredible tale of Kate's parentage.

"Good morning, my dear," Louisa, the dowager viscountess, greeted her, presenting a round, pink cheek for a kiss. "You must have risen with the roosters this morning."

Sophrina laughed. "Nearly. It is such a shame to miss even a moment of the morning on a day like this."

"It takes more than a few moments of sunshine to drag you from your bed this early." The dowager cast a speculative glance at Sophrina. "Now tell me your news."

"You will never guess whom I encountered yesterday!" Sophrina's eyes twinkled in anticipation of Louisa's reaction.

"Penhurst." The dowager's look of surprise rewarded her for the chilling morning trek.

"I had not known he was down. Goodness, he has not been at Talcott in ages. Wherever did you meet him?"

"He has brought his daughter to Talcott," Sophrina said, barely able to contain her excitement.

"Is she of an age with any of Mary's brood? They will be eager for a new playmate."

"She is almost four and a half," Sophrina explained, eyeing the dowager shrewdly. Did she know about Kate's parentage?

"She may rub along well with Susan then," Louisa decided, calmly pouring herself a cup of tea.

"She is William's child."

The dowager started, her teacup poised in midair. "How do you know?"

"Have you ever seen Penhurst? Hair as black as night. Kate's is nearly white."

"So was her mother's," the dowager pointed out, restoring her cup to its saucer with studied care.

"She has his eyes," Sophrina countered. "I thought there was something vaguely familiar about Kate when I first saw her, but I did not realize it until I met Penhurst. He confirmed my guess."

"So I have another grandchild," the dowager mused, a small smile teasing her face. Then she gave a guilty start as she glanced at Sophrina. "I do not mean . . ."

"Louisa, did you hear what I said? Kate is four-and-a-half! Do you realize what that means?"

The dowager looked blanky at Sophrina.

"She was born *before* I married William. I did not drive him into Lea's arms."

"Whatever are you talking about?"

Sophrina twisted her fingers together. "I always thought that it was some . . . some failing in *me* that drove William away."

"What a ridiculous notion!"

"What else was I to think?" Sophrina cried. "To discover, after a year of marriage, that my husband preferred the most elegant, beautiful woman of the neighborhood to the naive girl he married. I was a failure. I could not carry a child; I could not even keep my own husband in my bed."

"Oh, my poor dear. I had no idea you blamed yourself."

Sophrina smiled ruefully. "I realize now how foolish that was. Oh, Louisa, you cannot know how wonderful it is to discover I was wrong!"

"Be that as it may, I cannot comprehend what Penhurst was thinking to bring the child *here*. He must realize how awkward it would be for all of us."

Sophrina leaped to Kate's defense. "She has as much right to be here as anyone. I cannot help but admire Penhurst, for taking responsibility for the girl. It cannot be easy for him, having her as a constant reminder of Lea's betrayal.''

"True. Yet equally awkward for you, my dear.'' The dowager reached over and patted Sophrina's hand in a comforting gesture.

Sophrina laughed. ''Awkward is the *last* word I would apply to the situation. She is such an adorable girl. And terrified of Penhurst, poor thing. He is not much of a father, I am afraid. But he has promised Kate may come to visit me.''

The dowager gave Sophrina a skeptical glance.

"He is not at all what I imagined he would be.'' Sophrina was thoughtful. "He is much younger than I expected, and more formidable. After Lea's behavior, I anticipated a biddable, middle-aged gentleman—the type to indulge a young wife.''

"I do not think he is much above thirty,'' the dowager mused as she poured more tea. ''And formidable is not the word I would apply to a man who had such little control over his wife.''

"He was out of the country most of the time.'' Sophrina paused. How ironic to be defending Penhurst! But in the sudden discovery of her own blamelessness for William's actions, she was inclined to look more charitably on Penhurst. ''Perhaps if she had been with him, he would have ruled her with a firmer hand.''

Sophrina hesitated. The Charltons had no legal ties to Kate, since Penhurst had acknowledged her as his own. Yet there were the stronger ties of blood and family. She suspected that was something Kate was sorely lacking.

"Should you like to see her?''

"You always know how to cut to the heart of the matter, do you not?'' Louisa sighed, rubbing her ring-laden hands while she thought. ''She is all I have left of William, isn't she? But I think the matter should be up to Penhurst. Goodness, I do not envy him the task of deflecting gossip from the girl for the rest of her life.''

"People would not be so cruel as to bother her, would they?'' Sophrina was aghast and all her protective instincts rallied around Kate. ''How loathsome.''

"People are loathsome. You recall some of the more scurrilous whisperings about your own situation?''

Sophrina flushed. "I hate the way people are always so ready to think evil of anyone." Brightening, she continued, "It would do much to still talk, would it not, if you were seen to be on amiable terms with the girl? Other than for tattling to you or Bertram, I cannot see what interest her parentage would be to anyone here."

"Be that as it may, how do you plan to go on in this situation?"

"With Penhurst? I do not think our paths will cross often. Certainly, there is no reason both of us cannot be polite in social situations."

"I meant with the child. I am not so certain that close contact with her is a good idea."

"Why ever not?" Sophrina stared at her mother-in-law. "The poor girl is sadly neglected, I fear. And even Penhurst is not averse."

"Still . . ." The dowager frowned.

"Oh, Louisa, do not read anything more into this than my desire to befriend a child who is sorely in need of some attention. If she was Penhurst's own daughter, I would not feel differently."

"Besides," she added, cajolingly, "Edward and Susan are now firmly settled in the schoolroom and not available for larks, and Arabella and the baby are still too young to be companionable."

"What you need," said Louisa, with all the bluntness she was known for, "is a husband who will give you your own babies."

"Marriage is not high on my list of aspirations," Sophrina responded with determination. "Even if it would allow me to have a child of my own. There is no guarantee of that, you know; I lost the one. Mayhaps I am incapable of bearing a child."

"Nonsense. It is not an uncommon problem among young wives."

"Nevertheless, since I do not have any of my own, I see nothing wrong in borrowing others, be they Mary's or Penhurst's. I am most determined to have Kate visit. And it is perfectly normal for her to play with the other children in the district."

"There is some truth to that. But I do not think it is necessary to make a major push in this situation. Perhaps when you see Penhurst again, you might sound him out. He may be totally opposed to such a meeting."

"I do not expect to see him anytime soon."

"I thought Kate was coming for a visit." Louisa lifted a quizzing brow.

"It is highly unlikely he will escort her." Sophrina smiled. "But if the opportunity arises, I shall endeavor to speak to him."

After spending the remainder of the morning with the dowager, Sophrina briskly retraced the path toward her cottage. Louisa meant well, but she simply did not understand. William's unfaithfulness had not only destroyed Sophrina's marriage, it had also stripped away the veils of illusion covering her eyes. It enabled her to look with newfound insight at the people around her, and what she saw was rarely encouraging. Bertram and Mary were unique in the happiness of their union, yet even there, all was not smooth.

Most married couples Sophrina knew lived in situations little better than her own had been. A husband and wife who existed in bored toleration were said to have a happy marriage. How did so many couples manage to produce heirs to the title, when the husband and wife went their own ways so detrerminedly?

It seemed pointless to tie herself into that sort of union. Perhaps deeply buried inside her were a few vestiges of the romantic notions of her youth, the belief that it was possible to live in loving companionship with one's spouse. But her more practical self doubted the possibility. Sophrina firmly resigned herself to her status as widow and aunt.

Penhurst sent for his daughter following breakfast, determined to impress upon her the severity of her escapade the previous day. She entered the library hesitantly, eyeing him with the apprehensive expression she habitually wore in his presence. It pained Penhurst to think she was afraid of him. Granted, he had not been more than a shadowy presence during her short life. Since Lea's departure, oftentimes months had gone by without his seeing the girl. But he had never done anything to inspire fear.

"Do you know what I wish to say to you?" he asked sternly.

"I was bad," she said with a small frown.

"Yes, Katherine, you were."

"If I promise never, ever to run away again, will you let me visit Rina?" The pleading look on her face startled him. It was so reminiscent of Lea. "I promise I shall be a good girl always."

So that was it. Katherine was afraid he would not let her visit Lady Teel. How had the two formed such a fast friendship in such a short time? Lady Teel would have every reason to hate the girl, for was she not the physical evidence of Teel's adultery? Yet she had invited Katherine to visit *after* learning of her parentage. Was Lady Teel merely curious?

"Why did you run away?"

Kate remained stubbornly silent.

"I know you miss your old home, Katherine, but Talcott is to be your new home from now on." Penhurst attempted to interject some enthusiasm into his voice. "You will learn to like it here. It is where I grew up."

"I won't run away again."

"Very well, I shall take that as your solemn promise."

He intended his remarks as a dismissal, but the girl remained standing before him.

"Yes?"

"May I please visit Rina?"

He sighed. "I shall send a note to Lady Teel, Katherine. If she still wishes to invite you, I will allow you to go."

Kate bobbed a nod of thanks and warily slipped out of the room.

Penhurst frowned. Was it wise to throw Katherine and Lady Teel together? The girl wanted it very much, and there was probably little harm in a meeting. Lady Teel was surely curious about this child of her husband's, and another encounter with Katherine would satisfy that natural human response.

He knew there had been no children in Teel's marriage. With a trace of bitterness, Penhurst judged Teel too busy with Lea to tend to his own wife. Why then, would Lady Teel want a visible reminder of her husband's philandering? If he was in her place, he would never wish to lay eyes on the girl again.

He shifted uneasily in his chair at the thought. How often had he wished the same thing about Katherine? Had she been a boy, he would have divorced his wife and named the child a bastard at the same time. His decision to accept Katherine had been motivated less by charity than by the fact that he needed to be off on another lengthy diplomatic mission and did not want to be tied down by a messy court battle. A daughter could not inherit, so he need not fear a child of another's blood would carry on the St. Clair name. Lea had taken total charge of Katherine—which meant hiring a nurse and depositing the child at one of his lesser estates while she cavorted in London with her lover.

He had seen no reason to alter the situation when Lea eloped, or even after her death. But at his last visit, when the girl had talked of nothing but her sainted mama, he realized that changes had to be made. At the time, it seemed the easiest thing to bring her to Talcott while he searched out another nurse. If he intended to continue the charade that Katherine was his own, he needed to show a little more filial attention to the child, and moving her to Talcott would also accomplish that. The last person he had expected to find in the neighborhood was Teel's widow.

Penhurst gazed gently out the window, looking across the sun-drenched terrace to the park beyond. Had it been a mistake to bring Katherine here? She was unhappy in her new surroundings and distrustful of him. Her real father's widow was determined, for reasons known only to herself, to strike up an incomprehensible friendship. Her grandmother, uncle, aunt, and cousins lived only a short walk away. God, what could he have been thinking of to to such a thing?

But he had, and the damage was now done. It was his job to straighten out the mess. At least, he thought wryly, that was something he was good at, even if he usually dealt with other people's ill-founded efforts. The embarrassing presence of one small girl could not compare with the havoc wreaked by that mad Corsican in Europe.

Perhaps he should take Katherine with him if he resumed a Foreign Office assignment. Reaching out to the mounted globe sitting beside the desk, he gave the orb a vigorous spin. No end of countries to visit. Ten, fifteen years from now, no one would remember a very old scandal. Katherine would be a polished lady of nineteen, ready to make her debut into society. And he would be . . .

Older. Nearly fifty. With nothing to show for it but his signature scrawled across numerous documents that would be meaningless by then, and a daughter in whose veins none of his own blood flowed.

He could change that situation, of course. It would require little effort to procure a wife, spawn a few heirs, and ensure his name would live on for another generation, at least. But the thought of living in prolonged familiarity with anyone was a distasteful prospect. Oh, there was little danger he would find himself cuckolded again. He would be damn sure to choose a woman who would not dare.

But he was not certain whether the entire process was worth the effort it would take. Close intimacy with another required such an effort. He had a cousin somewhere who would inherit after he was gone, a spotted adolescent the last time Penhurst laid eyes upon him, but surely time had taken care of that. Perhaps when he got to London, he would call in the family solicitor and arrange a meeting. There might be some fatal flaw to his cousin that would be enough to force Penhurst into another marriage, but he fervently prayed it would not be so. A bachelor he was and a bachelor he would remain. It was too damn difficult having a wife.

Penhurst frowned, disgusted at his inability to shake off his ill humor. Surely he could find some other subject to occupy his mind. Lady Teel, for example. He had best do something to mend any fences he had damaged yesterday in his tirade against her. By responding as she had, the score was nearly evened, but a contrite note would certainly put him on the plus side. He had no intention of lingering long in the country, but he knew the value of amiable relations between neighbors. In a situation as awkward as this, the amenities must be strictly observed. Frowning, he reached for his pen and uncapped the inkwell on his desk.

Chapter 3

Sophrina found it difficult to connect the abject apology with the irate lord who had so thoroughly lashed out at her in the meadow. She could not suppress a smile as she scanned his note. Penhurst's long years in diplomatic circles had certainly not been wasted. But then, country ladies must pose little challenge after volatile Russians and acerbic Prussians.

Sophrina looked down at the spiky black letters scrawled across the paper. How like the man himself. Bold, impatient, quick to anger. He would be a worthy opponent at the negotiating table.

But this was not world affairs. It was only the fate of a small girl with wide blue eyes and hair the color of sun-bleached grain. Even if Sophrina had detested Kate, she would have invited her out of spite after Penhurst's odious reference to her willful ways and disobedient habits. How dare he apply such words to such an adorable child? The man obviously knew nothing of four-year-olds. Well, she would show him who did.

Sophrina's invitation to "milk and macaroons" was duly delivered to Lady Katherine St. Clair, who replied, through her papa, that she would be delighted to accept. Sophrina prepared for the anticipated visit as if expecting a royal personage. The always immaculate cottage was turned inside out for cleaning. To entertain her guest, she gathered up the various toys left at the cottage at one time or another by her nieces and nephews. The baking she left to her competent cook, who produced a heaping plate of macaroons that held the place of honor upon the table. All was in readiness when Sophrina heard the crunch of carriage wheels on the gravel drive.

Her casual glance out the window turned to a surprised stare when she saw Penhurst himself behind the reins of the sporting curricle, Kate perched in the seat beside him. Stepping back quickly from the window, lest he notice her ill-mannered gawking, Sophrina resumed her seat, smoothing out the skirts of her pale salmon taffeta gown. She may have looked like a rough country hoyden at their first meeting, but for reasons she did not analyze, she now wanted to show him she was a lady as well. And ladies did not get caught staring out of windows.

"Good day, my lord," she greeted Penhurst as he was shown into the spacious parlor. Was there a flicker of bemusement in his eyes as he took in her fashionable appearance? "This is an unexpected pleasure. Will you be joining us?"

"Thank you, Lady Teel, but I am merely delivering Katherine to your care." He gently urged the girl forward. "Say your greetings to Lady Teel, my dear."

The girl bobbed a clumsy curtsy. "Good day, Lady Teel." Her eyes widened as she saw the plate of biscuits on the side table.

Penhurst surreptitiously studied his hostess. The country dowd of the previous encounter had been transformed into an elegant lady. Was she always so full of surprises? She was not the diamond Lea had been, but neither was she an antidote. Her sun-reddened cheeks had faded to a fetching shade of pink and with her hair neatly swept up into a stylish coif, she was pleasingly attractive.

"And good day to you, Lady Kate." To Sophrina, the girl looked like a French fashion doll come to life. From the tips of her tiny blue shoes to the peak of her high-crowned bonnet, Kate was dressed from the pages of *La Belle Assemblee,* albeit in miniature. Penhurst had not stinted in that area.

Sophrina looked again to the earl. How stern he looked. Did the man never unbend? "Are you certain I cannot persuade you to take at least one macaroon before you leave?"

"Unfortunately, Lady Teel, I do not share your or Katherine's fondness for macaroons." His lips twitched in the hint of a smile. "I have business to conduct with my bailiff today as well. I shall send the carriage for my daughter in an hour."

"Oh surely she can stay longer than that," Sophrina protested, rising to her feet. "Two hours at least."

What could Lady Teel possibly find to do with a four-year-old child for two hours? But he was not willing to say no to her. Katherine had spoken of nothing else since the note arrived two days ago, and there would be an easier time of it in the nursery tonight if she was not vexed.

"Two hours then," he agreed. Turning a somber face to the girl, he said, "Now Katherine, you remember your manners." He gave a half-apologetic smile to Sophrina. "She has been sadly lacking in discipline, I am afraid. Her old nurse was far too indulgent and spoiled her shamefully."

Sophrina thought it shameful of Penhurst to say such a thing in front of the child. Kate needed her even more than she first thought. But if she wished to continue seeing the girl, Sophrina needed to remain on amiable terms with Penhurst and so chose to hold her tongue.

"I am certain Lady Kate will do all that is proper," Sophrina said, giving the girl an encouraging smile. Kate returned a very shy one of her own.

"Very well then." Penhurst bowed his way from the room.

Kate visibly relaxed after he left, Sophrina noticed with a pang. Poor girl. Penhurst was perhaps not deliberately callous in his treatment of her, for he surely had little experience in the matter of children, but his attitude still grated. Kate was an adorable child and deserved to be surrounded by love and kindness, no matter who her parents were.

"Well," began Sophrina, reaching out to untie Kate's bonnet. "What shall we do first? I myself am rather hungry, but if you would prefer to wait . . ."

"I would not mind if we eat," Kate said, her gaze drifting again to the macaroons.

"Very well, then," said Sophrina and she rang for the tea tray. Setting Kate's bonnet on a chair, Sophrina bent to undo the tiny fastenings on the expensive blue pelisse while they waited for the tray to arrive. Two china pots sat upon the gleaming silver platter brought by Jenny; one for Sophrina's tea and another with milk for Kate.

"Have you been invited to tea before?" Sophrina asked, hoping to set Kate at ease.

Kate shook her head.

"As I am the hostess, I pour, and then hand you your tea with a saucer, and than a plate with your biscuits. Normally you balance the plate on your knees and the saucer in your hand. But I always found that rather difficult, myself, so I thought we could sit around this table." While she talked, she prepared

Kate's milk and macaroons and presented them with a flourish.
Helping Kate into the chair, Sophrina took her own seat at the
small oval table.

"Now we are to engage in a lively discussion of all the news,"
Sophrina explained.

"What kind of news?" Kate asked.

"Oh, any sort. You might tell of a conversation you had
yesterday, or a visit you made. Did you pay any visits
yesterday?" At Kate's denial Sophrina continued, "Then I shall
tell you about mine. The Dowager Viscountess Teel lives near
here, and I spent the morning with her."

"Is she pretty?" Kate asked.

"I think so. She has the loveliest silver-white hair and deep
blue eyes."

"I have blue eyes."

"So you do. They go very nicely with your blond hair. My
eyes are brown to match my brown hair."

"Why aren't my eyes blond then?" Kate wore a puzzled
frown.

"Blond would not be an easy color to see next to the white
part, would it?"

"No," Kate admitted after a moment's thought.

"Now it is your turn," Sophrina prompted. "What did you
do yesterday?"

"Cook let me watch in the kitchen while she fixed dinner."

"That must have been fun. Did she let you have a taste?"
Kate nodded.

"My cook always let me do that when I was a girl, too,"
Sophrina confided. "And sometimes, if I am very good, my
cook still allows me a taste."

Kate giggled.

Sophrina kept a careful eye on Kate and, after judging the
girl had eaten enough macaroons for the time being, suggested
they play a game.

"This is one of my niece's favorites," Sophrina explained
as she brought out the box and spread the pieces on the table.
"We always call it Faces. These poor ladies have gotten their
faces all jumbled up and it is our job to match them up again.
First you find a chin, then the nose, and then the eyes."

"Why are their faces all chopped up?" Kate asked.

"So we can have the fun of putting them back together. Now, do you think this nose belongs to this lady?"

Sophrina gazed wistfully at the tiny blond head bent over the table in concentration. The child she had lost would have been a year younger than Kate, but it might have had its father's same white-blond hair and clear blue eyes. Even now, nearly four years later, the pain of her loss could still throb like a raw wound. Did one ever really get over losing a baby?

From experience gained by playing with her nieces and nephews, Sophrina was able to judge at what point Kate's attention began to wane and presented her with a new entertainment at the critical moment. Kate was adept at catching a ball in the cup, confiding that she had a very similar one at home.

"Now these are our alphabet cards," Sophrina said, when it was time for a new diversion. "Do you know your alphabet?"

"No," said Kate.

"Well, this letter is 'A,' which is the first letter in the word apple. That is why there is a picture of an apple on the card." She held up the "B." "What is on this card?"

"A ball."

"Right. And that is the letter B." Sophrina quickly ran through the remaining cards. It was another sign of Penhurst's lack of attention to Kate; a child her age should know most of her letters. Why, Edward had been reading at three-and-a-half!

"Now I will show you something else." Sophrina laid down the cards to spell Kate's name. "K-A-T-E. Do you know what those letters mean?"

Kate shook her head.

"That is your name. Kate."

Sophrina swept up the cards and then spelled her own name. "This is my name. Sophrina. And here is your papa, Penhurst. All these letters can be combined together in ever so many ways to make any word you want."

"Spell 'Kate' again," Kate requested. She clapped her hands gleefully when Sophrina complied. Pointing to each letter, she made Sophrina name it, then repeated the letter to herself. "K-A-T-E!" she announced proudly.

"That's right. What a bright girl you are. I think you should have a macaroon as a reward."

Kate was very sharp, Sophrina noted with satisfaction. What a joy it would be to teach her. Suppressing a sigh, she held out the biscuit plate. How she longed to have Kate in her charge.

Kate gratefully accepted the proffered macaroon and was munching away contentedly when Penhurst reappeared.

"Goodness, is it two hours already?" Sophrina asked, truly amazed the time had gone by so quickly.

"Past that, I'm afraid," he said ruefully. "I am sorry to be late."

"I had not even noticed the time."

"Guess what I can do, Papa?"

"What, Katherine?"

She went to the table and looked through the cards, retrieving the desired ones. Placing each one carefully upon the surface, she spelled out the word Sophrina had taught her. "K-A-T-E. That spells Kate. That's my name!"

"Yes, it is," Penhurst agreed. "And a very good thing for you to know. Did you thank Lady Teel for teaching you that?"

"Thank you, Lady Teel."

"You are most welcome, Lady Kate."

"You must get your pelisse, now, Katherine, for it is past time for us to return to Talcott. We have imposed on Lady Teel far too long today."

"Nonsense, we had a wonderful time, didn't we, Kate?" Sophrina rose and retrieved Kate's bonnet and pelisse. "You must promise to come back again."

"Oh, I will," Kate assured her.

"Now, Kate, you remain here for a moment. My lord, may I have a word with you?"

At Penhurst's acquiescent nod, she led him into the hall.

"I thought this would be a convenient time to speak. I took the liberty of explaining Kate's history to the dowager viscountess. I felt it best she hear the news from myself before it became common gossip in the village."

Penhurst scowled. "I would hope the people of the town could find a more worthy subject of conversation."

"Nevertheless, it is human nature to gossip, I fear. And the awkward connection between our families is well known. If it is seen that neither I nor the dowager is uncomfortable with Kate, much speculation would be stilled.''

"I concede your point."

"She would also like to meet Kate."

"I am not sure that is wise."

"Oh, she does not intend to do so in an encroaching manner. I was going to suggest that Kate be allowed to visit with my nieces and nephews. I am sure she would enjoy playing with the other children. Louisa—the dowager—could easily look in on them in an unobtrusive manner.''

Penhurst hesitated.

"Kate is her granddaughter," Sophrina reminded him softly.

He nodded. "I still can see no purpose to be served by a meeting. I only fear Katherine's presence will be a painful reminder . . .''

"Nothing can erase the past, my lord. But we cannot live our lives under its domination, either." Sophrina took a deep breath to regain her composure. "Do not deny Kate the company of her family, even if she is unaware of the connection.''

"I appreciate your interest in the child, Lady Teel, but I do think I must deny your request." He cloaked his rejection in his most diplomatic tones. "I do not see where it would benefit either party."

Sophrina accepted this defeat as only a temporary setback. A minor skirmish in the struggle over Kate's happiness.

"I do thank you, Lady Teel, for entertaining Katherine." Penhurst forced himself into amiability. "I hope she was not too wearing on you."

"It was my pleasure. She is a very bright child and a delight to have. I should like her to visit often, if you do not object.''

He hesitated, suddenly suspicious of her motives. What did Lady Teel have to gain by seeing Katherine? Why such interest in the child? After years of dealing with the enigmatic workings of the diplomatic community, he was averse to accepting any action at face value. What did she want?

In a blinding flash of insight, he realized the answer. Of course! Katherine was Sophrina's last tie to the man she had loved and lost. Her only physical connection to her dead husband. With a flicker of sympathy, he understood Lady Teel's motives. Yet he still was not certain a close connection would be best for either her or the child.

"I am sure there will be ample opportunities in the future," he said, refusing to make a firm commitment.

Sophrina sensed his underlying reluctance and did not press him further. The strongest ally to her cause lay within the enemy camp, and Sophrina did not think Kate would fail her.

Sophrina insisted on cleaning the parlor herself after Kate and Penhurst drove away. Putting away the games and toys, she was plagued by a lingering sadness that it was always the children of others who graced her chambers. Those laughing voices always departed eventually, leaving her alone and wistful. If only . . .

A tremendous sense of loss filled her as she thought back on the last years of her life. Married, abandoned, and widowed, all in three short years. Her token period of mourning had been less for society than an excuse to remain here in the country. Rarely did she have doubts about the course her life was taking, her refusal to contemplate another marriage. But on days like today, with her ears still ringing with Kate's bright laughter, she knew she was only fooling herself. She would give anything to have a daughter such as Kate for her own, or a bright, lively son like her nephew Edward. By holding on to her foolish, romantic dreams, she was denying herself the joy of mothering a child. Yet always there was the remembered pain of William's betrayal holding her back.

Pouring herself a cup of tea from the freshly brewed pot, Sophrina slowly sipped the hot brew and thought. Penhurst did not want Kate visiting Charlton, but there were other ways of arranging a meeting between the cousins. A sly smile curved at her lips as she began to lay her plot. It would be worth facing Penhurst's wrath to bring some happiness to Kate.

Chapter 4

Sophrina bided her time, waiting for a propitious moment to see Kate again. In the small neighborhood, it did not take long for the news of Lord Penhurst's departure for London to reach Sophrina's ears—particularly when it was news she had actively sought. Now she could deal with Kate as she thought proper, without her father's interference.

Sophrina presented herself the following morning on the front steps of Talcott. Penhurst's butler appeared nonplussed at her arrival, particularly when she insisted she was there to see Lady Kate, not the master. But he allowed her to enter and Kate was brought down from the nursery.

"Rina!" she cried in pleasure as she ran into the drawing room, flinging herself into Sophrina's arms.

"Hello, Kate." Sophrina gave her a warm hug. "I thought you might be lonely with your papa gone, so I came by to say hello."

"Can you stay and play?" the girl asked eagerly.

Sophrina untied the ribbons on her bonnet. "I think I can manage that." She reached into her reticule. "I even brought the cards for Faces and Alphabets."

Kate clapped her hands in excitement.

The morning hours passed in a flash of enjoyment for Sophrina. When she at last glanced at the clock on the mantel, the time startled her.

"Goodness, the entire morning is gone." She gathered up the scattered cards. "I must take my departure, Kate."

"Don't go," Kate pleaded. "Stay and play."

Her importunings tempted Sophrina, but she did have other obligations today. "I shall come back tomorrow," she promised.

"I do so like to play with you," Kate said, giving Sophrina a hug.

"I like to play with you, too, Kate." Sophrina paused. "Would you like me to leave the cards here?"

Kate's eyes glowed in delight. "Oh, I should like that."

"Very well, here they will stay. I shall bring something else when I come tomorrow. And I think I can persuade my cook to bake up another batch of mararoons."

"I wish it were tomorrow," Kate said a bit sadly.

Sophrina laughed. "Tomorrow will come soon enough. Now I must go, for if cook does not have the ingredients to make the macaroons, I shall have to go to the village for them. I will return in the morning. If the weather is pleasant, you can show me the garden."

Sophrina was smiling to herself when she climbed back into her gig. She had breached the first wall of Penhurst's defenses—the house. The next hurdle would be taking Kate out into the neighborhood. She would speak with Penhurst's housekeeper tomorrow, for Sophrina understood that woman had at least the nominal job of supervising Kate. If the housekeeper could be won over, Kate would soon be visiting her cousins at Charlton.

Indeed, Sophrina's worries were unfounded. Mrs. Gooch, the housekeeper, was more than delighted to have Sophrina entertain Kate.

"Keeps the young'un out of my way—not that she's a problem, mind you, a very well-behaved girl she is—but none of us has the time to play with her." The housekeeper smiled sadly. "I can already tell your visits are doing her a world of good."

So it was that only three days after Penhurst departed for London, Kate sat next to Sophrina in the gig on the road to Charlton. It had shocked Sophrina to discover that Kate had never been in contact with other playmates before. Remembering her own childhood, filled with the close companionship of siblings, Sophrina found it hard to envision the solitary life Kate had led. She railed against the indifference of both the girl's parents.

She gave little heed to Penhurst's clear opposition to Kate's contact with her relatives at Charlton. He knew too little of children, Sophrina rationalized; he did not understand how important it was for Kate to have playmates. The issue of cousins and aunts and uncles was not the point here. What was important was the happiness of a little girl. Certainly, even Penhurst would be able to see that!

Sophrina could tell that Kate was nervous, for she uttered only a few words during the short drive. A twinge of doubt assailed Sophrina, but only for a moment. Children were remarkably adaptable; Kate and Susan would soon be fast friends, Sophrina was certain.

When they arrived at Charlton, she hastened her charge up the stairs, knowing Susan would be waiting in the nursery. Kate's arrival was doubly welcomed, for it had earned Susan an early reprieve from the morning's lessons. Edward, at eight, was not granted that luxury.

The first thing that came to Sophrina's mind, as the two cousins silently examined each other, was how much more a Charlton Kate looked than Susan. Bertram was darker than William had been, and combined with Mary's brown locks, Susan's hair was more brown than blond. Kate's light hair and blue eyes easily matched many of the family portraits lining the walls of the house.

"Do you want to see my dolls?" Susan asked.

Kate nodded and Susan took her hand, leading her across the room to the overflowing shelves. Within minutes, they were chatting away and Sophrina uttered a sigh of relief. Matters looked to be going well.

"I am going to find your mother, Susan," she said. "I will put Kate in your charge."

"Don't leave me!" Kate wailed.

"I will only be downstairs," Sophrina reassured her. "You stay here with Susan and her dolls. I shall be back soon."

Kate looked at her doubtfully, but said nothing more as Sophrina walked across the room to the door.

Mary and the dowager waited for her in the drawing room.

"Susan is regaling her with the detailed history of every doll in her collection," Sophrina announced as Mary poured her a cup of tea.

"They will be occupied for hours, then," the reigning viscountess laughed. "I do not think there is another girl in England with so many dolls."

"Quite true," Sophrina agreed, taking the proffered cup. "How is Thomas today? Are his teeth better?"

Mary nodded. "He slept most of the night, finally. I do not understand why it seems to get worse with each child. Why, Edward never uttered more than a whimper when he was cutting teeth."

"Each one is different," the dowager said, and launched into a tale of the comparisons between William and Bertram.

Sophrina listened to their conversation with a touch of sadness. They never did this deliberately to hurt her, she knew, but at times it was excruciatingly painful to listen to their cheerful talk of motherhood and babies. It was a charmed circle that she could never enter; she was forever doomed to watch from outside the ring. No manner of nieces and nephews could ever make her a mother.

As if realizing how they had unintentionally shut out Sophrina, the dowager turned back toward her other daughter-in-law.

"When does Penhurst return from town?"

Sophrina shrugged. "I do not know. I am not privy to his plans."

The dowager eyed her warily. "Is he aware of Kate's visit, Sophrina?"

She flushed. "No."

Louisa uttered an exasperated sigh. "You are being very foolish, girl, going against his wishes."

"I fail to see what possible harm there is in introducing Kate to Susan." Sophrina set her mouth in an obstinate line. "She needs a friend near her own age."

"That is not the issue and you know it. Penhurst will be furious when he finds out you have disobeyed him."

"It is over and done with now. I am certain Penhurst will recognize that fact when he returns. And if not, well, I am not afraid of his ire."

"You very well should be, my dear. I have no intention of taking your side in this matter. The earl has every right to take you to task for this. Do not expect me to defend you from Penhurst's anger."

Sophrina's retort was cut off by Kate and Susan's entry, their hands clasped tightly together.

"Why is my papa angry?" Kate asked, her blue eyes wide with curiosity.

"Your papa is not angry," Sophrina quickly reassured her,

casting aside her own apprehensions. She glanced quickly to the dowager. The elder woman was staring sharply at Kate, searching her face intently for what Sophrina knew was a glimpse of the man who had fathered her.

Sophrina rose and took Kate's other hand. "Kate, I should like to present you to Susan's mama and grandmother. This is Lady Teel—"

"But that is your name!" Kate protested.

"Yes, it is," Sophrina said. In a lower whisper, she prompted, "Curtsy, if you please."

Kate executed a wobbly dip before Mary and turned to the dowager.

"And this is also Lady Teel."

Kate giggled. "Three Lady Teels! Why do you all have the same name? Are you sisters?"

Sophrina saw both Mary and the dowager stifle smiles. "Not sisters, but we are all part of the same family," she explained. "Susan's grandfather was Lord Teel. His son was my husband, and after his father died, he became Lord Teel. When he died, his brother, Susan's papa, became the new Lord Teel."

Kate looked at Sophrina. "Your husband is dead? Just like my mama is dead?"

Sophrina winced at how closely Kate had come to the truth of the matter. She nodded.

"Oh." And, with the fleeting attention span of a child, Kate turned to Susan. "Can I see the baby now?"

With the first-floor windows thrown open to catch the breeze, the sounds from the street below filled Penhurst's town house. London never ceased to amaze him. Even now, when anyone who could afford to had fled the city for the country, the streets teemed with life. No matter what the time of year, it was always the same. Not like the European capitals, when either the heat of summer or cold of winter dampened the normal rhythm of life.

Penhurst smiled wryly. Why then, if London so fascinated him, had he been dogging the halls of the nearby deserted Foreign Office, hinting broadly that he would like to be put back in harness? Nothing that blunt had been said, of course, but everyone understood that was the reason he was paying a call at such an unusual time of year. Spying out the lay of the land.

From the modest inquiries he had made, it seemed there would be little difficulty in getting a post somewhere. But the certainty of that, coupled with the lack of drama on the Continent now that Napoleon was safely away, made him suddenly wonder if he really wanted to go back to the arcane twists and turns of the diplomatic trade. Without the great military treaties to haggle over, without the added drama of competing offers, spies, bribes, and even death, life in a foreign embassy would be little different from life in London. Social events would once again predominate, and although the intrigues on the dance floor and in the saloons would be fierce, they would not involve anything more complex than who was, wasn't, or wanted to be sleeping with whom. Did he really want to leave this island again?

He leaned back in his chair, tipping the front legs off the floor. What would be best for Katherine? He was under no illusions that her parentage would remain a secret once she was out among society. Still, there was little likelihood she would come to the attention of anyone at such a young age. It would not be necessary to hide her across the water. Talcott was as out-of-the-way as St. Petersburg as far as he and the *ton* were concerned.

Yet Talcott no longer represented the safe haven he had once thought it. All due to the presence of an exasperating young widow who seemed determined to involve herself in Katherine's life. He tried to sympathize with Lady Teel. In cherishing the memory of her dead husband, of course she would have an interest in his child. But was it his obligation to further that connection? Would not her very interest only broadcast the truth of Katherine's birth? Lady Teel's presence made things damnably awkward. How much better it would have been for all concerned if she had taken up residence elsewhere!

At any rate, he had ample time to decide his course. Right now, he wanted a good glass of brandy within the deserted confines of his club. This huge, empty house held too many echoes of the past.

His club was not quite deserted, he noted with pleasant surprise. One familiar face sat at the far side of the room.

"Mind if I join you?" Penhurst asked, a broad grin cheering his face.

"Elliston!" The man in the chair rose to his feet, hand outstretched. "What are you doing in town?"

"Taking care of a few business matters," Penhurst explained as he took his seat. "You're the last person I expected to find here this time of year."

Seb Cole, younger brother of the Earl of Wexford, laughed. "I must confess I am escaping the family gathering at Lawton. Pressing business in the city, you know, must toddle off. Richard knows I cannot abide his in-laws, so he finds it a relief to have me gone. Never has to hold his breath worrying if there will be a dustup."

Penhurst poured himself a glass from the decanter and stretched out comfortably in the chair.

"Saw Harley yesterday," he offered.

Seb raised a brow. "Intentionally?"

Penhurst nodded. "To my chagrin, I discover I am bored, now that the Continent has settled back into normality. I fear I am not cut out for the life as a bucolic country squire." He directed a pointed glance at his friend.

"Still crave the excitement, eh? I should bring you home with me. Perhaps you could arrange some sort of truce between myself and my sister-in-law. We could certainly use someone with your skill to negotiate a settlement."

Penhurst smirked. Seb was known to be as thick as an inkleweaver with his elder brother, but his antipathy toward his sister-in-law was well-known. The feeling was totally mutual and the source of much consternatiaon to London's hostesses, who had to be particularly careful when arranging the seating at their dinners.

"I wouldn't mind going abroad again," Penhurst confessed.

Seb gave him a searching look. "Running away?"

Had any other man suggested it, Penhurst would have heatedly denied such an accusation. But Seb had been his closest friend ever since they were students at Eton. Even when their respective lives separated them, they kept in close contact by post. Seb had agonized with Penhurst over the unpleasantness of the Crim. Con. trial. He knew, perhaps even better than

Penhurst himself, just how much that whole episode had cost him. He was also the only person, apart from the Teels, who knew the whole story about Katherine.

"There's nothing to run from," Penhurst shrugged. "Perhaps it is running toward. I miss the activity. And the routine. You cannot imagine what a disordered mess Talcott has become since I returned. Katherine did not take the move well, I am being criticized on every side for the way I deal with her and . . ."

"And?"

"Teel's widow lives about two miles away."

"Good God. Had you no idea?"

Penhurst shook his head. "The thought never occurred to me. I imagined she would be in town, or remarried and living elsewhere. What's worse, she has taken an inordinate interest in the girl."

"Does she know?"

"I think anyone in the neighborhood with eyes would know," Penhurst admitted with a rueful grimace. "But I did acknowledge it to her. It seemed pointless to lie; she was bound to discover the truth sooner or later. But it made me realize what a difficult time Katherine may face in the future. I thought if we both went abroad, by the time we came back everyone will have forgotten—or no longer care."

His friend took a long swallow of the amber liquid. "I doubt anyone outside the families would care much these days, anyway. Too many new scandals have replaced it. Might be a bit awkward when she gets married—you are honor bound to disclose the situation to anyone who wants her hand."

"I had never even thought of that," Penhurst groaned.

"Well, it is years away," Seb said with forced cheerfulness. "Nothing to worry about now."

"Encouraging thought," said Penhurst morosely.

" 'Course, if you did take her to the Continent, they are more understanding about that sort of thing. Might not be a bad idea after all."

"Any posts opening up?"

Seb frowned in concentration. "Well, this is very much rumor, mind you, but there is some talk about Brompton being recalled. Seems he is paying too much attention to a certain native lady, whose husband—a count—has begun complaining to his prince. Brompton's wife is said to be furious and threatening to come home without him. You know how Castlereagh detests scandals."

"Well I do," Penhurst agreed. "He gave me a mild set-down about Lea, as if there had been anything I could have done about *that* situation."

"I can drop a few words in some ears if you think you might be interested," Seb volunteered.

Penhurst nodded. "I would appreciate that."

"Any plans for the evening?"

Penhurst shook his head. "There seems to be a dearth of dinner parties in town at the moment."

"Thank God." Seb motioned for the waiter to bring them another bottle. "Then you will not have any objections to dining with me. I'll give you tips about dealing with sniveling brats—from my vast experience with my nieces and nephews—and you can tell me how to handle the tartar."

"Agreed," said Penhurst with a grin.

Spending most of the day with Kate became a part of Sophrina's daily routine. She had always been a doting aunt to her nieces and nephews, but as she had pointed out to the dowager, the older children were growing too busy with their own pursuits to spend very many lazy summer afternoons with their aunt. Besides, with attentive parents, an adoring grandmother, and ample siblings, they simply did not *need* her like Kate did. If Sophrina needed Kate as well, it was something she did not dwell upon at length. They whiled away many an afternoon playing boisterous parlor games, often enlistening Sophrina's maid as an extra player.

There was no inkling of when Penhurst would return, and as the days passed, Sophrina ceased to even think of him. This suited her perfectly, for she could not dismiss the slight discomfort she always felt when he came to mind. Perhaps it was the awkward connection between their respective spouses that made an easy friendship difficult. Or perhaps it was Penhurst's nature. He did not strike Sophrina as a man who was easy to know.

"Rina?"

"Yes, Kate?" They were snuggled on the sofa at Talcott, Kate listening to Sophrina read.

"Can I come live at your house?"

Sophrina wished Kate could. Giving the girl in her lap an affectionate squeeze, she shook her head. "Your place is here at Talcott, with your papa."

"But he is never here," Kate pointed out.

"Your papa is a very busy man and he has to go to town to take care of his business on occasion. But this is his home, and he will always return here."

"I know! You could come live here, too. Then you would always be here to play with."

"That would not be possible, Kate." Sophrina suppressed a smile. "I need to have my own house. Besides, if I lived here, you would never be able to visit me, and think how much fun that is. I'd be plain, boring old Sophrina in no time if you saw me constantly."

Kate giggled. "Is my papa coming home soon?"

"I do not know, Kate. Have you asked Mrs. Gooch? She is more likely to have heard."

Kate shook her head. "I do not mind, really, that he is not here. You are more fun."

"I am certain your papa is fun, too, Kate. Sometimes, when people grow up, they forget what it was like to be a child and how to play. You will need to remind him."

"You mean Papa would go hoop rolling with me?"

"I daresay he would," Sophrina replied, secretly amused at the thought of the haughty Lord Penhurst rolling a hoop. Actually she held little hope that Penhurst would ever unbend enough to play with Kate, but it was worth the attempt to have the girl encourage him. They both might be pleasantly surprised, but she doubted it.

Sophrina was mildly pleased to hear Kate asking about Penhurst. Perhaps he had done something to make amends for the abrupt way he had removed Kate from her old home and brought her to Talcott. Despite her reservations about Penhurst's fitness for fatherhood, Sophrina hoped he and Kate would grow close. It was encouraging that she showed an interest in his return. It meant she was learning to accept him. Sophrina hoped that these tentative threads of filial respect would be nurtured and furthered by Penhurst.

She wondered again at Penhurst's continued absence. She daily expected to arrive at Talcott and find him in residence again, but he still had not returned. For Kate's sake, she hoped he would make an appearance soon. As far as Sophrina was concerned, Penhurst could stay away forever. She had no doubts he would throw a damper on her activities with his daughter.

Chapter 5

Kate tightly grasped Sophrina's hand as they made their way from the stables to the house. Sophrina smiled at how well the two cousins had played together this morning. Both girls enjoyed the almost daily visits to Charlton. Perhaps one day Susan could come to Talcott . . .

Sophrina's eyes widened in alarm as she watched Penhurst swiftly crossing the lawn toward them. That which she had dreaded was now going to be acted out. Thank God, she and Kate had come home early from Charlton today. Sophrina did not even want to think about the scene that would have ensued had Penhurst been forced to collect his daughter there.

From the taut lines of his body and his lengthy stride, Sophrina knew he was angry. Every instinct in her body cried "flee," but she knew she could not. If nothing else, she had to protect Kate from his wrath.

"Papa, Papa," shouted Kate, jumping up and down in uncontrolled enthusiasm. "Wait until you see what I have!"

"And what is it that you have, Katherine?"

His tone was warm, but the icy look he flashed Sophrina chilled her thoroughly. His barely restrained anger was clearly in evidence.

"A kitten!" Kate pulled the basket from Sophrina's hand and lifted back the lid. "See? Isn't she beautiful?" Reaching inside, she pulled out the fuzzy creature and thrust it into her father's unprepared hands.

Sophrina smothered a nervous laugh as Penhurst fumbled with the squirming ball of fur. He shot her another black look.

"Edward and Susan gave her to me!" Kate prattled. "They let me have first pick 'cause they both already have kittens and 'Bella is too little to have one of her own.'"

"I think the kitten would rather be back in the basket, Kate," Sophrina suggested, cutting off the excited explanation. "Remember, she is in a new place and might become easily frightened."

Kate yanked the kitten out of Penhurst's hands.

"Ow!" he yelled involuntarily, eyeing the sharp scratches across his hand with dismay.

"Oh, did she scratch you?" Kate was all solicitous concern. Holding the kitten up to her face, she scolded her sternly. "Naughty kitty. You are not to hurt Papa like that."

Sophrina struggled to contain her amusement, clinging to the last vestiges of decorum by firmly biting down on her lower lip.

"Take that infernal creature away," Penhurst thundered.

Kate stepped back at her father's angry words, confusion and disappointment flitting across her face. Sophrina deftly took the kitten from her hands and returned it to the safety of the basket.

"Run along and take the cat to the kitchen," she advised. "Tell cook you want a saucer of milk."

Kate cast one last, doubtful look at Penhurst then hastily walked toward the house, the basket banging awkwardly against her legs.

Sophrina turned to face Penhurst.

"I think," he said icily, "we have some matters to discuss. If you will permit me to escort you into the house where we can be private?"

Sophrina did not fear Penhurst in the least, for he could do naught to her, but she did fear for Kate and their friendship. She resolved to keep her words under control, accept the tongue-lashing Penhurst was certain to give her, then do what she could to restore the damage.

Penhurst ushered her without ceremony into the small study. It was the one room at Talcott where Sophrina had never set foot. Lea had always dismissed it airily as "Penhurst's retreat" and showed no inclination to display it to guests.

Sophrina looked about with unchecked curiosity. It was a very masculine chamber. The rest of the house featured Lea's impeccable taste in decoration, but it was obvious she had not had a hand in this room. Dark wainscoting melded with the deep green silk stretched across the walls, and the room would have been cloaked in gloom if not for the light cast by the bright, modern oil lamps. The furniture was upholstered in rich leather; Penhurst's desk was polished mahogany.

Penhurst gestured for Sophrina to be seated in one of the chairs flanking the fireplace. Disdaining the comfort of the matching twin, he rested his arm on the mantel, one booted foot braced against the fender. Sophrina saw it as a pose calculated to intimidate her. She met his gaze without flinching. She would show him she was made of sterner stuff.

"You may imagine my surprise, Lady Teel, when I arrived home earlier today and was informed that my daughter had been in your company since the early morning." His eyes narrowed. "Furthermore, I was told the situation was not at all unusual, that you and Katherine have been together for the better part of each day since I left for London. And it is your frequent practice to take her to Charlton."

Sophrina formed her face into a bland mask of attentive interest.

"Does that bother you, my lord?"

"Damn right, it bothers me," he exploded. "I had thought, Lady Teel, that I made myself perfectly clear about my desire to keep Katherine away from Charlton. Nothing can be served by opening old wounds."

"The only wounded people involved here are you and myself," she returned. "Kate is lonely in this huge barn of a house. At Charlton she has the opportunity to play with other children."

"I take it Edward, Susan, and Bella are her *cousins*?" His sarcasm bit deep.

"They are."

"What right do you have to contradict my wishes? You have no connection whatsoever with Katherine; she is not your responsibility."

Sophrina's thin control snapped. "Do you realize the kind

of life that poor child has led? Lea was a poor excuse for a mother, but I fail to see where you have been much of an improvement. Until I took her to visit her cousins, Kate had never, *ever,* played with another child in her life. That borders on the inhuman, my lord."

"I have done what I thought best," he retorted, anger coloring his face.

"Well pardon me, my lord, but your best has been highly inadequate."

"And you presume, after such a short acquaintance, to know what is best for her?" He took a step toward her.

"I am certain, my lord, that I have spent more time with Kate in the last two weeks than you have during her entire lifetime."

His lips tightened.

Sophrina rose to her feet. "Children are not pieces of furniture, or books, to be locked away and brought out only on occasions for display. They are living, breathing creatures who need love and attention, just as we adults do."

"She has the nursery maid, and Mrs. Gooch to attend to her."

"They are servants. She needs a parent, a *father* to show her love and affection. Instead she has a stern stranger who either criticizes or ignores her *when* he is home at all."

"Why are you so determined to take charge of Katherine's life?"

"Kate is as much my child as yours."

He blanched at her words, then, as his anger rose, his color returned. "I hardly agree. I seem to recall you were not the one who took in your husband's bastard child. Let's see . . . Kate would have been almost two months old at the time of your marriage. Perhaps I should have sent her to you as a wedding gift."

"It is not her fault, what Lea and William did. Blame yourself, or blame me, for their actions, but not Kate. She is the only innocent one of us all."

"What is your all-consuming interest in the child?" he persisted. "Are you so devoid of entertainment here in the country that you need amuse yourself with a four-year-old?"

"I like children," she said bluntly.

"Have one of your own."

"With my husband dead, that is not a very likely occurrence," Sophrina retorted.

"You could find another husband easily enough," he sneered. "Then you can have as many brats as you like."

"That may not be possible," she said quietly, turning away. "My only pregnancy ended in a miscarriage."

Oh God, he had gone too far again. How did this woman goad him into forgetting every rule of diplomacy? "I am sorry, Lady Teel," he said stiffly. "I had not intended to bring up a painful subject."

She slowly turned to face him again. "Kate needs someone who cares for her in a motherly way, my lord." Sophrina tried to keep the anger from her voice. She had already destroyed whatever chance she had of helping Kate, but she was determined to show Penhurst the path he must take. "I am not attempting to be her mother, nor would I wish that role. But since you are so busy, I thought it would not be wrong of me to give her some of the attention she craves."

Penhurst ran his hand through his thick, black hair in frustration. How did this slip of a woman manage to make him feel like a bumbling fool every time they spoke? He had intended to upbraid her for disobeying his wishes regarding Katherine, and now she had twisted things to the point where he was the guilty one. He had crossed swords with some of the wiliest diplomats in Europe. How could this diminutive widow continued to best him?

"I am not an experienced parent," he admitted, bitterly, reluctantly. "There is some wisdom in what you say."

"I realize that raising a child is a formidable task, my lord. Allow me to offer my assistance." Sophrina formed her mouth into a conciliatory smile. "Kate needs a great deal of attention right now, while she adjusts to her new home. I have the time to spend with her. And I truly do enjoy her company."

"I shall think on it, Lady Teel. What I will ask of you now, is that you respect my decision, whatever it may be."

"I can do naught else," Sophrina replied, fervently praying he would decide in her favor. Kate needed her; it was obtuse of Penhurst not to see that. But she would not grovel before him.

"Allow me some time to consider the matter," he said, stepping away from the mantel to indicate the interview was at an end.

Sophrina nodded and walked toward the door. Grasping the handle, she turned briefly to face him again.

"May Kate keep her kitten?"

Penhurst gave her an incredulous look. What did the kitten have to do with anything? "Yes, she can keep the damned kitten!"

"Thank you, my lord," said Sophrina with a mischievous smile and she slipped out into the hall.

Sophrina fled to the Dower House after her interview with Penhurst. She paced the floor of the dowager's drawing room, her hands waving about in agitation.

"You would not believe the arrogance of that man," Sophrina complained to Louisa. "He is totally unfit to be a parent. He has no sense whatsoever of how to raise a child."

"And you do?" Louisa's mouth curved into a quizzical smile.

"I certainly would do a better job than Penhurst." Sophrina turned indignantly to her mother-in-law. "He still has not replaced Kate's old nurse with a new one or hired a governess. There is only a nursery maid to keep an eye on her. I thank the Lord that the housekeeping staff likes Kate, for they watch over her as much as they can manage."

"Sophrina, Kate is his daughter."

"Piffle." She waved a dismissive hand. "She is no more his daughter than she is mine. You have a stranger claim to her than Penhurst does. He pretends he is making such a noble sacrifice, taking William's child into his house, then he treats her worse than a dog."

"Now dear, you are exaggerating. She is adequately cared for."

"But she needs more than just a roof over her head," Sophrina protested. "You saw how delighted she was to play with the children. Can you imagine being four years old and never having played with another child? It is almost criminal."

"You cannot blame Penhurst for everything. Lea must accept some of the blame."

"The woman should not have been allowed to bear a child,"

Sophrina said with disgust. "William may have been unsuited to marriage, but at least he had the makings of a good father. I think he would be appalled by Kate's situation."

"Still, Sophrina, there is little you can do to remedy the matter, unless Penhurst agrees. And it seems you have been going about it all wrong, ignoring his strictures. I warned you."

"He did not absolutely forbid me to bring Kate to Charlton." Sophrina defended her disobedience. "He merely said he did not think it was a good idea."

"A sentiment I concurred with, as you will recall." The dowager sighed. "Sophrina, I know that your marriage to my son was a disaster. I grieve daily for that failure. However, I cannot help but think you will never be content until you have a doting husband at your side and a houseful of children to pamper and spoil."

Sophrina scowled. "That will do nothing to solve Kate's problem," she reminded the dowager.

"Neither will angering Penhurst. You are going to have to show some forbearance on this, my dear. You rushed your fences and took a tumble."

"And is it not recommended that one immediately climb back into the saddle after a fall?"

"Not if the hunt has passed you by." Louisa smiled fondly. "Be patient. Penhurst will very likely come around to your manner of thinking. But he has to do it in his own way and his own time. Men like to think they are in charge."

"Even if he finally accepts my views?" Sophrina's eyes twinkled with merriment.

"Exactly. As long as he thinks it is his idea, he will be content."

Penhurst was determined to show Lady Teel that he did not need her help in dealing with Katherine. Certainly he could handle a four-year-old girl without outside interference. How difficult could it be to play a few games and listen to childish prattle? He set his plan in motion the following morning, sending for the girl right after breakfast.

"You may come in, Katherine." Penhurst nodded toward the chair. Noting the solemn look in the girl's eyes, he waited until she was seated. "I know I have been very busy of late, and my trip to London took me away longer than I planned. I thought that perhaps we could spend some time together this morning? You can show me some of the games you have been playing with Lady Teel.''

The expression on Kate's face was wary.

''We could play Faces,'' she offered doubtfully.

''That sounds like a capital idea,'' uttered Penhurst with false enthusiasm. ''You may explain the game to me.''

''I will get the cards,'' said Kate, slipping off her chair and dashing out the door.

For a moment Penhurst wondered if this plan of his was folly. But no, he would show Lady Teel, or anyone else for that matter, that he was a competent father, capable of dealing with Katherine on his own. It was preposterous to think that he was unable to effectively handle a slip of a child.

''These are the cards,'' Kate announced upon her return, handing them to Penhurst.

''How is the game played?'' he asked.

''You put all the cards out on the table and then make faces out of them,'' Kate explained.

''That sounds easy enough,'' said Penhurst and began laying out the cards in neat, orderly rows. ''Would you like to go first?''

Kate nodded and picked out a card displaying only a chin. From the arranged cards, she pulled out a nose and eyes, and then a forehead. Placing them against one another, she looked to Penhurst with a look of triumph as she presented her first face.

''That is very interesting, Katherine,'' said Penhurst. ''But I do not think you have it quite right. Are you certain that is the proper nose to go with that chin?''

Kate looked at him with puzzlement. ''Does it have to match?''

''All things must match,'' Penhurst said gently, reaching for the proper piece and substituting it for Kate's choice. ''Now, doesn't that look better?''

''It is not supposed to look better,'' Kate complained. ''My nose was funnier.''

''But it was not the right nose,'' Penhurst persisted.

''Rina does not care which nose I use,'' Kate pouted.

''I cannot help it if Lady Teel does not play according to the rules," Penhurst muttered. "The object, Katherine, is to put the cut-up faces back together. The three pieces make up a 'set.' And I am certain that the person who has the most sets at the end of the game wins."

"That is not how Rina does it." Kate scowled.

"Then Lady Teel is not playing the game correctly," Penhurst reiterated, holding back his irritation. "Now, here is another chin. Try to find the nose that matches."

"I do not want to match the nose," Kate said petulantly. She grabbed an obviously unmatching piece. "I want to use this nose."

"You cannot," said Penhurst sternly.

Kate threw the piece down onto the table. "Then I do not want to play," she said, crossing her arms determinedly across her chest.

"Fine!" Penhurst stood up. "You can go back to the nursery then."

Kate reached out to gather up her cards.

"Leave the cards here," Penhurst ordered. "You may not have them until you are willing to play with them properly."

Kate burst into tears. "I want my cards!"

"Stop it, Katherine," he ordered. "You are not a baby any longer; stop acting like one. I think you had best stay in your room for the rest of the day if this is how you are going to behave."

Kate scrambled off the chair. "I hate you!" she cried as she raced out of the room.

This was all Lady Teel's fault, Penhurst fumed, stifling his own childish urge to sweep those stupid cards onto the floor. Imagine allowing Katherine to make up her own rules to the game! How would the girl ever learn anything if she was taught in such a slapdash manner? The sooner she learned that every aspect of life had rules, and they must be obeyed, the better off she would be.

Yet the following morning, he was not so certain of his ability to impart that knowledge to Katherine. Waiting in the study while Mrs. Gooch summoned his daughter, Penhurst frowned. His attempts at companionable fatherhood the previous day had been a complete disaster. If he had looked deep within himself, that should not have surprised him, for he realized he would never have the easygoing nature that a child would desire. His friend Seb Cole was far better suited for fatherhood. But Penhurst had committed himself to that role when he acknowledged Katherine as his own, and he now must make the best of it.

Of course, it did not help in the least that Katherine had attached herself so quickly to Lady Teel. He would never be able to match her easy way with children. Yet for his sake—and Katherine's—he had to make the attempt. He had never before failed at anything he had set out to accomplish, and he was not prepared to accept defeat now.

Katherine entered the room timidly, if anything, more wary than she had been yesterday. Penhurst cringed at her subservient expression.

"I am sorry that we did not deal well together yesterday, Katherine," he began. "I was only endeavoring to teach you a much-needed lesson—that our lives are guided by rules, and they must be followed. You cannot indulge your personal whims. Do you understand that?"

"Yes, sir."

"There will be no more emotional outbursts like the one yesterday, is that clear?"

She nodded, eyes downcast.

Penhurst's expression softened. "I do not intend to be harsh, Katherine. However, you are old enough now to begin learning how to comport yourself. You are the daughter of an earl. It is a position of much honor, but it also brings great responsibility as well. I mean to ensure you are properly prepared."

Katherine looked at him silently, her hands folded neatly in her lap.

Penhurst sighed. His words meant nothing to a four-year-old. It was absurd to think she would understand her future obligations at this age. "That is all I had to say, Katherine. You may run along now."

He doubted he had accomplished much with that conversation. Had Lady Teel been right? Was he totally inadequate as a father? He turned glumly to the pile of mail that had accumulated during his absence, but he was not able to keep his thoughts from straying to Lady Teel. Her excessive interest in Katherine bordered on an obsession. What drove that woman so?

Of course! He had been a fool not to see it before. Naturally Lady Teel was enamored of Katherine—she was the child she had never had. He winced at remembering his blunt suggestion that she marry to have children, and her pained revelation of a miscarriage. The girl fathered by her dead husband was the closest thing Lady Teel would ever have to a child of her own unless she remarried.

But why was it *his* responsibility to indulge her maternal fantasies? Lord knows, he had not asked to become a father. Now he was stuck for life with a miniature version of the woman he despised, all because he had been too full of St. Clair pride to admit to the world he had been cuckolded. What a fool he was. And now he was to be pestered by the other member of this ill-fated foursome, who only wanted to hold onto the offspring of her dead husband. God, what a coil.

Scowling, Penhurst poured himself another cup of tea and wished he kept the brandy decanter in the breakfast room. He normally was not much of a drinker, but today he felt the need for the soothing solace of France's best. Scott's lines came to mind: "O, what a tangled web we weave, when first we practice to deceive." Lea and William had woven their web, and now he, Lady Teel, and Katherine were tangled up in the threads. He hoped there was a special torment in hell for his dead wife and Teel. Something akin to the torment their actions were putting the others through. Something with hot knives and scalding oils.

Embarrassed at the vehemence of his anger, Penhurst took another long sip of milk-laced tea to steady his mind. Whatever retribution the two faced, it would have no impact on his life. As he began to seriously examine the avenues open to him, he realized he had been neatly boxed into a corner. Lady Teel had effectively trapped him in as clever a plot as he had ever seen.

If he forbade any further contact with Katherine, he would be labeled the ogre by both his daughter and his neighbors. He uttered a rueful laugh. Lady Teel should have gone into the diplomatic service. For she had nicely tricked him into accepting her fait accompli. He shook his head in begrudging admiration. One must never underestimate the power of an Englishwoman bent on achieving her own ends. He raised his cup in a silent salute.

Well, if Lady Teel wanted to dote on her dead husband's daughter, let her. It would only be sheer spite to keep the two apart, and Penhurst prided himself on being above such childish actions. She had neatly bested him in this encounter and he would accept his defeat gracefully. But he would be damned if he did not watch her like a hawk from now on. She would not get the jump on him again.

Chapter 6

Sophrina anxiously awaited a response from Penhurst, fearful she had angered him beyond repair, but days went by with no word from Talcott. She seethed with frustration, toying with the idea of marching over to the house herself to demand an answer. Remembering the dowager's counsel of "patience," Sophrina resisted her impulse. To still her frantic energy, she filled page after page of her sketchbook, as she tromped about the neighborhood for hours each day, drawing images of everything in her path. She ruefully admitted most of her efforts were not very good, drawn with too much haste and little interest, but at least they occupied her time.

Returning from one of these sketching expeditions, she found the long-awaited note from Penhurst lying on the hall table. Eagerly she tore open the seal and scanned the contents.

Luncheon! What did that mean? Sophrina decided it must be a favorable response, for she could not imagine him politely offering food to a guest and then telling her she would not be welcome at the house again. She breathed a deep sigh of relief. She had missed Kate terribly these last few days.

Sophrina could not rid her mind of her disheveled appearance at that first meeting with Penhurst, and she had looked little better the last time they exchanged words. Determined to erase that image from his brain, Sophrina dressed with great care the following day in a new summer frock of pale primrose muslin, with a white lutestring spencer and a flower-bedecked bonnet. She might be only a country widow of moderate means, but she would show him she was the equal in dress to a London lady.

In the back of her mind remained the nagging feeling that he always compared her to Lea. It was a futile effort to compete, she knew. William had made the same comparison and found his wife wanting; Penhurst would certainly have the same response. But she was female enough not to avoid the temptation to try.

Sophrina had just stepped across the threshold of Talcott when Kate bounded down the long, formal stairway into the marble-tiled entry hall.

"Rina, Rina!" she cried in joy, flinging herself into Sophrina's welcoming arms.

"Katherine!" Penhurst's voice was stern but not angry.

Kate immediately released her frantic hold on Sophrina as Penhurst reached the bottom of the stairs.

"I should like you to show Lady Teel a more ladylike welcome," he said.

Kate stepped back a pace and executed a wobbly curtsy. "Good day, Lady Teel."

"Good day, Lady Kate. My lord." Sophrina strove to keep her face solemn.

"Papa says I may eat with you today." Kate grabbed Sophrina's hand, leading her toward the door. "And we are going to sit at the big table in the dining room."

"I am greatly honored," Sophrina replied, casting a quick glance at Penhurst. She thought his lips twitched in a hint of a smile.

"You have to see my kitten after lunch. She is bigger already. Cook says it is all the milk."

"What have you named her?"

"Twinkle."

"That is a very good name for a cat," Sophrina agreed. She caught the look of amusement on Penhurst's face.

Sophrina listened with delight to Kate's animated conversation during lunch, suspecting even Penhurst appreciated the girl's enthusiastic chatter. At least he never offered a word of criticism, as was his usual wont. Following the meal, Kate dragged Sophrina down to the kitchen to see the kitten, then Penhurst gently but firmly detached his guest from Kate's hold, sending her out in the garden to play with the animal.

"If you do not mind, Lady Teel, I would like to have a word with you. I promise I shall not keep you overlong."

Sophrina nodded. He had not yet said a word about her relationship with Kate. This was obviously to be the topic of conversation. Steeling herself with a deep breath, she walked with him down the hall to his study. A shiver of apprehension raced up her spine. What if he did plan to forbid her to see Kate again? Did he resent the close connection between the two?

She would never willingly do anything to alienate Kate from her papa, but with a twinge of guilt, Sophrina admitted she had shamelessly wormed her way into Kate's affections. Penhurst had seemed so indifferent to the child, and she was such a winsome creature . . . But perhaps, in Penhurst's view, Sophrina had gone too far, and he was going to urge a retreat to more formal ties.

Sophrina shook her head to rid herself of such worrisome thoughts. There was no point in getting exercised over something that might not even be on the earl's mind. Firmly pushing her concerns aside, Sophrina followed him into the study.

"Would you like a glass of sherry, Lady Teel? Or brandy?"

"Sherry would be fine, thank you," replied Sophrina, taking her seat in one of the richly upholstered chairs he indicated. She took a breath. "I would prefer that you not call me Lady Teel, my lord. Apart from the confusion arising from three women in the neighborhood holding that title, it is not a name I associate with pleasant times."

"What do you rather I called you?" He handed her the wine and took his own chair, brandy in hand.

"Sophrina would suffice in this situation."

"Then I must insist you call me Elliston instead of 'my lord.' "

"I believe I can manage that." She flashed him a conciliatory smile.

"Good. Now, I did not mean to attach such an air of mystery to this talk," he said, with a hint of a apology. "It is only that I wished to speak of Katherine, and as you are the one most well acquainted with her situation, I thought you could give me some advice."

"I shall do my best."

"I fear I was overhasty in my judgment last week." He shifted uneasily in his chair. "It has become quite clear that Katherine has grown attached to you. It would please me, and cause her untold delight, if you would resume your visits with her."

"I would be more than pleased to spend time with Kate, my—Elliston." She noted the marked look of relief that crossed his face. She stifled her smile of triumph. One must always remain gracious in victory.

"It is obvious, due to your infinitely patient instruction, that Katherine is ready for a formal course of education. I had not realized that girls were ready to begin their schooling at such a young age, else I would have looked into the matter earlier."

"We are, as a sex, capable of picking up at least the rudiments of knowledge at a tender age," Sophrina said evenly.

"Touché. I never had any sisters, so I am unaware of how girls are raised. And from what I could tell, my wife was not taught anything beyond flirting, dancing, and spending money."

"Ah, but think how capably she learned her lessons. Had she been instructed in matters of more substance, she might have learned them also."

"I suppose you think I should have Katherine learn Latin and Greek?"

"Not unless she expresses a desire to. Knowledge forced is knowledge resented." Sophrina paused. "I am needling you, to be sure, Elliston, but I do agree with your point. Kate is at the stage where she needs a governess who can give her formal lessons."

"How, exactly, does one go about finding a governess?" He leaned forward in his chair.

"That is an odd question to put to a woman who has no children!" Sophrina laughed lightly. "I suggest you would do better to ask my sister-in-law, or Lady Groves."

"I had thought, since you are so much better acquainted with Kate . . ."

Sophrina shook her head at his pleading expression. "I can see that in addition to Latin and Greek, you men should be taught something about household management and child rearing as well. As near as I know, governesses are found through word-of-mouth, in the adverts, or through the London employment agencies."

"How shall I know if the person is competent?"

"You must interview them. Ask for their references to see if their previous employers were satisfied with their services. Ask them what they would teach a four-year-old girl. And try to get a measure of them as people. In my experience, governesses are either angels or horrid women who hate children."

"Why would anyone become a governess if they hated children?" His expression reflected his puzzlement.

"What other avenue of employment is open to gently bred women?" Sophrina shook her head in sympathy. "Goodness, as much as I love children myself, I know I should be a bit resentful if I knew I was dependent upon them for my bread and butter. I think you should offer a handsome salary, to still that resentment."

Penhurst sighed. "Seems a deucedly complicated procedure just to find someone to teach Katherine her ABC's."

Sophrina laughed. "I am sure you thought children managed themselves. But, unfortunately, they do not, and it is your job as her parent to oversee the situation."

He gave her a searching look. "You think me a poor father, don't you?"

"No," Sophrina replied, surprised at his obvious desire for her approval. "I do not think anyone can deny you are in a very awkward situation. I admire you for accepting Kate as your own. As you grow more confident in dealing with her, I think you will do marvelously as a father."

"How should I deal with Katherine? I do not think she likes me very well."

"That is because she hardly knows you. Remember, she had a difficult time. Kate adored Lea, and her departure and death were a blow. Then you were away when she very much needed someone else to latch on to. She chose her nurse, only to have her sent away as well."

"I sound like some kind of monster." Penhurst ran a hand through his thick hair. "I only tried to do the right thing. Katherine's nurse was perpetuating Lea's memory, building her into an angel who bore no relation to the real woman."

Sophrina agreed that Lea was no angel. A more unfit mother she could not imagine. She felt an onrush of sympathy for Penhurst. He honestly wanted to do well.

"I think a governess would be a marvelous thing for Kate. She is a very bright child. I think with some care and attention she would blossom. As she grows more confident, I think she will be more open to you also."

"Do you think she would like to have her dinner downstairs with me on occasion?" He hesitantly voiced the idea.

"I think that would be a wonderful plan." Sophrina flashed him a broad smile. "You could make it a very special evening. Kate would like that."

"I insist that you join us. I am leaving for London again in a day, but perhaps after I return . . . ?"

"I would be delighted to join you and Kate for dinner." Sophrina thought for a moment, and added, "If you would like, I could take charge of Kate until you find a governess for her."

"I cannot ask you to do that."

"You did not ask, I offered. Truly, it would pose no difficulties. I can easily walk over in the morning. We can continue our little lessons and have fun."

"It is a pity you do not have any children of your own." She paled. "I have often thought it so."

"I am sorry, Sophrina." He had meant it as a compliment, but instead caused her pain. "That was impertinent. I would be most grateful for your assistance with Katherine. I shall take all your advice to heart, and if I am lucky, I can return from London with a governess who will suit your exacting standards."

"Kate deserves the best." She looked down at her hands, self-conscious at her obvious affection for the girl.

"I had thought to look for some toy for Katherine while I was in London. Do you think she would like that?"

Sophrina suddenly realized how unsure he was in his role of father. Despite his veneer of arrogance and assurance, when it came to Kate, he was as uncertain as any first-time father.

And in a rush of empathy, she viewed Elliston St. Clair in a more sympathetic light.

"I am certain Kate would."

"What should I purchase?"

Sophrina hid a smile. He agonized over the simplest matters!

"There is so little in the nursery, anything would be welcome. What toys did you enjoy as a child?"

"I hardly think . . ." He broke into a boyish smile. "Toy soldiers. I was mad for them, as I recall. But hardly the thing for a girl."

"I think a doll would be an appropriate choice."

He nodded. "Now, I have certainly taken up enough of your time for one day, Lady—Sophrina. I will rest easier in London, knowing that you will be watching over Katherine while I am gone."

"Kate," suggested Sophrina softly. "Save 'Katherine' for the day when she lengthens her skirts and pins her hair atop her head."

He shook his head ruefully. "As you can see, I have not a clue how to go on with her. You must not hesitate to make suggestions."

"I think all your new ideas are quite good. Having her join you for dinner and bringing her a present are admirable steps."

Penhurst escorted Sophrina to the garden, where she said her good-byes to Kate and promised to come again in the morning.

As she reviewed that most illuminating conversation in her mind during the carriage ride home, Sophrina was filled with a rush of sympathy for Penhurst. He truly wanted to do his best. A few more gentle nudges from her and he would be well on the road to becoming a model father for Kate. She doubted he would ever be the type to romp on the floor with little ones, as Bertram had been known to do, but she was certain he would at least capture Kate's affection.

She wondered about Penhurst's childhood. He had stated he had no sisters; had there been any brothers? If he was the only child, it would do much to explain his lack of knowledge about children. With five siblings of her own, she certainly had enough experience. It was the one part of her childhood she would not trade for anything.

Chuckling, Sophrina recalled the dowager's counsel. Penhurst had not only adopted Sophrina's plan, but now looked to her for guidance on how to go along in the future. And it had been her deliberate disobedience that had spurred him into this new outlook. That was certainly counter to Louisa's advice, but Sophrina held to her tactic. Had not Wellington himself espoused the doctrine of attack? She had attacked and achieved her goal quite nicely.

A broad grin lit her face. Now that she had free access to Kate, there was no limit to the things they could do. Her mind began spinning lengthy plans as the carriage gently rolled toward home.

Kate looked at Penhurst doubtfully.

"I may eat in the dining room with you?"

"That is what I said." She did not look nearly as enthused as Sophrina had predicted. Was this whole idea a mistake?

"It is not very entertaining for me to eat alone," he explained, hoping to coax some enthusiasm out of her. "I had hoped you would keep me company."

"All right."

Kate was ushered into the drawing room at half past six, dressed in the blue gown she had worn to Sophrina's.

"That is a pretty dress, Kate." Penhurst smiled warmly.

She raised her eyes in surprise.

"What should you say when you recieve a compliment?"

"Thank you, Papa."

"What did you do this afternoon?"

"I played in the garden. Rina has been teaching me the names of all the flowers and . . ."

"And?"

"Is Rina going to come back?"

"Not tonight. She will come in the morning, remember? I have to go to London again tomorrow, and she promised she would look in on you every day while I am gone." That news brought a smile to her face, at least. He cleared his throat. "Is there anything you should like me to bring you from London?"

"Something pretty for Rina."

Penhurst let out a long breath. "What do you think Sophrina would like?"

"Maybe a ribbon. Or . . . or a pin. Susan's mama has the prettiest pin. That is what I would like for Sophrina."

And the current Lady Teel's pin probably came from Rundell and Bridge, Penhurst thought ruefully. "What did it look like?"

"It was all pretty with sparkly stones."

"What color stones?"

Kate wrinkled her brow in concentration. "They were red-and-white ones."

Penhurst thought quickly. There were probably several pins among his mother's jewels, lying in the vault in London. Lea had not dared to take any of them with her when she departed. Perhaps there would be something that would meet Kate's standards. It was her jewelry, really. With no wife to give it to, it would eventually pass to his daughter. Let her dispose of it as she wished.

"I shall do my best to find something similar," he promised. "Shall we go into dinner?" Kate was too short to take his arm, so he extended his hand. After a moment's hesitation, she reached out and took it in her own.

Chapter 7

While Penhurst dealt with his business in London, Sophrina spent most of her time with Kate. They played in the garden with the kitten, Sophrina teaching Kate the names of the flowers while they romped. During walks through the meadows, they recited the alphabet until Kate could sing out the letters with ease. Her ability to soak up knowledge constantly amazed Sophrina. She wished she had told Penhurst more about the type of governess to look for. Kate needed a woman who would spark her curiosity and fill that little head with more than the rudiments of a lady's education. Kate might have no need for Greek or Latin, but she deserved more than needlepoint and deportment.

One rainy afternoon, they enlisted the aid of several footmen and conducted an expedition into the cavernous attics of Talcott.

Sophrina suspected there might be a relic or two from Penhurst's childhood lurking in some dark corner—a rocking horse perhaps, that Kate would enjoy. And if not, it would be a capital adventure to retain Kate's interest on a day when they could not go outside.

Sophrina surveyed the dim and cobwebby attic. The boxes, trunks, shadowy-draped furniture, and odds and ends of discarded possessions had probably not seen daylight since the earl's grandfather's time. Kate was at first reluctant to enter, but after Sophrina held her hand, they both ventured forward. They spent the better part of an hour poking among the hidden treasures. One of the footmen did unearth a rocking horse—much the worse for wear. Sophrina hoped the estate carpenter might be able to repair the broken right rocker, and there was no shortage of horsehair to fill out the bedraggled mane and tail. She smiled as Kate inspected the ancient toy. Had Penhurst once galloped across the nursery floor on this beast?

They were winding up their search, having uncovered nothing more of interest to a small child, when Kate drew Sophrina over to a small trunk.

"Look, Rina, all sorts of tiny men."

Sophrina looked over Kate's shoulder. She had discovered Penhurst's collection of soldiers.

"These were your papa's, I believe," said Sophrina. "He played with them when he was a boy."

"Can I play with them?"

"I think we had better ask your papa first," Sophrina cautioned. "But we can take them out of the attic, in any case. What do you suppose he will say when we tell him we found them?"

"It will be like a present." Kate laughed and clapped her hands. "Just like the present Papa is bringing from London."

Sophrina smiled. That had been a wise tactic on Penhurst's part, telling Kate he would bring her a present. It encouraged her to look forward to his return.

The next day was as gray and rainy as the previous, so Sophrina and Kate were forced to amuse themselves inside again. They were both sprawled across the thick Aubusson carpet in the front drawing room, engrossed in an intense game of spillikins, when Penhurst arrived.

He stood in the doorway, watching Sophrina with amusement. He had never before seen a lady of his acquaintance romping on a drawing-room floor with a child, wispy ends of hair escaping her neat coiffure. She looked half her age, at least. Certainly not like a respectable widow. A faint smile flitted across his face.

"Am I interrupting?"

Sophrina froze in horror at his words and scrambled into an only slightly more dignified sitting position. Kate dropped her sticks and ran across the room to Penhurst. Grabbing his hand, she pulled him into the room.

"We were up in the attics yesterday and guess what we found?"

"I cannot imagine, unless it was enough cobwebs to stuff a mattress."

Kate giggled. "Wait until we show you."

"I am agog with curiosity," he replied. "But first, perhaps we can help Lady Teel from the floor. She looks deucedly uncomfortable." He smiled at the blush his teasing provoked.

"It is difficult to play spillikins anywhere else," she said, accepting his proferred hand and rising to her feet with as much dignity as she could muster.

"It must have been an exciting game," he murmured, tucking an errant lock of hair behind her ear. "I do not recall spillikins being the kind of game to destroy a lady's hairdo."

"It is sometimes difficult to maintain one's dignity when playing with a four-year-old," Sophrina retorted archly.

Penhurst laughed. "I am roasting you, Lady T—Sophrina. You look quite unexpectional. Now Kate, where is this surprise for me?"

She took him by the hand and led him across the room to the chest.

"My soldiers!" he exclaimed after lifting the lid. "You found these in the attic, did you?"

Kate nodded. "I wanted to play with them but Rina said I had to ask you first."

"I think we can arrange that," he said, pawing through the wooden box with the eagerness of a child. He pulled out one conical-hatted grenadier. "Look at this fellow! I had some royal battles with his comrades."

"What kind is this?" Kate held out a kilted Scot.

"My Highlanders," he exclaimed. "Now there's a fearsome group of soldiers for you, Kate."

Sophrina stood back, struggling to suppress her mirth as she watched Penhurst dig through the box with childish delight. She saw the stern Earl of Penhurst transformed into a small, likable boy again, filled with excitement and enthusiasm. What had transpired during the intervening twenty-odd years to change him? Mere age was not enough to have turned him into such a starched-up shadow of his former self. If it had been Lea's betrayal that altered him so, Sophrina wished she could wring that lady's neck.

Absorbed in memories and pleased by Kate's interest, Penhurst forgot about Sophrina's presence for several minutes. Not until he glanced up and saw her standing there, a wide grin upon her face, did he recall himself. With a sheepish smile, he put down the soldier he held.

"I fear we are ignoring Lady Teel," he whispered to Kate.

Sophrina laughed aloud at last. "That is quite all right, for it is time for me to be on my way."

"The surprise!" Kate cried.

"I almost forgot," he said. "You wait right here." In a moment he was back, an enormous paper-wrapped package in his arms. "This is for you, Kate."

"For me?"

"Open it so we can see what it is," Sophrina suggested.

Kate eagerly tore at the wrapping, opening the lid of the box and staring in transfixed wonder at what lay inside.

"What is it?" Sophrina asked.

"A doll," Kate breathed as she carefully lifted the elegantly garbed lady from her box. "She is so pretty!"

"Oh, she is," Sophrina said. She flashed Penhurst a congratulatory nod. "I do not think I have ever seen such a lovely doll."

"What is her name?" Kate asked.

"You can give her any name you wish," Penhurst said.

"Is she as beautiful as my mama?" Kate asked.

Penhurst sucked in his breath. "No, Kate," he said slowly. "I think your mama was even prettier."

"Then I shan't name her after Mama," Kate decided.

"You could name her Georgianna, or Caroline," Sophrina suggested helpfully. "Those are nice names."

"Where is Sophrina's present?" Kate demanded.

Penhurst looked embarrassed. "I thought you would like to wait and present it to Sophrina when you two are alone."

"I want to give it to her now."

"Very well," he said, taking a small packet out of his inner pocket. He turned apologetically to Sophrina. "Kate insisted you must have a present from London as well."

"How nice of you to think of me," Sophrina said to Kate as she untied the pink ribbon that surrounded the package. Folding back the tissue, she stared first in amazement and then in growing agitation at the garnet-and-diamond brooch that lay inside. She cast Penhurst a look of dismay. "My lord, I cannot . . ."

"Let me see." Kate pushed up next to Sophrina. "Oh, it is pretty. Just what I wanted."

Penhurst gave Sophrina an apologetic smile. "You would not wish to disappoint Kate, would you?"

It was pure blackmail, Sophrina thought. But he was right. To refuse would hurt Kate's feelings. She gave the girl a hug.

"It is the loveliest brooch I own, Kate. Thank you very much."

"And you can wear it Thursday evening for the dinner party I am having," Penhurst interjected.

"Do I get to be there?" Kate asked.

"Not this time, I am afraid. But you may come down before the meal and meet the guests. Now Kate, we have detained Sophrina long enough. I am sure she would like to go home to her cottage."

"Come back tomorrow and we can play with the soldiers."

"I am not certain Sophrina wishes to play with the soldiers, Kate. Not all ladies enjoy that."

"Of course I do," Sophrina said with feigned indignation. "I will have you know that Edward trusts me to handle his cavalry units."

"My apologies. We shall see how well you can handle the grenadiers then."

"Bye, Rina." Kate gave her a hug.

"I shall have one of the footmen escort you home," Penhurst announced when he and Sophrina entered the hall.

"That is not necessary," Sophrina replied. "I am quite capable of walking on my own. About the brooch . . . I cannot accept—"

"Consider the matter closed." His voice was firm. "It was my mother's, and so most rightly belongs to Kate now. If she wishes to give it to you, that is her privilege."

"It is far too valuable." She looked at him doubtfully.

"May I remind you, Lady Teel, that the will of a four-year-old is not to be thwarted." The teasing look in his eyes betrayed his mock-serious expression.

Sophrina nodded in acquiescence. "Accept my apologies for being such an ungracious recipient, my lord."

"Consider yourself forgiven."

It was absurd to feel nervous, Sophrina chided herself, unconsciously smoothing the skirt of her claret-hued gown as the coach rattled down the lane the following Thursday. It was not as if she never went out in society, even if it was only among the comfortable circle of her country neighbors. And certainly she and Penhurst were long past the stage where each interchange led to an argument. Why then, was she so unexpectedly anxious about this dinner party?

She knew all eyes would be on the two of them, looking for any sign of awkwardness. The situation was a gossip's delight, with the scorned wife and the cuckolded husband at the same party. Sophrina hoped that once curiosity was satisfied, it would turn into an unexceptional evening.

What preyed more heavily on her mind was the date. Penhurst could not have planned it, but the night of his party fell two years to the day that William had run away with Lea. How appropriate to spend such a landmark in Penhurst's company! There must be a poetic justice in it all.

As the carriage pulled up in front of the long, low stairway gracing the front of Talcott, Sophrina struggled to gather her thoughts. Resolving to enjoy the opportunity of fine conversation and food, she stepped from the coach with a light tread.

She was grateful to discover Bertram and Mary had already arrived. It had been tactful of Penhurst to invite them. They could not ignore the awkward connection between the two families; presenting an amiable front was the best way to dampen any neighborhood gossip. Sophrina crossed the drawing room to warmly greet her in-laws, exchanging kisses with Mary.

"I am so glad you are here," Sophrina said. "I feel absurdly nervous about this evening."

"That would not happen if you went about more," Mary pointed out. "I believe we shall forcibly drag you to London with us for the Little Season this year."

"Perhaps," Sophrina demurred. She had no desire to go over the old argument again. Mary was determined to see her sister-in-law wed again, and Sophrina equally determined not to.

The entry of Lord and Lady Ferris captured her attention. The two newcomers began to survey the drawing room with mild curiosity, but Sophrina saw the looks of amazement that crossed their faces when they espied her, Bertram, and Mary. Taking a deep breath, Sophrina stepped forward. Better to have it over with quickly.

"Good evening, Lady Ferris. My lord."

"How wonderful to see you, Sophrina dear. I own I had not expected to see you here—or Teel and Mary."

Sophrina smiled disarmingly. "It is silly to allow other people's actions to interfere with neighborly relations, don't you think?" She was grateful to have Penhurst appear at her side at that moment to add emphasis to her words.

"How kind of the three loveliest ladies in the county to grace my hall," he greeted, nodding at Ferris and Bertram.

"I was just telling Sophrina how pleased I am to see her," said Lady Ferris, casting a curious glance at Penhurst. "She had become so adept at declining invitations, I despaired of finding her anywhere but at Charlton."

"Lady Teel is a welcome guest at Talcott," Penhurst said, sharing a knowing smile with Sophrina. "She has been most kind in entertaining my daughter during my trips to London."

As if on cue, Mrs. Gooch ushered Kate into the drawing room.

Penhurst turned to Lady Ferris. "I do not believe you have met my daughter, Lady Katherine?"

Kate bobbled a creditable curtsy to Lady Ferris, then turned eagerly to Sophrina.

"You are wearing my present!" she exclaimed, eyeing the brooch pinned to Sophrina's gown. "Doesn't she look pretty, Papa?"

"Yes, Katherine, she certainly does." Penhurst's eyes gleamed appreciatively as he carefully noted all the details of Sophrina's appearance. She did look very fine in that ruby-hued gown, which revealed a great many curves he had not been aware of before, as well as two shapely, snowy white shoulders. A pleased smile stole over his face.

Sophrina blushed under his careful scrutiny. She could not help but notice how fine Penhurst himself looked in his tailored evening clothes, the black coat a near-perfect match to his hair. Formal clothing suited him very nicely indeed.

"We are embarrassing Sophrina," Penhurst whispered conspiratorially to Kate, secretly delighted at the heightened color in her guest's cheeks. "We should go around the room and compliment all the other ladies on how nice they look as well."

"I still think Rina is the prettiest," Kate whispered loudly as he drew her away.

"Well, Sophrina, at least one member of this household is certainly under your spell," said Lady Ferris archly.

"Little Kate is a treasure," Mary put in hastily. "She and Susan are becoming devoted friends." Her voice faced as the two women moved away.

Sophrina remained next to Bertram, watching the progress of Penhurst and Kate through the crowd as she sipped her punch. What exactly had Lady Ferris meant? That Penhurst viewed her with interest? The idea was ridiculous.

Yet watching him now, unobserved, she was forced to admit he was a very attractive man. He moved with grace and fluidity, an impression only enhanced by the skillful cut of his clothing. There would be no extra padding in those shoulders, nor in the calves. Those pantaloons were far too snug to cover anything but the man beneath.

Sophrina blushed an even deeper red as she realized the wayward train of her thoughts. Whatever was she thinking of? She had not thought about men in that way for years and to think such things now—about Penhurst? The man who less than a fortnight ago had been ready to wring her neck? If she had not known better, she would have sworn it was not ratafia she was drinking.

Yet perhaps it was an indication that she was ready to shed the cocoon of isolation with which she had surrounded herself in the country and return to a more social life. A life where she could view men as interesting and attractive creatures—even if she did not want one for a husband.

"That went rather well, I think." Penhurst handed Sophrina a glass of wine, then settled himself into one of the comfortable chairs arranged before the fire in the study. Now that the other guests had departed, he could take some minutes to relax and chat with Sophrina. His duties as host had left little time for private conversation with her.

"Did you think it would go otherwise, my lord?" She raised a brow.

"It has been an age since I entertained here at Talcott," he said, crossing one taut, muscular leg over his knee. "I have held countless soirees in foreign capitals, but I find entertaining one's neighbors a much more intimidating prospect."

"They were an amiable group," Sophrina said. "Once they swallowed their astonishment at finding our two families on speaking terms."

He laughed. "Lady Ferris could not have looked more surprised if the Prince of Wales had made an appearance."

"I own I have not been seen overmuch at the local entertainments."

"I am honored, then, that you chose to grace mine." And grace it she had. He realized he had spent far too much time arguing or discussing his daughter with Sophrina to have taken much notice of her in a physical sense. When she played with Kate, Sophrina had a girlish mien. But in that flowing dress, with her curled locks looking as if they might tumble from atop her head at any moment, he acknowledged that she was very much a woman. His lips curved in a appreciative smile.

Discomposed by his attentive glance, Sophrina took a sip of her wine.

"You will discover that it is a very friendly neighborhood. There are no feuds or neighborly hostilities to mar the peace."

"Has it been awkward for you here? With your situation . . ."

"Everyone was most kind here. Particularly when the news of William's death arrived." Yes, Sophrina thought, they had been kind. There had been few who criticized her refusal to wear mourning for the man who had deserted her.

Penhurst swirled the liquid in his glass, watching the light of the blazing candles reflecting in the ruby liquid. "I tried to dredge up some grief over Lea when I heard. But all I felt was an enormous sense of relief," he admitted. "It was a neat ending to a deucedly awkward situation."

He looked sharply at Sophrina, feeling a twinge of guilt at his callous revelation.

"I suspect you think me coldhearted," he began, but Sophrina objected.

"Not at all," she said smoothly. "I think I know exactly how you felt."

Their gazes met and held.

Penhurst shifted in his chair, swinging his other leg across his knee. "I have spent countless hours thinking about my marriage. Where I went wrong. What I could have done to salvage things." He shook his head. "I made so many mistakes."

"How long were you married?"

"Four years, all told." He uttered a long, drawn-out sigh. "I wonder now why I ever married her, although it seemed the thing to do at the time."

"Were you in love with her?"

"I was fond of her, certainly. She was beautiful and witty, and if she had the vanity to match, I did not observe it until it was too late. I was impressed by her demeanor. She was entertaining without the giddiness of most young ladies. I anticipated we would have the usual *ton* marriage—not a grand passion, but an amiable relationship. Unfortunately it was not enough for Lea. I accept the blame for driving her away."

"Do you not think you are being too harsh with yourself?" Sophrina asked. It astounded her to hear Penhurst voice such doubts.

"Lea was the type of woman who needed to be cosseted and petted. She thrived on adulation." He took a slow sip of claret. "As my government duties grew more onerous, as my absences became longer, she felt neglected. I did not have the time to constantly reassure her of her charms. And as my attention dwindled, her demands increased. It was a never-ending spiral. By the time I received my first assignment abroad, it was almost a relief to leave her at home."

"Was that when she and . . . and William . . . ?"

"I believe so." Penhurst shrugged. "If not Teel, there was another. In retrospect, I can see that. When I returned for a brief visit, she had changed. She was happier, content. I put the cause down to her relief at my return." Penhurst uttered a wry laugh. "How we salve our egos."

"Did you ever think to take her abroad with you?"

"I asked her, that first time I returned, but she demurred. I did not try to argue with her much; it was not the best location to take a young bride. I thought perhaps later, in a more hospitable capital . . . But by then it was out of the question."

He looked absently ahead, as if forgetting Sophrina's presence. "Mayhap if I had insisted . . . In a strange city, without the distractions of London, thrown into each other's company . . . we might have developed a comfortable marriage. But I was too busy with my own work to give any thought to her needs and wants. So she found someone else who would."

"I do not think you can place all the blame on yourself, Elliston," Sophrina said soothingly. "It sounds as if you and she were not well suited from the start. The marriage might have failed even if you had never set foot off this island."

"No, but I certainly hastened its demise with my absences." There was a trace of bitterness in his voice.

"I thought much the same about my marriage," Sophrina confessed. "That somehow I had failed William. That I was too unsophisticated, too naive to hold a man like him. Had I been wittier, prettier, patronized a better dressmaker, not lost the baby . . ."

"You, of all of us, are the blameless one," Penhurst protested. "Your marriage was a blatant sham to disguise Teel's affair with my wife. Believe me, she swore when Kate was born that it was all over, that your upcoming marriage was proof that the affair had ended."

"I wish I had known . . ."

"So do I. It would have spared you much hurt."

Sophrina was moved by the sympathetic expression in his eyes. He was capable of tender feelings, she thought, even though he did not often show them. That, and his obvious pain at his failed marriage, made him appear suddenly more human and eminently more likable than the cold, distant Penhurst she had seen previously.

"God, what a maudlin evening. I had not asked you to stay in order to listen to a recitation of my failings as a husband. I wanted to confess I have had little success in finding a governess for Kate."

"And have you looked very hard?" Sophrina meant to tease, and his sheepish expression delighted her.

"Not as hard as I ought, I know. I did interview three ladies in London. Two were the type you described—totally unfit to be with children. The other lady looked promising—but she refused to work in a bachelor household."

Sophrina clapped her hand over her mouth in dismay. "I had not thought about that problem," she confessed. "Perhaps you should stipulate an age requirement. Certainly a woman past fifty might consider herself free from your untoward advances."

"You underestimate the lecherousness of a bachelor, my dear lady." His dark eyes twinkled. "We are incapable of keeping our hands off anything in skirts."

Sophrina almost visibly started. Penhurst making a joke? This was a night for revelations.

"Perhaps my sister-in-law would be of assistance. She could supply you with a character reference that might satisfy the more wary."

He nodded in agreement. "Are you finding Kate a burden on your time? I realize my dillydallying is affecting you and—"

"I do not mind in the least. Kate and I are having a marvelous time together. You may take months to find a governess for all I care.''

"Perhaps I should hire you instead. I trust you feel safe in my presence, else you would not be here alone with me, sharing a glass of wine.''

Sophrina looked down to hide her blush. It was not precisely an irregular situation, for after all, she was a widow and did not need to be quite so mindful of her reputation. But her heightened color stemmed from her growing awareness of Penhurst as a man. It was rather shocking to discover she could once again find that sex attractive. Sophrina had thought that very human reaction was too deeply buried to resurface.

"By God, you are nervous.''

"No, no,'' she hastened to reply. "The thought had never crossed my mind, until you mentioned it.''

"Then forget it was uttered,'' he said abruptly.

Lord, he had not even given a thought to the impropriety of sitting here, alone, with Sophrina. He had only thought to snare her for a few moments of private conversation. Yet the scene had a decidedly domestic air to it, as if the lord and lady of the manor were discussing their own party. And with a pang he realized how much he enjoyed the experience.

As she watched him retreat into his customary distant manner, Sophrina felt a twinge of regret at the disappearance of the candid man she had glimpsed this evening. She liked the other Penhurst, who was a gracious host, a witty conversationalist, and an intriguing man. What would it take to bring that aspect of him into the open more often?

Penhurst spoke softly. "I am truly grateful for your attention to Kate. I realize it must be an awkward relationship for you.'' He paused at her bemused expression. "Being William's child, I mean. Her presence must be a painful reminder at times.''

Sophrina shook her head. "The fact that William is her father is a source of great joy to me.'' She looked down self-consciously. "I always thought it was some inadequacy on my part that drove William to Lea. When I discovered Kate was born before our wedding, it was like the lifting of an enormous weight. It had not been my fault the marriage failed.''

Penhurst was overwhelmed with sudden rage at William

Charlton, who had trampled so callously on the sensibilities of his young, innocent bride. Sophrina had deserved far more from her marriage.

Later, after Penhurst had seen Sophrina into the carriage, he returned to the study. He had enjoyed himself this evening. Not only at dinner, although it felt good to preside over a table consisting of more than himself and Kate. But it was the conversation with Sophrina he appreciated the most. Now that they were able to converse without shouting at one another, he found she was a pleasant companion. She had a sparkling wit and was, all in all, an attractive woman. It was not the heart-stopping beauty of Lea, whom he readily admitted was the loveliest woman he had ever known. Sophrina's beauty was more understated, but real nonetheless—particularly when set off by a dress such as she had worn tonight. He laughed aloud as he remembered her ragamuffin appearance at their first meeting. Quite a contrast to the silk and jewels she had worn this evening.

Apart from Seb Cole, she was the only person he knew who had any inkling of what he had gone through when his marriage collapsed. Indeed, her experience was a hundred times worse than his. For Lea's betrayal had only hurt his pride. Teel's unfaithfulness had shattered Sophrina's world. Amazingly she had not retreated behind a wall of bitterness and hate after such a revelation. He suspected she was a woman of untold strength, to have come through such an ordeal nearly unscathed.

It was unfortunate that their shared common experience was tied to the failure of their marriages. For no matter how amiable they found each other's company, there was always a slight awkwardness in their relationship. They could never forget the relationship between their two spouses. Would they ever be able to remove that barrier?

Chapter 8

"You are looking smug these days," Louisa remarked as she sat sipping tea in Sophrina's front parlor. "It is not becoming to gloat, you know."

Sophrina laughed. "I cannot help it. Penhurst has capitulated so thoroughly on the matter of Kate I cannot conceive how I was even concerned."

"The man is not a fool," Louisa countered. "He has the services of a governess without having to pay the wages."

"He is not taking advantage of me," Sophrina protested. "I asked to teach Kate her letters until he can hire a full-time governess. He is having a difficult time; apparently there are few qualified females willing to work in a bachelor household."

"Something that does not scare you off, I see."

Sophrina blushed, remembering her last conversation with the earl. "Really, Louisa, I hardly think I am in danger from Penhurst. I am certainly the last person he would consider for an untoward advance."

Louisa gently shrugged her shoulders. "Perhaps. Well, I must own I am curious. What is my granddaughter's latest accomplishment?"

A smile lit Sophrina's face. She knew she sounded more and more like Mary every day, trumpeting the successes of Kate as if she were her own daughter. But she did feel proud when Kate mastered each new task.

"She can write her name. And yesterday she counted all the way to one hundred."

"Admirable, admirable," nodded the dowager. "Charltons were always quick with their wits."

"I only hope Penhurst does not hire an incompetent woman who will only give her a 'young lady's' education. Kate has such an interest in everything around her I would hate to have that enthusiasm for learning crippled by some rigid martinet."

"Sophrina, I do not mean to throw a damper on your enthusiasm. I think Kate has done you a world of good. But I worry you are becoming too attached to her. Penhurst is by no means an aged man. Without an heir, it is very likely he may marry again one day. And his new wife will then be the one to oversee Kate.''

''I am certain I would weather the storm,'' Sophrina said with a conviction she did not feel. Goodness, she had never even thought about such an occurrence. The thought of turning Kate over to another woman sent a cold chill through her. A governess was one thing . . . but a stepmother?

''It will be a good thing for everyone concerned when Penhurst hires a proper governess. I will have Mary make some inquiries; perhaps she can unearth one.''

''I am sure Penhurst would be appreciative,'' Sophrina said and turned the conversation to other topics.

But Louisa's disturbing words stayed with Sophrina throughout the afternoon. Was she headed for misery, getting so involved with Kate? Perhaps it would be better for both of them if they did not spend quite so much time together.

Yet what else would either of them do with themselves? Penhurst was certainly taking a more active part in Kate's life, but a shared dinner a few times a week and an occasional battle with the toy soldiers did not take up an enormous amount of time. And truly, Sophrina did not think Penhurst was in any great hurry to remarry—if he ever did. She suspected he was as wary of that institution as she herself was. Kate still needed her, and until Penhurst procured a governess who could give the girl the attention she required, Sophrina would continue to do so. She would not allow Louisa's nebulous fears to cloud her judgment.

As the noise gradually penetrated Sophrina's sleep-fogged brain, it incorporated itself into the stange dream she was having. She was at Charlton, it was winter, and a loose shutter was banging against the side of the house. Sophrina wandered down all the corridors, checking in every room, but she could not locate the offending window covering.

''My lady, you must wake up.''

Why was Jenny here at Charlton? Had she found the banging shutter?

''My lady.''

Jenny's voice was too persistent. Sophrina attempted to listen.

"My lady, there is a man here from Talcott. They say Lady Kate is ill and you are wanted there."

Sophrina sat bolt upright, her eyes wide in alarm.

"What?"

"One of the footmen just rode over. Penhurst is sending the carriage behind him. You shall have just enough time to dress."

"Grab something out of the clothes press, Jenny." Sophrina was completely awake now. Gingerly stepping into the cool night air, she splashed water on her face to clear the last fuzzy cobwebs from her brain. With Jenny's assistance, she dressed in a matter of minutes and was downstairs, buttoning her warm pelisse, when the carriage arrived. Cook pressed a hastily prepared mug of tea into Sophrina's hands, and the coach set off for Talcott before she could even catch a breath.

The entry hall and several of the upper-floor windows were ablaze with light when Sophrina arrived, somewhat after one o'clock. The sleepy-eyed but correctly attired butler met her at the door, taking her wrap.

"My lord wishes you to meet him in Lady Katherine's room," he explained, unnecessarily, for Sophrina was already headed for the stairs.

Penhurst met her at the top.

"Thank God you are here! I heartily apologize for dragging you out of your bed, but she has been calling for you for the best part of an hour, we are still waiting on the doctor and I do not know what else to do."

The agitation in Penhurst's face stunned Sophrina. He was dressed, but his toilet had obviously been performed in great haste for he was in his shirtsleeves, without a cravat. The casual dress and disheveled hair gave ample sign of his distress.

"What is the matter?" she asked as they rapidly strode down the hall.

"She is burning with fever," he explained, pushing open the door as they reached Kate's room. "Mrs. Gooch said she was not feeling quite the thing at dinner, but I did not think . . . ."

"These childhood fevers come on very quickly," Sophrina reassured him.

"I want Rina."

Kate's choking sobs made Sophrina wince.

"Rina is here, darling," she replied, sitting gingerly on the side of the bed and taking Kate's hand in hers. Sophrina noticed her high color and glassy eyes.

"I'm hot," the little girl complained.

"And so you are," said Sophrina, laying her hand on Kate's forehead. The heat there was almost scorching. Sophrina looked at Penhurst. "Has anyone bathed her yet?"

Penhurst shook his head.

"That may be the best thing to do while we wait for the doctor. If you can get a basin, and some cloths . . ."

Penhurst motioned to the hovering housekeeper.

"I'm thirsty," Kate moaned.

"Of course you are," said Sophrina. Penhurst placed a glass in her hand before she could even ask. Slipping her arm behind Kate's head, she gently raised the girl until she could take a sip.

"We are going to give you a bath now, Kate," Sophrina explained, when the water basin arrived. She pulled back the covers. "It will make you feel much better. Can you sit up for me?"

Sophrina carefully removed the girl's nightgown and began stroking her skin with the cooling washcloth.

"This will help?" Penhurst asked anxiously.

Sophrina nodded. At least she hoped it would. She had seen enough minor fevers with her nieces and nephews not to be too alarmed, for children were wont to be deliriously ill at one moment and dancing down the halls an hour later. But on occasion, it was a serious matter. She prayed it would not be so with Kate.

Penhurst gladly handed Sophrina the cool, wet cloths, desperate to do anything to ease Kate's discomfort. She looked so small and tiny, even in the half-size nursery bed. When they had first awakened him to inform him of Kate's distress, he had been terrified. He knew nothing of sick children; knew only that England's churchyards were full of so many who had not passed beyond their tender years, like his own brother and sisters. He might despise Kate's mother, but for the girl herself he only felt a growing fondness. He did not want Kate wrenched away from him now that he had begun to appreciate her.

Sophrina set the washcloth back in the basin Penhurst held. "Does that feel a bit better, Kate?"

The girl nodded.

"I remember when Edward was so sick with the measles, the doctor bade him lie naked on the sheets," Sophrina said, turning to receive Penhurst's agreement. "If the doctor is to arrive soon, it may not hurt. I think she will be more comfortable."

"Do what you think is best," he said, grateful to have anyone tell him what to do.

"Don't go," Kate begged, grabbing Sophrina's hand as she attempted to rise.

"I will be right back," Sophrina said soothingly. "I thought to find a book to read while we wait for the doctor."

Kate reclined back against the pillow. Penhurst moved a chair into position, bringing a branch of candles to illuminate the book Sophrina returned with. He pulled up a chair of his own, content to wait and listen.

By the time Dr. Hammond arrived, Kate had drifted off again into a fitful sleep.

"It is always the children who drag you out of bed at the wee hours of the morning," the doctor grumbled good-naturedly as he entered the room. "Either coming into the world or making their way through it. Good evening—or morning—Lady Teel. So, the little one is feeling poorly, is she?"

"She was out of sorts at dinner, I understand," Penhurst explained. "I did not know anything was amiss until they woke me about midnight. She had been screaming and crying."

"I gave her a cooling bath about an hour ago," Sophrina explained. "It seemed to help some."

"Has she had the usual childhood ailments? Chicken pox? Measles?"

Penhurst shook his head. "I know of nothing."

The doctor bent over to examine his small patient. "Any of her companions ill?"

"The only children she plays with are at Charlton, and none of them have been ill."

"I see." The doctor gently poked and prodded Kate. "Has she been inoculated, my lord?"

Penhurst paled. "I honestly do not know. I was gone . . . out of the country . . . when she was young."

The doctor examined Kate's arms carefully. "I see no sign

of an inoculation site, but that means naught. Particularly when babies are treated, it can be nearly impossible to tell.''

"You think it may be the pox?''

"Unlikely,'' said the doctor. "There has not been a case in the neighborhood in years.''

Sophrina could have struck the doctor. How dare he frighten them so, then dismiss his conjectures out of hand?

The doctor rose, turning to Penhurst. "I see no sign for great concern, my lord. She responded well to the bath, and the fact she went back to sleep is encouraging. She is feverish, but not seriously so. Keep her cool, and I will leave some powders for her. She may very well be bouncing out of bed in the morning.''

He reached for the bag. "Childhood fevers are strange things,'' he explained as he drew out the medication. "They are often a very poor indicator of how sick a child is. I have seen the sickest children running through the garden the next day, and the ones only mildly ill buried in the graveyards the following week.''

"A comforting thought,'' Penhurst muttered under his breath.

"I will look in again in the afternoon,'' Dr. Hammond said. "Send for me, of course, if she worsens, but I have a feeling she will be much improved later this morning.''

Penhurst accompanied the doctor out into the hall, while Sophrina resumed her place beside the bed, clasping Kate's small hand in hers.

"See? The doctor says you will be feeling much better soon.'' She bent down and planted a gentle kiss on her brow. "Try to get some sleep now.''

"Will you stay, Rina?''

Sophrina nodded. "Of course I will, Kate. But only if you promise to go to sleep.''

Kate nodded contentedly and it was not long before she slipped into slumber again. Sophrina remained where she was, her hand still clasping the girl's.

"Is she asleep?'' Penhurst whispered as he reentered the room.

"It did not take long,'' Sophrina said.

"I cannot thank you enough for coming,'' he said, taking his seat beside her. "I feel father foolish now, with Dr. Hammond saying it is not a serious matter, but I have never been confronted with a sick child before.''

"I am glad you thought to send for me," Sophrina replied. "I do not think my presence has much of an impact on her illness, but at least I can feel that I am doing something to help."

"I think your being here has done all the world for her," he said softly. "She was so afraid and crying earlier. As soon as you arrived she calmed."

"It must be frightening to a child to be sick, not knowing what is happening. Particularly when the adults around you are worried as well."

"Overly so, it seems," he said ruefully.

She gave him a reassuring smile. "No, I do not think there is anything amiss in being too concerned for a sick child. Dr. Hammond was right, they can be fragile little beings. It is always best to err on the side of caution."

They talked quietly for some time, until it was apparent that Kate was sleeping peacefully again.

"I insist you remain here and sleep," Penhurst told Sophrina as they silently stole into the hall.

"It is just as convenient to return home," she said.

"Nonsense. What if Kate wakes and demands to have you at her side again?"

He did have a point. Sophrina could not quite stifle a yawn. It would be nice to be in a soft, warm bed in only a few minutes.

"You are a bully," she said. "But I will accept your offer. I do detest falling asleep in coaches and I fear I would not get past the drive before my eyes closed."

"I will have Mrs. Gooch tend to you," he said. "Thank you again for coming to my rescue tonight. I shall be in your debt."

"All I wish is to see Kate well again," she said. "Good night, Elliston."

"Good night, Sophrina."

It did not take more than a few moments from the time her head hit the pillow for Sophrina to fall asleep. She awoke, sometime after noon, feeling refreshed despite the excitement of the night. Not wishing to drag Mrs. Gooch away from her duties, Sophrina resolved to dress herself. She was surprised and pleased to find fresh clothes awaiting her. Penhurst must have sent to the cottage for them. How thoughtful of him.

Once dressed, she made her way down the hall to Kate's room. She knew the girl would be better; had there been a crisis, someone would have awakened her. But she wanted to see firsthand just how the patient was doing.

Tapping softly on the door, she entered and found Penhurst sitting beside the bed, reading to Kate. Sophrina paused in the doorway, studying the sharp physical contrast between the two. Kate's white blond locks and Penhurst's black hair were as dissimilar as could be, yet Sophrina sensed that a tie was developing between the two of them that would overcome the lack of shared blood. She smiled at the thought.

"And how is Lady Kate this afternoon?"

"Better," said Penhurst. "Is that not right?"

Kate nodded.

"I am certainly glad to hear that," Sophrina said, sitting down carefully at the edge of the bed. "You cost us quite a bit of lost sleep last night, you know. I shall have to take a nap every day this week to make up for it."

Kate gave her a small smile. "I am glad you came to take care of me."

"I am just glad you are well."

Penhurst eyed Sophrina with renewed admiration. She looked so fresh and rested after staying up half the night with his daughter, with only a few hours of sleep since. Lea would have taken to her bed for a week. No, he reconsidered, Lea would never have tended to Kate in the first place. Yet Sophrina had not demurred for an instant when his call for help went out. She was a remarkable lady.

Penhurst closed the book he held and stood. "I am sure Sophrina is famished, Kate, so I will take her downstairs and allow her to eat. You try to sleep some more."

"All right."

Sophrina bent down and pressed a kiss to her cheek. "I will come back later," she promised.

Sophrina followed Penhurst into the drawing room, where a cold collation awaited them. She reveled in the warmth of the bright September sun that flooded the room.

"I do not think I have ever felt more helpless in my life as

I did last night," Penhurst said, shaking his head in amazement. "Kate looked to me for help and there was nothing I could do."

"You did exactly as you ought," Sophrina assured him. "I know it is humbling to find we do not have all the answers."

"And yet she still wanted me at her side," he marveled, then smiled. "Not as much as she wanted you, of course, but it was amazing to me all the same. I did not think she particularly liked me."

"Of course she does. You were not here to see how much she anticipated your return from London."

"She was expecting her present."

"She was expecting her *father,*" Sophrina countered. "I think you have done a marvelous job of drawing closer to her in the last weeks. She enjoys sharing your table and playing games with you."

He looked at her with doubt in his eyes. "You think I am making headway?"

Sophrina nodded emphatically. "Kate has a very loving nature and it only took a little enthusiasm on your part for her to develop an attachment."

"But nothing like her feelings for you."

"Children often find women easier to talk with."

"She has been like a new person since she met you," he said. "I can always tell when you have spent time together, for she is bright and cheerful for the rest of the day. What is your secret?"

Sophrina ducked her head modestly. "I merely talk to her as another person, without condescension. If you take a sincere interest in their ideas and questions, any child will become your friend."

"You make it sound so easy." He leaned back in his chair, crossing one elegantly shod leg over the other.

"Does it still bother you that she is William's daughter?" Sophrina asked bluntly.

He shook his head. "It certainly did at first. But now . . . I chose to accept responsibility for her so I must make the best of things. And last night, when she was ill . . . well, I realized that it was suddenly very unimportant who her natural father was."

They both fell silent for a moment, Penhurst self-consciously turning his attention to his food, Sophrina marveling at the change in the man.

He hardly seemed the same person she had met two months ago. From a cold, glowering aristocrat he had turned into a well-meaning, if still somewhat awkward parent. Sophrina did not hold herself responsible for the change; she may have pushed him down the road faster than his natural inclinations would have led him, but she gave full credit to Kate for winning Penhurst over. In Sophrina's eyes no one could resist that winsome girl for long. Penhurst's heart had proven no more impervious than Sophrina's.

"What was your childhood like?" Sophrina asked softly.

Penhurst flashed her a look of consternation.

"Forgive me, I am being impertinent."

"No, it is a logical question to ask." He sank back into his chair. "You know I was an only child. And from an early age, I was brought up knowing I was the heir to an earldom. The responsibilities inherent in that position were thoroughly drummed into me."

"It sounds perfectly horrid!" Sophrina was aghast.

He smiled. "It was not *that* bad. Certainly I do not think my life was different from that of most boys of my class. Both my parents were sticklers for form and rules; there was a very clear code of conduct to be followed. Deviation was severely punished, but at least you knew where you stood at all times."

"No one can be perfect all the time," she protested. "In fact, that is how we learn best, by making mistakes."

"But it is so much tidier not to make the mistakes in the first place," he countered. "Then you do not have to contend with messy emotional scenes, chastisement and punishment."

Sophrina was filled with sadness. No wonder Penhurst had hidden himself behind his cold, unemotional shell. His parents were perfect monsters to turn what had once been a warm-hearted, likable boy into this dispassionate earl.

He tilted his head in query. "You do not agree?"

"Of course not! Humans *are* emotional creatures. It is what lifts us above mere animals. To stifle that aspect of a person is to stifle everything that is human."

His eyes narrowed for a moment, then he smiled easily. "You

are right, of course; I am just beginning to realize it. I certainly intend to raise Kate in a far different manner.''

"That is a wise course," Sophrina acknowledged. "Kate does have a trace of her mother's emotional volatility. Accept it, deal with her accordingly, and she will grow into a wonderful young lady.''

"How did you grow so wise in such a short space of years?" he teased.

Sophrina's cheeks pinkened. "I am only wise about a few things,'' she demurred.

"And in what areas is your wisdom lacking?"

"Oh, several," she replied airily. "I have a dreadful sense of fashion—I always defer to my sister-in-law in that area. I have a deplorable tendency to speak my mind at inappropriate times.'' She flashed Penhurst a sidelong glance, pleased to see his answering smile. "And, of course, my marriage was a distastrous mistake.''

"I must confess I do have an eye for ladies' clothing, and I am *capable* of being the perfect diplomat at times.'' His lips twitched as he suppressed a grin. "But I know nothing of children and made an equally abominable mistake in my marriage. So one could say we were evenly matched.''

The warmth in his tone flustered Sophrina and she quickly looked away. It meant little to acknowledge that their ruined marriages were their strongest common tie. Perhaps, over time, there would be other facets to their friendship.

Chapter 9

"I had almost forgotten how much fun this could be," Penhurst admitted as he lazily cast his fishing line into the pool at Talcott. "This pond has been ignored for so long, I am amazed there are still fish in it.''

Sophrina smiled at his realization. It was as if she had two pupils: Kate, who needed to learn the lessons required in growing up, and Penhurst, who needed to learn how to be a child again. She beamed at her success in both areas.

Kate lay beside Sophrina on the blanket, sleeping the exhausted sleep of a happy child. She had caught four fish, to her squealing delight, captured several frogs, and had eaten her fill of the massive picnic lunch prepared by Talcott's cook. It had all been too much for one day.

"I must confess I never was much of a hand at fishing," Sophrina said. "They are such slimy creatures. There were always more pleasant things to look at or do. And I fear I lack the patience."

Penhurst laughed. "You mean, you would rather be sketching. I have never seen such concentration as when you are working."

Sophrina blushed. "Well, perhaps I can concentrate some of the time." She stretched lazily. "I cannot believe we are having such a glorious fall. It seems as if it will stay warm forever."

"I think Kate snagged all the fish for today," Penhurst said ruefully. Carefully placing his pole on the ground, he sat down next to Sophrina. "What did you manage to sketch this afternoon?"

"Oh, just a few things," she mumbled. She knew that her sketches were good, but it embarrassed her to have others look at them and comment. With few exceptions, she considered her sketches private possessions.

"May I look?"

The gentle pleading in his rich brown eyes caused her to nod.

It was odd, really, she thought, as he slowly flipped through the pages of her sketchbook, how comfortable she felt with him now. The rigid, unbending aristocrat had shown that underneath the cold exterior, he was a warm and caring man, that his original boyish shyness had been molded into aristocratic aloofness by his stern parents. Here, in muddy boots and rolled-up sleeves, he exuded a youthful charm that she found unsettling.

She watched him while he looked through the pages and met his gaze when he looked up.

"These are better than good, Sophrina. You have a marvelous ability to capture a scene."

"It is only for fun . . ." she protested.

"Do not undervalue your skill," he chided. "Your faces, particularly . . ." He held up the book. "This one of Kate is wonderful. May I have it?"

She nodded shyly.

"Kate will treasure this when she is older. It captures her perfectly."

"Kate is easy to draw," Sophrina explained. "She is open and guileless and all is there in her face to see."

"Unlike us adults."

She nodded.

"It is odd," he mused, "for I was taught that it was a serious breach of etiquette to let one's feelings show, to become emotional in either extreme. It stood me in good stead in diplomatic circles, but in real life . . . I am certain it was off-putting to many."

"But you are improving, Elliston," Sophrina said lightly. "Or you never would have shown such enthusiasm for those miniscule fish you caught."

He glared at her with mock severity. "Do you not know it is dangerous to attack the quality of one's catch? Besides, it is not the size of the fish that counts, but the skill needed to land them. In that I excelled."

Sophrina giggled. "You would have been as pleased if you had caught nothing."

He laughed. "You are right. Lord, I haven't felt so free since I can remember. I fear you are a bad influence on me, Sophrina. Soon you will have destroyed all my aristocratic countenance."

"Would that be such a bad thing?"

He caught her eyes in a long, lingering look. "No," he replied slowly. "I do not think it would be bad at all."

Sophrina quickly looked away, unnerved by the intensity of his gaze.

They sat in companionable silence for some minutes, breathing in the heady scents of late fall and listening to the sounds of the woodland and meadow around them. Sophrina felt utterly content, as if she were sitting in front of a raging fire on a cold winter's night, snug and secure in the knowledge that the outside elements could not harm her.

After Kate awoke from her nap, they gathered up the picnic and fishing poles and ambled their way back to Talcott. If

Sophrina was not quite certain how her arm had become entwined with Penhurst's, it seemed the most natural thing in the world. Kate danced merrily at their side, stopping only to pet her kitten when they deposited their catch and the fishing poles in the kitchen. Mrs. Gooch herded Kate upstairs to the nursery for a much needed bath, while Penhurst insisted on driving Sophrina home himself.

"I am having a house party next week," he began hesitantly, once they had cleared the gates of Talcott. "Some very close friends, not too many people. I should like you to be a guest as well."

How long had it been since she had been in the company of any but their close neighbors? Before William and Lea had run off, she was certain. And to be suddenly catapulted into a house party of strangers, hosted by a man whose company she was beginning to find usettling?

"I am not certain . . ."

"They are all very pleasant, undemanding people," he hastily explained. "You know I am not one for casual society acquaintances. I had enough of that type of entertaining on the Continent. These are the type of people who do not mind if you wander off with a book or sketch pad for hours on end, and will not bore you to tears in the evening with their stories."

"Perhaps I can join you for dinner a few times."

"And will you abandon Kate entirely for a fortnight? I thought it would be much easier for you if you were not running back and forth between houses several times a day. You would not have time to enjoy yourself."

"You do have a point."

"I know. I shall expect you to arrive with your bags on Tuesday. And I will tell Kate immediately so you will not dare to go back on your word."

"You do know how to gain my acquiescence, don't you?" she responded dryly.

He laughed. "You are only lucky Kate is still too young to realize the power she holds over you. She would be overbearing, otherwise."

"Nonsense," said Sophrina, her hazel eyes twinkling. "I am firmly in control of matters."

He tossed back his head and roared with laughter.

The tantalizing echo of that laugh still rang in her head as Sophrina entered her cottage. She wondered what she had committed herself to. Elliston had said he was only inviting some close friends. Friends who undoubtedly had known his wife. No matter what transpired, Lea and William's shadow always loomed over them. Would their ghosts ever be banished?

Sophrina was not afraid to go out in society; it was only that she had felt no interest in doing so in the years since William's departure. At first she had hidden herself away to avoid the attention she would attract. Yet even the following Season, when new gossip would have laid that old news to rest, she had felt no need to accompany Bertram and Mary to London. William's death had given her further excuse to remain in the country.

Perhaps she had taken her self-imposed isolation too far. It was a bit much to be so nervous over a simple country-house party. She had always found the parties and gaieties of society pleasant. This would not be an onerous task. Hadn't she begun to realize it was time to step away from reclusive life?

Yet was the prospect of meeting total stangers the true cause of her apprehension? Or was she more nervous about spending two entire weeks in Elliston's house? Granted, she saw him nearly every day now, but often only for a moment as they passed Kate back and forth. But as his guest, they would be thrown together constantly. And she found that prospect unnerving. Precisely because she looked forward to it.

It was silly, really. They were merely friends, she rationalized, united by their mutual interest in Kate's well-being. He was no more interested in a romantic relationship than Sophrina was. They had both been burned by that fire once, and had learned their lessons only too well. It was ridiculous to think that two people in their particularly awkward situation would be attracted to each other in that way.

Yet for her part, she was. Oh, not in a silly, schoolgirlish manner. His presence did not put her to the blush, nor did his company reduce her to stammering inanities. Yet Sophrina readily admitted to herself that she liked him. At least she liked the new Penhurst, the relaxed and joking man who had replaced the grim and overbearing lord of their initial meeting. He was by no means a carefree soul, but he had come a long way since their first encounter. His new enthusiasm for entertainments, fighting mock battles on the drawing-room floor with Kate and the toy soldiers, all pointed to a man who was learning how to enjoy life.

Which did not necessarily mean she thought him a perfect match for her. Sophrina was not so blind as all that. She saw his faults perfectly well and they were ones that had no ready cure—and could make one's life miserable. He had a ready temper; he had controlled it with admirable restraint recently, but she knew it lurked beneath the surface, ready to explode at any moment. And traces of the old, starched-up Penhurst peaked out from time to time, often enough to let her know he would never be free of his repressive childhood. Kate drew him down to her level now, as only a four-year-old could. But as his daughter grew older and more ladylike, would he abandon his newfound relaxed demeanor and return to his old aloof manner? Sophrina feared he would. And she would not be able to abide a man like that.

Despite Kate's insistence that she come over first thing in the morning on Tuesday, Sophrina delayed her arrival until late in the afternoon. It would have looked too much like a cozy domestic scene for her to have been there to greet the guests with Penhurst. She did not want anyone to misconstrue the situation.

"I feared you had changed your mind," Penhurst said, taking her hands in greeting as he ushered her into the drawing room. His impatient wait for her arrival made him realize just how much he looked forward to this extended visit.

"Never say you think I am a coward," she teased.

"No, a brave lady," he whispered back and pulled her into the room. "And a lovely one as well," he noted approvingly, admiring the way the rose-hued gown complimented her coloring.

"Aunt Violet, this is a near neighbor, Sophrina Charlton. And Violet is, alas, nearly the last of my family, except for my cousin, Robert."

Sophrina nodded at the introduction. His aunt had the same dark, quizzing eyes as Penhurst. She would not miss much.

"Teel's widow, are you not?"

The lady did not waste time getting to the point. Yet it relieved Sophrina to have the awkwardness over with now, at the beginning.

"I am," Sophrina replied and was surprised at the look of approval in Penhurst's elderly aunt's eyes.

"Wretched situation, that. I am pleased to see you have weathered the storm. Never did like Elliston's wife. Not that I wished the poor girl dead, of course, but it was a relief to have her gone."

Amazingly the lady's pronouncements did not embarrass Sophrina. They only fueled her curiosity. If Lea and Penhurst had been so dreadfully wrong for each other, why had he married her in the first place? Had her beauty blinded him? Elliston did not seem like a man to throw his brains out the window at the sight of a pretty lady.

"I am certain you two would love to sit and tear my ex-wife's character apart, but there are other people here for Sophrina to meet." Penhurst smiled apologetically.

"I like her," Sophrina whispered to him as he led her out onto the terrace.

"She acts the part of a tartar, but a sweeter lady does not exist," he said with a fond look in his eyes.

Sophrina grew acutely aware that Elliston had not released her hand since he had first greeted her inside. She felt a stab of embarrassment, wondering what the other guests would think. Yet if she pulled free now, with all eyes watching them crossing the terrace, it would cause an even worse stir. Then, as if he realized her sudden discomfort, Penhurst released her fingers and gently grasped her elbow to guide her forward to greet the other guests.

He described Viscount Newby as his oldest friend and partner in crime at Eton and Oxford, and Sophrina liked the friendly face of the viscount's wife, Amelia. Penhurst's cousin and heir, Robert Thorne, was a personable young man of nineteen with a taste for shocking-colored waistcoats, but had a manner which indicated that it was probably his only serious vice. Richard Webb, a friend of Penhurst's from the Foreign Office, was there with his wife, Dorothea. Four more arrivals were still expected.

The balmy fall weather had continued into this first week of

October—a bane to hunters but a boon to house parties, which could become tedious if everyone was cooped up inside. It was not until late afternoon that the chill finally drove the guests indoors. Sophrina was engaged in a comfortable coze with the three ladies when a trilling female voice broke into their thoughts.

"Elliston, you horrid creature. Why have you waited so long to throw a party down here? You know everyone has been dying to know what you have been up to."

All eyes turned to the woman entering the room and Sophrina's spirits sank as she took in the sight of this elegantly dressed woman who so obviously was a close friend of Penhurst's. Despite her new gown, Sophrina felt suddenly dowdy in this lady's presence. *La Belle Assemblee* probably copied *her* clothes. Sophrina fought down the urge to grimace as the new arrival planted a kiss on Penhurst's cheek.

"As lovely as always, Willi," he said, bowing low. "And as blunt. I have been up to nothing, as I am sure you will soon discover. However, I am certain Talcott will be more lively now that you are here."

"Gad, if I am the entertainment, you must be sadly bored." She nodded at the remainder of the guests, whom she obviously knew and drew up in front of Sophrina.

"Wilhelmina, Lady Taunton," Penhurst introduced. "The Dowager Lady Taunton," he added with a sly smile.

"How horrid of you, Elliston. It makes me sound a veritable ancient."

Sophrina smiled in sympathy. "I am a dowager of sorts myself," she said, extending her hand. "Sophrina, Viscountess Teel."

Penhurst raised an eyebrow. He knew how loathe Sophrina was to use her title. And her tone of voice sounded deucedly peculiar to his ears.

Lady Taunton's eyes widened as she recognized the name and notoriety immediately.

"How interesting to find you here."

"Lady Teel is a near neighbor," Penhurst hastily interjected. He had been in the diplomatic corps long enough to recognize the underlying currents of hostility between the two women.

What the hell was going on? And why did he suddenly feel defensive about Sophrina's presence? There was nothing untoward about her inclusion in the house party. "Both the dowager and the viscount will be dining with us this week so you will have the opportunity to meet the entire family, Willi."

"I will look forward to it," she said with a look that belied her words. She turned to Penhurst as if dismissing Sophrina. "Who is yet to arrive? I hope I have not committed the unpardonable sin of being the last?"

"Belkirk and his lady are due still. And Seb."

"Darling Sebby," said Willi. "How is the dear boy these days?"

"Hale and hearty," said a deep male voice from the doorway. "Sorry if I'm late, Elliston, but the lead horse cast a shoe on the way down."

Penhurst crossed the room in long strides, clasping his friend by the hand.

"Trust you to make the grand entrance," said Penhurst, a wide grin splitting his face. "Do you ever do anything without a dramatic flair?"

"Hardly," the new arrival said with a haughty air, then he too grinned. "I see you have Willi here."

"All for you, Seb, all for you. Single men make such a deucedly awkward mess of things at a country party, you know."

"And I suppose you are saving that sprightly brunet for yourself?" His friend raised an impish brow as he observed Sophrina.

Penhurst managed to frown and smile at the same time. "Not like that at all, Seb. She's here because . . . well . . . that's Teel's widow."

"Good God! You must be planning a lively party. Complete with fireworks."

"No, no," Penhurst hastened to reassure him. "We have settled into neighborly amiability. She is a godsend when it comes to dealing with my daughter. I don't know how I could have managed without her."

"But such an intriguing situation," Seb whispered as he

finally allowed himself to be drawn into the room. "Is she comparing you to Teel or are you comparing her to Lea?"

"Neither," Penhurst growled before he forced his face into a bland mask for his guests.

Sophrina could not help but notice that whispered conversation, and it served to further whet her curiosity about the strange assembly Penhurst had arranged. The positively leering look with which Mr. Cole had greeted her did little to set her at ease. She had no difficulty in labeling him a rake from their first acquaintance and found it odd that he and Elliston were such close friends. Rakishness was *not* one of the qualities she would ascribe to Penhurst.

She dressed for dinner quickly, eager to further her acquaintance with Elliston's odd assortment of guests. One old school chum, a Foreign Office crony, a cousin on his best behavior, a very eligible bachelor, an aging aunt with a blunt tongue, and a radical MP. And a very attractive widow who was obviously on close terms with Penhurst.

The emotion that arose inside Sophrina when she thought of that connection could not possibly be jealousy. It was absurd. What did she have to be jealous of? She was very pleased with the easy friendship that existed between herself and Elliston, so different from the angry confrontation of their earlier encounter. She had no cause to be irritated if he wanted to pay his attentions to a dashing widow. For being jealous implied that Sophrina had feelings for Penhurst that went beyond friendship—and she most decidedly did not! It must be that Lady Taunton reminded Sophrina of Lea. They both had the same predatory traits.

Sophrina pulled her hairbrush through her dark locks with a violent tug. This was ridiculous. Elliston had invited her so she could enjoy herself, and she determined to do just that. No one, male or female, was going to cut into her appreciation of this party.

When she swept down the stairs for dinner, her head high, Sophrina was determined to find everything pleasing. She was glad Mary had insisted on updating her wardrobe during the summer. Sophrina knew that while she could not compete with Lady Taunton in the matter of high fashion, her frock dress of green satin and net, with its deep flounce, was as elegant as she could wish.

Penhurst's eyes widened in appreciation when he saw Sophrina hesitate for a moment at the open drawing-room door. He was no arbiter of fashion, but he knew what he liked and found her ensemble pleasing. She looked well in green, and the chestnut curls caught atop her hair revealed the graceful curve of her neck and shoulders. He caught her eye and saw the slight nervousness there. He gave her an encouraging smile—and a challenging glance.

Sophrina saw the challenge in his eyes. She drew herself up to her full height, put on her haughtiest expression, and swept forward imperiously into the room.

Seb Cole immediately made his way to her side.

"You are looking lovely this evening, Lady Teel," he said with practiced smoothness.

Sophrina was not so far removed from society that she did not recognize the ways of a skilled rake. Her eyes danced with mischief. During her come out, she had been too inexperienced to participate in any but the most innocent of flirtations. But in her years as a married woman, she had seen many skilled practitioners of that art. She felt a wicked impulse to indulge in the practice herself.

"Spanish coin, Mr. Cole," she replied, tapping him lightly on the arm with her fan. "I know that an insignificant country widow cannot hope to hold a candle to the elegant ladies of London."

"Ah, but it has been ever so long since I was in London," Seb retorted in a drawling tone, delighted to see some spirit in Elliston's lady. For he was very certain that was what she was, even if they both denied it.

"Then I will accept your praise as genuine," she said with a smile. Seb offered his arm and they made a gradual circuit of the room.

A less perceptive observer would have missed the slight narrowing of Sophrina's eyes when Willi entered the room, but Seb, burning with equal fires of curiosity and mischief, noted the brief reaction. He had been pleased with the invitation to the house party, for it obviously marked an end to Elliston's

self-imposed isolation. The potentially inflammatory circumstances were an intriguing surprise. Had Elliston been in full
possession of his senses when he planned this party? This might
be the most entertaining fortnight in years.

On the basis of experience and skill, the average observer
would give the match easily to Willi. However, Seb had learned
long ago never to underestimate a woman. He had glimpsed
the steel that lay beneath Lady Teel's placid exterior. Willi
would have her hands full if she expected to come out on top.

And if the contest began to tip in a way he did not wish, Seb
was not above dabbling in the fray himself. Oh yes, a very
interesting fortnight. His eyes gleamed with mischief as he
escorted Lady Teel into the dining room.

When the gentlemen rejoined the ladies after dinner, the
conversation turned to the next day's activities. Sophrina found
herself irritated and annoyed at Lady Taunton's attempts to
organize their schedule.

"I would like to see more of Elliston's lovely estate," Willi
announced, casting a winsome smile at her host. "With the
weather so lovely, an early morning ride would be just the
thing." A chorus of acceptance greeted her suggestion.

Seb noticed Lady Teel's silence. "Do you not wish to join
us?"

"I do not ride," Sophrina replied.

"Oh, what a pity," replied Willi in a tone that belied her
words. "But certainly, you could follow behind us in one of
Elliston's carriages. Perhaps you and his aunt could travel
together."

"I prefer to walk," said Sophrina. "I find it much easier to
appreciate the beauty of nature from a closer vantage and slower
pace."

Point to Lady Teel, thought Seb, glancing quickly at his host
to ascertain his reaction. Penhurst's face showed his
bemusement.

"Ah yes, I forget how in the country life is paced slower than
the city. One can afford to indulge oneself with the more bucolic
amusements." Willi's voice carried a sharp edge.

Sophrina was not oblivious to Lady Taunton's declaration of
battle. A few years ago, Sophrina would have backed away from

confrontation—as she had in the matter of Lea. But she was no longer the naive, sheltered woman she had been at the start of her marriage. She would not allow this elegant woman to rattle her.

"Yes, we are hopelessly countrified here in Wiltshire," said Sophrina with a disarming smile. "However, I much prefer it to London. One has more of an opportunity to develop close friendships away from the city and its innumerable distractions. Here, people tend to be more straightforward and sincere."

"Perhaps I should spend more time in the country," said Willi smoothly. She shot a challenging glance at her host.

A vague sense of confusion plagued Penhurst. He sensed a trace of animosity between Sophrina and Willi that surprised him. He had invited Willi deliberately for Sophrina's sake, thinking the two would have more in common with each other than with the married ladies present. Were they not both widows? And Willi, despite her brashness, was an entertaining woman. He had not stopped to consider that it was usually the men, not their ladies, who were clustered about Willi at the *ton* parties.

Seb guessed Penhurst was puzzling over the veiled confrontation between his two guests. Penhurst was a crack diplomat, but he knew little about women. He expected deviousness in politics, but not in personal relationships. The man had much to learn. And Seb guessed Penhurst was about to have his first lesson.

Sophrina rose abruptly. "While you plan your ride, I will chat with Lady Newby. I promised I would share my lesson plans for Kate with her. She has a daughter of the same age." She could not suppress a smug smile. She would like to see how well Lady Taunton handled Kate!

Penhurst watched her departure with regret. He had insisted Sophrina stay at Talcott so he could spend more time in her company. Yet one day was nearly gone and he had been able to enjoy no more than a few minutes in her presence. Would all his plans go awry? No, he determined. He was the host, and he had the right to organize their entertainments to suit his desires. He would make certain to arrange matters to enable himself to spend as much time with Sophrina as he wished.

Chapter 10

Penhurst lay back lazily in his chair, watching the fire burn low in the grate. The brandy decanter resting beside him was two-thirds empty, and Seb did not look inclined to pour another glass. After a week of convivial association they had exhausted the commonplace gossip, the traded stories of who had seen whom and how so-and-so was doing. They had swapped reminiscences of previous adventures and house parties. Now, in the early hours of the morning, it was time either for bed or for the deeper confidences that seemed only to emerge on late nights like these.

"I like your lady."

Seb startled Penhurst from his musings.

"My what?"

"I wasn't born yesterday, Ellis. I have eyes to see and ears to hear. If you are not top over tails in love with her, I will eat my coat."

"Of whom, precisely, are we speaking?"

Seb uttered a short laugh. "Don't try your wily diplomatic tricks on me, Ellis. They just won't fadge. It has not escaped my notice that you contrive to be at her side at every opportunity."

"I think your romantic notions are getting the better of your common sense, Seb." Penhurst took a sip of brandy.

"Do you deny you care for her?"

Penhurst was about to ask again whom Seb referred to, but decided against it. There was no need for games.

"I admire her. Appreciate her. She has a magical way with children, particularly Kate." He tilted his head thoughtfully. "She is no antidote, I have certainly noticed. But neither am I planning another trip down the aisle, Seb. One venture soured me on that for a long time. Forever, perhaps. Besides, the situation between us is highly irregular, to say the least."

"You know how it is with widows—take our Willi, for example. Perhaps a little playtime between the sheets is called for. It might do both of you a world of good."

"I do not think so," Penhurst said in clipped tones. Seb's rakish nature had never disturbed him before, but he did not like to hear Sophrina spoken of in such a way.

Seb crossed his hands protectively over his breast. "Egad, you sound like an outraged father. Will it be pistols at dawn?"

Penhurst pierced him with a withering stare.

"Well, if you are not interested that way, perhaps I shall investigate the possibilities. She is a trifle quiet, but they say that can hide a fiery nature underneath. And certainly she has been a long time without a man. Isn't it over two years since Teel ran off?"

"As long as she remains a guest in my home, she will not be subjected to your untoward advances," Penhurst said icily, quietly consumed with anger. "Satisfy your lust with Willi."

"Ah yes, the lovely and amiable Willi. Since you profess not to be interested in Lady Teel, I assumed you were keeping Willi for yourself. Or have you sworn off women entirely?"

"That very well may be."

Seb smiled enigmatically. "You seem so sure of yourself, never doubting your course. Do you ever cease to be the perfect Elliston St. Clair and act like a mortal man? Does nothing ever ruffle your composure?"

"All the time. You should have seen me a few months ago. Kate was driving me mad—I had no idea of how to deal with her. I was convinced she hated me—she ran away once, you know. Then Sophrina stepped in and . . ." his voice trailed off in selfconscious awareness.

Seb flashed him a knowing smile.

Penhurst ignored him. "So what of you, Seb? Are you going to elude the parson's mousetrap for the remainder of your days?"

"Undoubtedly," his friend replied. "Unlike you, I do not have a domestic crisis on my hands that needs the healing powers of a woman. No, I quite enjoy my bachelor existance. I am a welcome guest at every house party, for one always needs a single man to make up the numbers. I can sleep where I will, when I will, and with whom I will. I enjoy the freedom."

"You and Willi would be well-suited."

"Ellis, I am shocked that you would suggest such a thing.

What kind of friend would I be, to seduce a guest under your own roof?''

"I find the idea of seduction and Willi at odds with each other."

"Now I should call you out for blackening the character of such a fine lady!" Seb's voice dripped amusement.

Perhurst sighed. "Since I am not up to lurking in the halls until all hours, peering around corners to see who dashes into what room, I will have to take your word for it."

"Willi is a good friend," Seb mused. "She reminds me a lot of myself, I fear. We are enjoying ourselves far too much to even contemplate a permanent arrangement."

"Until, of course, you are caught in the noose and could not wriggle free even if you wished," Penhurst grinned. "I think you are ripe for a fall, my friend."

"I will lay you a hundred guineas that it will be you wearing the leg shackles again before I do."

"Agreed." Penhurst knew the both of them were halfway to being foxed if they were engaging in such folly, but what were old friends for if not to enjoy a bit of castaway foolishness?

They traded sallies far into the night, and it was not until Penhurst at last stretched out upon his bed, his brain comfortably fogged from the late hour and the brandy, that he thought back on Seb's words. Seb knew him well—perhaps even better than he knew himself. His friend's observations were usually right on the mark.

Penhurst frowned into the darkness. He did not love Sophrina. They were friends, surely. He had never thought much about the possibilities of unencumbered friendship with a woman, but his relationship with her seemed remarkably free of the awkwardness a more tender emotion would engender. Perhaps because of what they had both been through in their marriages, they no longer looked at members of the opposite sex as potential partners. Which freed them up for the infinitely more satisfying role of friend. Friends were less demanding, less cloying, less intense than a spouse. They could come and go with relative ease, leaving perhaps regret but not dramatic upheaval and destruction in their path. Friendship was much safer.

Let Seb go on thinking he knew all. Penhurst uttered a low chuckle and let sleep claim him.

Penhurst had less charitable thoughts for Seb later that morning, when his head throbbed with an abominable ache. Why, oh why, had he drunk so much brandy? Kate's bright chatter during his mid-morning visit to the nursery had nearly sent him running for the door. But he gritted his teeth and remained long enough for her to show him her latest artwork and read a few sentences aloud from her primer.

"I cannot stop marveling at how much you have taught her in such a short time," he said to Sophrina as he escorted her back to the drawing room at the conclusion of Kate's morning lesson. "I fully expect her to be spouting Latin next week."

Sophrina laughed. "I am afraid you will be sorely disappointed, for Latin is not one of my accomplishments. Still, you can hire for a tutor later for that."

"You are sure you still do not mind playing the role of governess?" he asked, stopping her with a staying hand. He searched her face for an inkling of her true thoughts. "I feel as if both Kate and I are taking advantage of you."

"It is odd," said Sabrina, "for until Kate tumbled into it, the slow pace of my life never bothered me. But I fear I would be sadly bored now without having her as a pupil. I honestly do not know what a I would do with all the hours in the day."

He tucked her hand in his arm and they continued their slow walk down the hall. "Are you enjoying the house party as well?"

She smiled. "You have a very amiable group of guests. They have a wonderful knack of making one feel as if they had been lifelong companions."

He nodded in agreement. "I see you and Lady Newby are already fast friends."

"I like her," Sophrina said. "She dotes on her own children, and thinks Kate is adorable. What could better recommend her?"

"I had thought you and Willi would get along better," he said ruefully.

Sophrina dissembled. "I fear she is far too fashionable a lady for a country widow like myself. I find I am more comfortable with the matrons than the eligible ladies."

Penhurst hesitated, half-afraid to ask the more important

question. "You seem to be taken with Seb Cole's amusing prattle."

Sophrina's cheeks turned rosy. "He is a dreadful flirt, isn't he? But I own it is a trifle gratifying to think anyone would care to flirt with me."

Penhurst suddenly halteld and turned her to face him. "Do not devalue yourself simply because your husband was a fool."

Sophrina was taken aback by the intensity of his words.

"I will take care not to," she whispered.

"Good," he said abruptly, holding open the drawing-room door.

A light, misting rain descended on Talcott that afternoon, spoiling plans for an alfresco lunch on the terrace and canceling all outdoor activities. Penhurst considered slipping off to his study to take a glance at his correspondence and leaving his guests to their own amusements. Starting for the door, he paused to exchange a few words with his aunt.

"I propose a rousing game of billiards," Seb announced, when the conversation turned to alternative activities. He smiled winsomely at Sophrina. "Do you play, Lady Teel?"

"Very badly, I am afraid."

"Then I shall appoint myself as your teacher." He rose and took her hand. "Anyone else care to join us?"

Penhurst's earlier intentions to review his papers went out the window. He would not permit Sophrina to be alone with Seb, even for something as potentially innocent as billiards. Sophrina lacked experience with Seb's rakish ways and he did not want to see her hurt. He turned to Lady Taunton. "Willi?"

Penhurst reckoned himself a tolerable billiards player, but his game was off the mark this afternoon. Whenever he looked up, Seb hovered over Sophrina like a possessive suitor. Penhurst's innards twisted in apprehension every time Seb inclined his blond head toward hers, with some whispered remark that brought a smile or gentle laughter to her lips. The rakehell insisted on helping Sophrina with her game, putting his arm around her in a most proprietary manner as he guided her motions with the cue.

"Elliston!" Willi's voice assaulted his ears. "Pay attention. It is your shot."

He left off glaring at Seb long enough to make a disgracefully poor shot. Willi flashed him a withering stare and Penhurst retreated glowering into the corner.

"What is your problem?" Willi hissed at him. "You look like your best friend has died."

"He just might," Penhurst mumbled.

A smile tugged at the corners of Willi's mouth and she laid a hand on his arm. "Do not tell me you two are having a slight disagreement over the delicate Lady Teel?" She uttered a throaty laugh. "How amusing."

"It is not that," he said stiffly, turning his scowling countenance on her.

"In that case, I think you have been neglecting me shamefully, Elliston. When you invited me here, I thought . . ."

He heard Sophrina laugh again and glanced up, consternation in his eyes. Damnation! There was Seb again, his arms around her in a disgracefully intimate clasp as they leaned over the table for a difficult shot. Seb's lips were only a fraction of an inch away from that delicately formed ear . . . Penhurst clenched and opened his fists reflexively. He felt the urge to plant Seb a facer.

Sophrina could not arrest her sidelong glances at the other couple in the room. She knew that Elliston and Lady Taunton were old friends. But just how old and how friendly? Watching them now, with Lady Taunton's hand casually resting on Penhurst's arm, Sophrina suspected it was a very close relationship. As it had the first day she had been introduced to the lady, a stab of some very unpleasant emotion stole through her.

That woman was all wrong for him. She was an incorrigible flirt, for had she not been dividing her attentions between nearly all the men of the party since the first day? Sophrina could not believe Elliston would be taken in by someone like her. She was Lea all over again; could he not see that? He must have a blind spot where forward women were concerned. Sophrina did not want to see him make the same mistake he had made with Lea. Lady Taunton would only bring out all of his faults and would do little to encourage the traits Sophrina had promoted—his growing desire to be a good father, his newfound inclination toward relaxation and pleasure.

Lady Taunton's low, sensual laugh grated on Sophrina's ears

as she watched Penhurst incline his head to hear some whispered comment. She turned away with an imperceptible sniff. What did it matter to her whom Penhurst consorted with? If he wanted to make a fool of himself over such a brazen creature, let him. Sophrina did not care. She looked back at Seb Cole and flashed him a radiant smile.

"I believe it is my turn?"

The first dinner bell had just rung when Penhurst slipped silently into his daughter's room, unobserved by the two persons on the bed. Sophrina's dark head was bent close to Kate's as they both looked at the book in Sophrina's hands. He leaned casually against the door frame, listening to the sound of her voice as she regaled Kate with a fairy tale. The bedside candles cast an amber hue over them and for one moment he ached to be an artist, in order that he might permanently capture the vision that appeared before him.

"Papa?"

Sophrina looked up from reading to see Penhurst at the door. Her cheeks reddened. How long had he been standing there listening?

"Hello, Kate," Penhurst said, walking into the room. "I hoped you would not mind if I shared in your bedtime story."

"That is all right, Papa," Kate said. "You can sit at the foot of the bed. But you have to listen very carefully because we are coming to the best part."

"The best part?" He arched a quizzing eyebrow.

"The part where the prince rescues Snow White," said Kate, with a hint of exasperation.

"Ah yes, dear Snow White." He eased himself down onto the bed, then looked expectantly at Sophrina. "Well?"

She was embarrassed, but firmly resolved to hide her state from both Kate and Penhurst.

"Now, when the prince first saw Snow White, lying in her glass coffin, he was overcome with love. He begged the dwarfs to sell him the coffin, but they were loathe to part with their beloved Snow White." She paused and glanced up, to find Penhurst gazing at her intently. Sophrina dropped her eyes to the page. "However, the prince finally persuaded the dwarfs to allow him to take Snow Wite back to his kingdom. The servants of the prince picked up the coffin and began to carry it away. Suddenly, one of them stumbled! But, wondrously, the shock dislodged the piece of poison apple from Snow White's throat. She opened her eyes, lifted off the lid of the coffin, and sat up.

" 'Where am I?' she asked. The prince, full of joy, said, 'You are with me,' and he told her all that had happened. Then he said 'I love you better than all the world; come with me to my father's castle and be my wife.'

"Snow White agreed and went with him, and their wedding was celebrated with great magnificence."

Kate clapped her hands with glee as Sophrina closed the book. "And they will live together forever and ever."

Sophrina smiled at Kate's enthusiasm.

That joyful smile finally lifted the blindness from Penhurst's eyes. He had been foolish to deny and ignore what had been stealing up on him for so long. Seb, with the wisdom of an outsider, had seen it quite clearly, as had Willi, yet still Penhurst had dismissed the idea as nonsense. But now, just as the tiny girl he had once thought to cast from his life had stolen his heart, so had the elegant lady beside her. With dawning realization, he acknowledged that all his protestations of friendship and esteem were nothing but a screen of smoke to hide from his deepest self the knowledge that he loved Sophrina Charlton, as he had never loved another woman before.

Almost in fear he glanced again toward the two figures on the bed. Kate was still holding the book, absorbed in the picture of Snow White and her prince. He shifted his gaze and met Sophrina's eyes. What he saw there both startled and elated him. He would have sworn an unspoken message passed through them and he could barely believe his senses.

Sophrina was startled by her reaction to Penhurst's gaze.

She should have known, of course. It was so clear now, as she looked into his eyes. Yet like so many other things, it was often the most obvious that was the last to be comprehended. It *was* jealousy that had been plaguing her these last days, for Penhurst meant far, far more to her than merely being Kate's father and a friend. It was not only admiration she felt for him. He represented all that she had once longed for, before William's betrayal had destroyed the childish dreams of her youth—love, happiness, security, peace. Dear God, she loved him so. For being the doting father he was rapidly becoming, and more importantly, for being the self-assured, witty, and caring man he already was. And strange as it all seemed, he needed her as much as she needed him.

As their glances locked, a thrill ran through her, for what she saw in his eyes was a mirror of what she was certain shone in hers. Sophrina could barely draw a breath.

They would have sat there, frozen, perhaps for eternity, had not Kate's voice interrupted.

"Are you going to kiss me good night, Papa?"

"Certainly, Kate," he said, tearing his eyes away from Sophrina.

Sophrina bent down and gave Kate a kiss on the brow. "Sleep well, dear." Fearing to look at Penhurst again, she rose and stepped toward the door.

In the darkened safety of the corridor, she leaned against the wall and took several deep breaths. This was happening far too quickly. Of course, her feelings had been building to this point ever since the day Penhurst had found her and Kate in the field, but she had always thought that falling in love would be a lengthy, gradual process that one would be aware of as it unfolded. Not this bolt out of the blue that hit like a hammer blow, taking away one's breath and leaving one stunned and confused in the bargain. Torn, Sophrina did not know whether to flee or wait for Penhurst. There was so much she wanted to say, and hear, yet she feared to stay.

"Sophrina?"

His voice was a bare whisper, but the sound sent chills up and down her spine. In the shadowed hall, with the wall sconce at his back, she could not see his face clearly. Sophrina knew she must look like a trapped rabbit and she felt the veriest fool.

"The second dinner bell has rung. We should return downstairs before they send out a search party," he said gently, knowing that he would rather stay in this wide, drafty hall forever as long as she was there. He reached out his hand and caressed her cheek.

"Sophrina, I—"

"Lost your way?" Seb's drawling tones met their ears.

"No, but it looks as if you have," Penhurst retorted irritably.

"Bets were being laid on what was delaying you two," Seb chastened. "I feared something might be amiss."

"Nothing was," said Penhurst coolly as he turned Sophrina toward the stairs. "Until you arrived," he whispered under his breath to Seb.

Seb only grinned and took up his station on Sophrina's other side.

Sophrina was glad the darkened hall hid the blush that rose to her cheeks. Seb's untimely interruption allowed her to rein in her racing emotions. By the time they had descended the stairs and stopped outside the drawing-room doors, she had herself firmly under control once again. It was only a temporary escape from the confrontation that she knew would come eventually, but she would at least have some time to control the panic rising within her. For she was elated and frightened at the same time, and woefully unsure of how to deal with her newfound feelings—and the man who engendered them.

Chapter 11

The light tap on her bedroom door did not surprise Sophrina. She had half hoped, half expected it for some minutes now, ever since she had said her good nights in the drawing-room downstairs. Yet for a moment she hesitated, suddenly nervous and uncertain. She was heading into the unknown and a tremor of apprehension shook her. She clutched her robe closer about her. In the next breath she cast all the ingrained rules aside and in a clear but low voice, called, "Come in."

Sophrina's eyes widened fractionally at the sight of Penhurst's undress. Even in a robe of dark claret brocade, he appeared as distinguished as he had earlier in his fashionable evening clothes. His look of eager expectancy gave him an air of uncommon vulnerability, a boyishness she had not often seen in him.

Penhurst shut the door behind him, the soft click of the latch punctuating the silence. Despite the dim light of the candles, he had no difficulty spotting Sophrina as she sat before the dressing table across the chamber. Her dark hair lay unbound in waving curls about her shoulders and in the lacy night robe she looked delicate and enticing. He crossed the room with hesitant steps.

"We did not have much opportunity to talk tonight," he explained, setting the decanter he carried on the table. He plucked two goblets from his pcoket. "Would you care to join me in a glass?"

"Yes, thank you, Elliston." Sophrina rose and stretched out her hand in greeting. She felt his slight tremor as he clasped it and realized with a start that he was as nervous as she.

After Penhurst filled the glasses, they took their places on the long, low sofa that Sophrina had always thought such an odd piece of furniture for a bedroom. She had never imagined the necessity of such a piece for a late-night tête-à-tête. Sipping her wine slowly, willing her nerves to calm, she waited for Penhurst to speak.

"You did such a marvelous job of putting Kate to bed tonight, I felt I should return the favor. I thought you might like a bedtime story of your own."

"I would feel privileged," she replied softly.

He cleared his throat with a nervous cough. The flickering candlelight bathed her face in its soft, golden light. Sophrina looked so young, so untouched by all the pain she had endured. She deserved to be happy. He prayed he could make her thus— and in so doing bring happiness to himself as well.

"Very well," he began with a slight hesitation. "Once upon a time there was a beautiful princess. She was married to a handsome prince, who was as wicked as he was handsome. He treated the beautiful princess cruelly, but was justly punished for his crimes, leaving the beautiful princess all alone. Then one day she met another prince. He was not so handsome as the first prince, but he was good and kind."

He stopped suddenly, all his carefully planned words sounding inane in his ears. He waited to hear her laughter.

"And?" Sophrina prompted with a teasing smile. "I cannot

predict much of a future for you as a storyteller if that is how you plan to stop, for I assure you it is a very poor ending.''

''How would you end it?''

''It is your story.'' Sophrina knew with a deep certainty how *she* would end the tale, but Elliston must speak his own words.

He impatiently ran a hand through his thick hair. ''All right then. The not-so-handsome prince fell in love with the beautiful princess. He married her and took her home to his castle where they lived in happiness forever and ever.''

''Forever?'' she whispered, hardly daring to breathe as she raised her eyes to his face.

''Dash it all, Sophrina, this sounded right when I first thought it out,'' he grumbled. ''Now I sound like a spotted adolescent in the throes of calf love.'' He took her hand in his. ''I love you, Sophrina. I have been slow to realize it, but now that I do, please know that I mean it with all my heart. It is as if a whole new life has opened up before me since I met you. You have shown me so much, how to be a father, how to play. How much I can need someone. I want you to be my wife, my companion, to share my bed and raise our children. Please say you will marry me.''

A sharp pain tore through Sophrina at his words. Sadness filled her eyes.

''Elliston, I . . . You know I miscarried once. It is possible I could never give you a child.''

He gently stroked her cheek with his fingers, reassuring her with his gaze. ''If we are not so blessed, we will have to accept that. It will not dim my love for you, or make my needs less.''

His mingled look of love and pleading cut through Sophrina's fears. How she could ever have thought him cold and austere? Her heart swelled with joy at the thought of a life with him.

''I should very much like to become your wife, Elliston,'' she replied with a shy smile.

Releasing her hand, he crushed her to his chest. ''I am no saint,'' he explained, with a wry grin, ''and I am certain I shall say things when I am in a temper that I will regret, but you can be assured I will never be false to you, my love. It is the one thing you need never doubt.''

''I shall endure your temper, for without it you would be such a paragon of perfection I could not bear to live with you."

"Liar," he said fondly, releasing her fractionally so he could look down into her eyes. "I will never be able to thank Kate enough for bringing you into my life."

"This will truly make her our child," Sophrina said.

"And you will be such a marvelous mother. To her and to the others I hope we will have."

He continued to gaze into her eyes for a long moment, then bent his head to gently brush her lips with his. But the moment their skin touched, he knew that the chaste betrothal kiss he had planned was an impossibility. Her soft, warm lips were too pliant, too inviting beneath his, and before he could recover his thoughts, his kiss turned demanding, passionate. And to his great delight, Sophrina responded with equal passion.

It was all she had wanted his kiss to be. Sophrina felt the blood surging through her veins; her skin tingled at every molten point of contact. Her lips responded hungrily to his, moving, shifting as their mouths met. At the tentative probing of his tongue, her lips parted in invitation, welcoming his entry. She clasped his shoulders, holding him to her.

Penhurst was lost to all rational thought, his senses filled to overflowing with images of Sophrina. He heard her labored breathing, barely audible above the pounding of his own heart. The spicy scent of carnations tantalized his nostrils; her mouth tasted sweet from the wine. Even with his eyes closed, he easily pictured her in his mind, her hair in tumbled disarray around her shapely shoulders. But it was the feel of her that drove him close to madness. He luxuriated in her soft curls, the curving tendrils feeling like strands of silk beneath his fingers. Encircling her waist, pulling her close, he marveled at her exquisite shape. Despite the clothing that lay between them, he felt her breasts pressed against his chest, her nipples hard and erect.

The burning ache in his groin finally intruded into his consciousness, bringing Penhurst back to a sense of place. He suddenly realized where he was and what he was doing. With a Herculean effort, he wrenched his lips from Sophrina's, planting gentle kisses on her face, stilling his roaming hands while he struggled to regain his composure.

Gulping in air, Sophrina fought her way back from the heavenly place his embraces had taken her. Never once had she lost the sense that it was Elliston who held her so close, Elliston whose hands traced a burning path across her body. It was him for whom her body ached.

"My apologies, Sophrina," he began, his words as broken as his breathing. "I had intended to seal our betrothal, not provide a preview of our wedding night."

Sophrina took a deep breath. "Why ever not?"

She felt him tense against her.

"Rina, love . . ."

Sophrina lifted her head from his chest and looked directly into his dark chocolate eyes.

"I am no virgin bride, Elliston, to be carefully initiated into the mysteries," she said plainly, a fond smile tugging at her lips. " 'T'would not be a mortal sin to antedate our wedding night."

"Are you so very certain?" he asked, marveling at the warm glow in her soft hazel eyes.

"As certain as I am about how much I love you." To show her determination, she fumbled with the belt of his robe. "Love me now, Ellis. Tonight."

He did not hesitate, but led her to the old-fashioned, curtained bed on the far side of the room. Lifting her onto the high mattress, Penhurst kissed her softly, tenderly, while his fingers struggled at the ties of her robe.

"I feel like a blundering virgin," he whispered in her ear before he ran his tongue along her earlobe. "How I want you, Rina."

His touch sent shivers up Sophrina's spine. Her hands, too, were busy, unfastening the buttons on his shirt.

In scant moments, robes and clothing lay in crumpled piles on the floor, and Penhurst pressed his naked form against hers as they lay between the smooth linen sheets. He marveled at her softness, her skin feeling like velvet beneath his hands. Touching, caressing, he began to explore the body he wished to know better than his own. He wanted this to be so perfect for her, to destroy any vestiges of doubt she had about herself as an exciting, desirable woman. He hoped this precious art of love would forever banish the demons of guilt and failure for them both.

God, she was shaped so exquisitely, from her tiny waist to

those deliciously full breasts that felt so marvelous in his hands. Groaning at his self-imposed restraint, Penhurst stroked his hand across her flat belly, inching ever closer to the junction of her thighs. As his hand feathered ever lower, he felt her legs part slightly, and he slipped his fingers toward the base of her curling triangle. He moaned a deep expression of desire as his probing fingers found her as damp and ready as he could ever want.

Elliston's gentleness was a delight to Sophrina. His hands and mouth stroked and kissed her until her body was screaming for release. She arched against him, her hands buried in his thick hair while he expertly suckled her aching breasts. Whispering his name, she held him to her, feeling such a mix of love and desire she thought she would burst.

Sophrina opened her eyes as she felt Ellison shift his body. Their gazes met briefly, then his mouth crushed down on hers in a bruising kiss. Without hesitation she parted her thighs and drew him to her, begging for this final expression of intimacy and love. As the tip of his rigid manhood touched her, she opened herself to him, crying out in delight as he slowly sheathed himself inside her welcoming body.

"Oh, Rina, Rina, my darling Rina," Penhurst whispered in her ear before planting kisses across her face and brow. It was agony to lie here motionless when his body begged for movement, but he did not want to hurt her. With iron control he held himself still until he felt the tenseness leave her body. Ever so slowly he began to move with a gentle cadence, keeping his pace steady until he felt the impatient urging of Sophrina's hips.

"I cannot bear it," she whispered, arching her body against his and wrapping her long legs about his hips to draw him deeper. She wanted him, needed this physical affirmation of love and joy. The heat built up inside her with explosive force, radiating out from that secret part of her, building and swelling until she could no longer contain it. With a long, low cry she shuddered beneath him.

All of his self-control broke at the realization of her pleasure and he lost himself in the joy of their union. He moved with her, their bodies instinctively matching rhythms as if they had long been lovers. He could only murmur her name as he buried his face in her hair, unable to consciously direct the motions of his body. He was lost in a world of sensation and delight that he had never thought possible; a world that only Sophrina could have shown him. As his own release burst inside her, he was inarticulate with joy.

Penhurst knew he was crushing her with his weight, but he could not move. Chest to chest, he felt their hearts pounding in unison and listened to the ragged tone of their breathing. At last, when he thought he could finally move, he raised himself onto one elbow. Brushing back a strand of her wayward hair, he looked down at the face of the woman he loved.

"That was beyond all that is wonderful, Ellis," she whispered, reaching up to stroke his face lightly with her fingers.

"So I thought." He planted a tender kiss on her lips then rolled to his back, pulling her into his arms. They lay together, talking and whispering of their newly acknowledged love, in voices that grew drowsier and drowsier until sleep claimed them both.

How warm and cozy her bed was this morning, Sophrina thought as she blinked back sleep. She stretched drowsily, then her eyes snapped open as her foot made contact with the man sharing her bed. A slow smile stole across her face as remembrance dawned and she snuggled back against his naked form, listening to his slow and regular breathing. Oh, how wonderful life could be!

After several minutes she grew impatient with Ellis's inactivity. Turning, she examined his sleeping face. He looked so untroubled, so unguarded. Much like a little boy, with his dark hair tousled about his head. Overwhelming love swept through her. He had brought it all back for her: hope, dreams, trust. She prayed she had been able to do as much for him. They had both been battered and bruised by life; it was not too much to ask that they be granted a little happiness.

Leaning over, Sophrina planted an airy kiss on his cheek. Receiving no response, she trailed her lips down his neck, then back up again, ending with a nibble on his earlobe. He uttered a muffled groan. Drawing back, Sophrina saw his eyelids flick open in widening surprise, before those chocolate eyes softened as he recognized her.

"I would like to awaken this way every morning," he said, pulling her face down to his for a long, drawn-out kiss.

As his hands began moving down her back, in long, sensual strokes, Sophrina's body tingled in newly awakened anticipation. She could never have imagined what a passionate man lurked beneath the dispassionate exterior. She ached to have their bodies joined again. Dear God, this must be what heaven was like.

When Penhurst at last reluctantly withdrew from her arms, it was with the whispered promise of a hasty return. They both were eager to share the news with Kate.

"Where have you been?" Kate demanded as Sophrina entered the nursery, followed closely by Penhurst. "I have been waiting forever."

"Your father and I had a very important matter to discuss," Sophrina explained, kneeling down to give Kate a hug.

Kate looked at Penhurst. "Was it about me?"

"Partly," he replied. "But mostly it involved Sophrina and myself. I have asked her to be my wife and she has accepted."

Kate looked quickly from Penhurst to Sophrina and back again. "You mean Rina will come here to live with us?"

Penhurst nodded.

Kate clapped her hands in joy, then flung her arms around Sophrina. "We will be able to play every day! And you can tuck me into bed every night."

Sophrina laughed. "That I will do gladly, Kate."

The girl looked thoughtful for a moment. "Does this mean I should call you 'Mama' now?"

"You may call me anything you want, Kate," Sophrina said softly. "If you want to keep the name 'Mama' for your own mother, I will not mind. I rather like Rina."

Kate's face broke into a relieved smile. "I am glad you will be my new mama, Rina." She gave Sophrina a damp kiss.

Over her shoulder Sophrina looked at Penhurst. As their gazes met, they both broke into broad smiles.

When they announced their intentions in the drawing room later that morning, Penhurst's guests greeted the news of their precipitate betrothal with amused congratulations. Lady Taunton accepted the news with a disinterested nod. Seb professed to be heartbroken, threatening to cast himself into the Thames in despair upon his return to London. In a quieter moment he drew Sophrina aside to offer his sincere congratulations.

"You are the best thing that has ever happened to Elliston," he confided as they sipped tea in a corner of the drawing room. "I could tell the moment I arrived that something about him was different, and now I know what it was."

"You make me sound like a paragon," Sophrina laughed. "When I would turn your words around and say the same of Ellis. I can still barely believe it is all happening."

"Do you plan to wed from Talcott or London?"

Sophrina blushed. "We have not had time to discuss that yet."

"I warn you, Seb, she is no longer available for your flirtations." Penhurst's teasing tone belied his stern expression as he approached.

"And so ends my last valiant attempt to win her away." Seb flung his hand to his brow in mock despair. "Alas, I am lost forever."

Penhurst pulled a chair close to Sophrina. "If he is bothering you, I can have him shown to the door."

"No, I do not think it will be necessary. I am certain he will behave himself in your presence."

"I was trying to elicit the details of your upcoming nuptials from your intended, but she roundly informed me you haven't any as yet."

Penhurst winked ostentatiously as Sophrina. "Good girl. With any luck, he will never learn the truth."

"I've always found weddings deucedly boring, myself," drawled Seb. "It only is of interest to the couple, and perhaps their relatives. Why people insist on inviting half the island, I will never understand."

"Good," said Penhurst. "Then you will not be cast down if we do not invite you."

Seb projected such an air of wounded sensibility that Sophrina was forced to laugh.

Penhurst looked at Sophrina, delighting anew at the love he saw shining in her eyes. "Perhaps we should discuss such 'boring' matters, my love."

"Oh, pray tell, do," urged Seb, settling himself back in his chair. "I am all ears."

"De trop, Seb, definitely de trop." Penhurst managed to glare and smile at the same time.

Seb rose chuckling to his feet. "If you grow bored with his arrogant ways, Lady Teel, before the fatal die is cast, you need only summon me and I will come to your rescue." Bowing low, he sauntered over to join the Newbys.

"He is horribly brash," said Sophrina, "but I do like him."

"So do I," Penhurst agreed. He took her hand in his, running his thumb over her knuckles. "We should talk about the wedding. Do you wish a grand affair?"

"Oh, no." Sophrina shook her head. "I would like to be married here at Talcott, if that suits you."

"It does," he said, drawing her hand to his lips.

He flashed her a look of such smoldering heat it brought a blush to her cheeks.

"I should like to take you to London, first," he said. "The lawyers will need to draw up the settlement papers and we can enjoy ourselves while they do the work. With the theaters open again, town will be lively and I am certain we can find ample amusements. I want you to look at the town house. You will want to redecorate it to your own taste and this way it will be ready by spring."

"And I thought I was marrying a man who enjoyed the peace and quiet of country living."

Concern crossed his face. "I only thought it would please you."

She squeezed his hand. "I am roasting you, Elliston. I would love to go to London. Yet will it not engender some comment if I accompany you?"

He looked puzzled.

"We are not yet wed," she pointed out.

"Ah, yes. Propriety. I am certain Aunt Violet would not be adverse to accompanying us—that is, if you would be amenable to her company."

"She would be very welcome," Sophrina said.

"But do not think I shall allow her room to lay between ours," he whispered softly. "One can carry propriety too far, you know."

"Yes," she said, with a warm smile, "one can. I should not

like to become a pattern card of behavior if it means giving up what we shared last night—andthis morning.''

His breath caught briefly at the remembrance of their passion. ''Do you think if I asked the houseguests to depart this very instant, they would comply?''

Sophrina laughed. ''It is hardly possible to ask them, Elliston. You must be patient, I fear.''

''I shall have to wait, then, since I have no choice,'' he said reluctantly. As he rose and extended his hand to her, he added in an undertone, ''but be assured I detest delays. I want you for my own, soon.''

Chapter 12

''A decidedly unfashionable time to visit London, I am afraid.'' Penhurst murmured softly in Sophrina's ear as the carriage rattled over the nearly deserted cobbled streets of Mayfair. ''I promise you we shall descend on the city in style during the spring.''

''I did not come to London for the amusements, Ellis,'' she whispered in reply. ''Only to be with you.''

He squeezed her gloved hand. ''I promise not to let you out of my sight.''

Sophrina could not restrain a twinge of dismay as she crossed the threshold of Penhurst's London house. Like Talcott, she had visited it often during the first months of her marriage, and even after three years she half expected Lea to be presiding in the drawing room. Sophrina shivered involuntarily.

''It is chilly in here.'' Penhurst was all solicitous concern as he ushered her into the front drawing room.

''No. It is only . . . this house is so tied with Lea in my mind.''

''We'll stay at Grillons,'' he announced, pulling her toward the door.

''No, no,'' Sophrina protested. ''I got over this feeling quickly at Talcott and it will pass here was well. I think it is only because I did not anticipate it."

He drew her into his arms. "Dearest Sophrina. You are much more deserving to be mistress here than she. Gut the interior. Redecorate to your heart's content. I want this to be *our* house."

"It will be," she promised, kissing him lightly on the cheek.

The bedroom would be the first place to start, Sophrina determined. She could not resist the temptation to peer into Lea's old room. Propriety dictated that an affianced bride should not yet sleep in the wife's chamber, sparing Sophrina from that awkwardness. But after taking a brief look, she resolved to have the room in readiness for their next trip to London.

For a fleeting instant Sophrina had the crude desire to burn the bed as well, but she dismissed the vengeful thought in an instant. Whatever physical intimacies Ellis and Lea had shared, they had not stemmed from a love such as she had now. And that was all that mattered.

Yawning slightly, Sophrina sank down onto the bed. There would be time enough to look for furniture, hangings, and paper in the next weeks. Penhurst had promised her carte blanche in redecorating the house, and she firmly resolved to take every opportunity of imprinting her image on their London home. She would exercise Lea's ghost here as easily as she had at Talcott. Sophrina eyed the heavy velvet draperies with undisguised loathing. When she finished with it, there would be no hint of the room's former occupant.

The days in London sped by with incredible swiftness. True to his word, Penhurst rarely left Sophrina's side. They traversed the town like tourists, viewing the paintings at the Royal Academy, inspecting the Elgin marbles in their new location at the British Museum, and crisscrossing the newly opened Waterloo Bridge. He escorted her to every manner of shop, waiting patiently while she made her choices, offering a suggestion if it was solicited, delighting Sophrina with his excellent tastes.

Penhurst was overwhelmed at how much Sophrina's presence changed his view of the city. In his earlier trips, he had endured the city as a necessary part of his visit, but he had not particularly enjoyed it. But with her at his side, it all seemed fresh and exciting. He delighted at her interest in all that was new and different, and shared her rediscovery of old favorites.

Even more blissful were the nights, when they could lie in each other's arms and talk about all their plans and dreams. Penhurst could not wait to introduce Sophrina to the sights of the Continent, where they would spend their wedding trip. The Foreign Office was keenly interested in his willingness to return and had virtually promised him a senior European post when he adjusted to the enchantment of his marriage. Sophrina assured him she was thrilled at the idea of living abroad, and he knew Kate would enjoy the experience.

It was at times like these when he could hardly believe that it was all happening to him. Watching Sophrina sleep next to him, her chest rising and falling with each soft breath, his happiness threatened to overwhelm him. Penhurst fervently prayed he would be worthy of Sophrina's love and trust.

He willingly left her side only once, to buy the special gift that would proclaim his love to all the world. There would be no family heirloom gracing her finger—he wanted a ring chosen especially for her.

Penhurst looked forward in eager anticipation to their first formal appearance as a betrothed couple. Their presence at the theater tonight would draw many eyes.

"I am sorry to be late," Sophrina apologized as she entered the drawing room. "We had a frightful time with the clasp of this necklace."

"The wait was well worth it."

"We shall miss the first act if we do not leave now."

"I assure you, that prospect does not dismay me in the least." Penhurst eyed Sophrina with undisguised admiration. The flowing blue satin gown did little to disguise her delightful figure and the low-cut neckline, set off by the dazzling Penhurst sapphires, revealed such an expanse of snowy bosom that he suddenly felt far too warm in his tailored evening dress.

"Do you like it?" Sophrina twirled about.

Penhurst nodded in appreciation.

"I was admiring how well the sapphires match."

Sophrina caught the gleam in his eye and rapped him lightly on the arm with her fan. "You were looking at what lies beneath the sapphires," she chastised. She glanced briefly in the mirror.

"I owe it is a trifle revealing. I have not had such an elegant evening gown in an age—do you think the modiste went too far?"

"Not at all. As long as you keep your shawl firmly wrapped about you, I have no complaints."

"T'would be a shame to hide such an expensive gown," she teased, delighted at his jealous possessiveness.

"Let us hope the next fashion is for high-necked frocks," he said in mock dismay. He reached for a small package on the table. "This is for you."

Sophrina carefully unfastened the silver-gilt paper, calmly noting the Rundell-Bridge imprint on the small, cube-shaped box. But she could not suppress her gasp of surprise and delight as she viewed what lay within.

"Oh, Ellis, it is lovely." The glistening diamonds twinkled in the light, their brilliance setting off the subdued hue of the large sapphire in their center.

"I sent the notice to the papers today, so I thought you had best appear with a betrothal ring tonight."

She pressed the box into his hands.

"You put it on."

Setting down the box and wrappings, he took her left hand in his and slipped the diamond-and-sapphire ring on her finger. Bringing her hand to his lips, he kissed the symbol of his love.

"Let us go back to Talcott tomorrow, Ellis," Sophrina said suddenly. "We could be wed this week."

He shook his head. "I promised you a shopping trip in London," he said with mock sternness, "and you have not yet bought nearly enough." He wagged his finger warningly. "It does not do for you to deliberately disobey me."

"Wait until you get the next round of bills from the dressmaker," she countered. Sobering, she reached up and cupped his face in her hands. "I love you so much, Ellis. I cannot wait to become your wife."

He allowed her to draw his face to hers, reveling in the gentle touch of her lips on his. Then Penhurst ran his hands down her sides, stopping at her tiny waist.

"Hang the theater," he said, pulling her roughly against him. "I think your new gown should be reserved for my eyes only."

"You are forgetting your aunt," Sophrina whispered, shivering with delight as he trailed slow kisses down the slender column of her neck.

"What does she have to do with it?" he whispered, his fingers teasing along the top of her bodice.

"She wanted a full report on who was in attendance tonight."

"But it is so fashionable to arrive late," he persisted, his hands growing more and more insistent. "I am certain Mr. Kean would not mind if you missed the first act."

Sophrina cautiously sipped her morning tea, watching with amusement as Penhurst's aunt poured over the society news in the morning papers. Even two weeks in London had not dimmed that lady's voracious desire for the latest *on-dits*.

"I would have thought your head had been filled with a week's worth of gossip at Lady Lyndhurst's last evening," Sophrina said.

"One can never have a surfeit of gossip," Violet retorted.

"Unless it is about oneself," Sophrina pointed out. "I own it was a great relief to discover that no one regards my upcoming marriage with more than cursory interest."

Indeed, it had been a pleasant shock to find the old scandal all but forgotten. Reaching for another piece of toast, Sophrina gratefully acknowledged that the last, lingering presence of William and Lea was finally exorcised from their lives.

She looked up as Penhurst hastened into the room, his face grim.

"Have you heard the news?"

"What news?" Sophrina looked puzzled.

"Princess Charlotte is dead."

"Oh, Ellis, no!" Sophrina half rose from her chair. They had all heard the sad news yesterday of the stillborn son, but the medical reports on the princess's condition had been encouraging.

"If you ladies do not mind, I think we should plan to leave for Talcott in the next day or so. The city will be shut down by the end of today, I am certain, and there will be no point in staying on."

"Will you be required to attend the funeral?"

"I doubt it," Penhurst replied. "I shall have the staff put up black hangings and a wreath today. I do not think there is a need for us to worry about obtaining full mourning for ourselves if we are leaving for Talcott.''

''Such a sad day,'' murmured Violet, excusing herself from the room.

''Since we are returning to Talcott early, should you like to move up the date of the wedding?'' Penhurst eyed Sophrina carefully.

Her face broke into a broad smile. ''I would not have any objections to that plan.''

''You have purchased enough items to keep you content?'' His voice was teasing.

''I believe I can survive for a short while,'' she replied.

''I will go out today and obtain the license, then. Shall we leave on Sunday, after services? That will allow us a few days to settle in. We could schedule the ceremony for Friday.''

She nodded in agreement. ''I think I can endure the wait until then.''

He bent over and kissed her gently. ''Friday it is, then. One week until you become my lady.''

''You look lovely, dear.'' The Dowager Countess Teel beamed approvingly at her.

''You are certain?'' Sophrina anxiously scanned her image in the mirror, fidgeting with the rich blond lace at the dress's bodice.

''I doubt Penhurst will even be able to give a coherent description of what you are wearing.'' Louisa shook her head with a smile. ''I have seen bridegrooms of nineteen act with less giddiness than he has displayed this week.''

''Oh, Louisa.'' Sophrina took the dowager's hands in hers. ''There are still times when I have to shake myself to believe this is truly happening. I am so happy, yet I have this horrible fear it cannot last.''

''Nonsense. Bridal nerves.'' The dowager took the diamond earrings from Sophrina's fumbling fingers. ''Let me help you.''

Sophrina sat quietly while the dowager fastened the jewelry to her ears. In only a short time she would be the new Countess of Penhurst. *Ellis's wife.*

''Are you ready?''

Sophrina nodded. She picked up the intricately carved ivory

fan that had been delivered to the cottage that morning. "For my bride on the happiest day of my life," his note had read. Tears misted in her eyes. In less than an hour, she would be his, forever.

Sophrina sat quietly during the short carriage ride to Talcott. She was grateful for Louisa's help today. The marriage would sever their formal ties to one another, but nothing could ever alter the friendship Sophrina felt for her mother-in-law. The walk from Talcott to the Dower House was only slightly longer than that from the cottage. They would remain close companions.

Bertram waited at the front stairs to hand them down from the carriage.

"Nervous?" he teased.

"No," Sophrina replied, realizing it was now true. "Anxious."

"As is your groom. He has been looking at his watch nearly every minute for the last hour."

"Then let us not keep him waiting further."

Penhurst heard the carriage as it swept up the gravel drive and fought against the impulse to rush out to meet Sophrina. Steady, he told himself. In a short time she would be his forever. Still, he could not help peering out the window as the carriage pulled in front of the house, but a bush effectively blocked his view.

With a sigh, he turned back to the assembled guests. Quite a contrast to the eleborate wedding with Lea seven years ago. Only his aunt and Bertram's wife waited with him today. He gave Kate an encouraging wink. She was so pleased at the small part she was to play today—handing Sophrina her flowers. Dressed in her flounced pink dress, her white-blond hair decorated with matching ribbons, she looked like a delicate piece of confectionery.

Voices in the hall outside the drawing room caught his attention and he turned expectantly to the door. First the dowager, then Bertram, then . . .

His breath caught in his lungs as Sophrina stepped into the room. Her eyes found his immediately, and the radiant smile she flashed him caused a painful lurch in his chest. He quickly crossed the room to be at her side.

"I thought you would never arrive," he whispered, placing her arm in his. He could not tear his eyes from her face.

"Nor did I." She smiled.

"Here are your flowers." Kate handed Sophrina a collection of delicate pink and ivory roses.

"Thank you, Kate." Sophrina bent to breathe in their aromatic fragrance.

The vicar cleared his throat. "Shall we begin?"

Penhurst led Sophrina across the room. They stood together, hands clasped, the pale light of late fall shining through the windows upon them.

"Dearly beloved . . ."

Sophrina heard the familiar words as if they were spoken at a great distance. She heard Ellis speaking beside her, found her mouth forming the requisite words at the proper time. She was aware of Penhurst drawing the requested ring from his pocket and handing it to the vicar, when a loud disturbance in the hall startled everyone. Sophrina found herself turning, as did Ellis, to look toward the door.

As they all turned toward the doorway, the butler appeared. "Excuse me, my lord, but there is a man here who insists—"

"Out of my way, you fool." A light-haired, deeply tanned man elbowed his way into the room.

Sophrina sensed the flowers slipping from her hands and heard, as if from a far distance, someone's in-drawn breath. But as she sank into oblivion, she recognized as her own the voice that wailed a long, drawn-out "Wil . . . liam."

Chapter 13

Penhurst caught Sophrina's crumpling form in his arms and quickly carried her to the sofa. Gently laying her down, he began chafing her wrists, whispering her name.

Behind him, the room was in commotion. The dowager countess sank into a chair, her face white with shock as her eldest son knelt beside her. Bertram guided Mary to the sofa, while Penhurst's aunt hastily whispered a quick explanation to the puzzled vicar. Kate looked around the room in bewilderment. Frightened by the strange behavior of all the grown-ups, she burst into tears.

Penhurst turned around in frustration. "Aunt Violet, can you take Kate to the nursery?"

"I want Rina!" Kate wailed, rushing across the room and flinging herself at Penhurst.

He gave her a soothing hug. "Rina is all right, Kate. She has just had a very bad shock. You go with Aunt Violet now, and I will come and talk with you later."

"Promise?"

"Promise." He gave her a brief kiss on the cheek.

Kate accepted Violet's hand and allowed herself to be led from the room. She gave the mysterious stranger who had caused such a commotion of curious glance. He returned it with a weak smile.

Mary was the first person to recover her wits and rummaged in the dowager's reticule for some hartshorn. Penhurst gratefully accepted the offered stimulant, waving it under Sophrina's nose.

As her eyes blinked open, Sophrina gradually focused on Penhurst, hovering only inches away.

"William?" she croaked.

He nodded grimly, offering her a sip from the glass of brandy Bertram handed him.

"Can you sit up?"

Sophrina nodded. She felt a trifle dizzy as she raised her head, but the sensation soon faded. She could not help glancing over Penhurst's shoulder at William. Their eyes met briefly before he turned back to his mother.

"I will take you upstairs now," Penhurst announced.

"But I—"

"You will go upstairs and lie down," he ordered. "I do not want you taking any more upset this afternoon."

She nodded. Leaning heavily on his arm, she rose to her feeet, swaying slightly with the effort. This could not really be happening. It was all part of some horrible nightmare and in a moment she would awaken on the morning of her wedding day . . .

William could not be here; he was dead. Yet the man who stood across the room from her looked exactly like him. By some twisted miracle he had survived and was standing here before her, threatening to destroy all her happiness again. Sophrina shivered and felt Elliston's reassuring touch on her arm. She fought the urge to bolt for the door and walked calmly at Penhurst's side. William's eyes met hers again and he took a step toward her, but she quickly averted her face. She could not bear talking with him now.

In the privacy of the hall, she sagged against Penhurst.

"Oh my God, Ellis, what are we going to do?" Despair filled his eyes. She searched his face, desperate for some sign of hope, of encouragement.

"Hush," he soothed, kissing her forehead, pulling her into his arms. "We will find a way out of this fix, I am certain."

Mary followed them into the hall.

"You go back and speak to . . . to Teel," she told Penhurst. "I will take Sophrina upstairs."

Penhurst was torn. He wanted to stay with Sophrina, to reassure her and himself that there *was* a solution to this mess, that they could find a way to marry. And he desperately wanted to hold her and be held in her comforting arms. God, how he needed her now. He had not realized until this very moment how much he did. The mere thought of life without her . . .

But he itched to confront Teel. To demand to know why he was not dead, why he was only now returning to wreak havoc in all their lives again. He nodded briefly to Mary.

"I will come to you soon, darling," he whispered, pressing a soft kiss to Sophrina's lips. "Do not worry."

The long stairs and halls seemed to go on forever to Sophrina. Her feet felt like lead, but she did not wish to lean too heavily on Mary, who had to be suffering from shock as well. Sophrina barely had enough strength to push open the door to her room.

Mary turned her toward the bed and rang for the maid. "Lie down, Sophrina. After a glass of brandy and a cold compress you will feel much better."

"William is alive," Sophrina said in a dull monotone, finally acknowledging the awful truth. "Oh, Mary, how can this be happening?"

"I feel as if I am being torn in two," she confessed. "To

find William is not dead—Louisa will be so relieved. But for you and Penhurst . . . And Bertram . . . I do not know what will come, Sophrina dear, but I pray there will be a happy conclusion to this mess for all of us."

Sophrina gulped the arriving brandy, wincing briefly at the hot burn sinking down her throat, then sank back across the counterpane. She allowed Mary to place a cold cloth across her eyes and forehead. It did nothing to relieve the knot in her chest, but it was a relief to lie in the calming darkness.

"You return downstairs," Sophrina insisted. "I shall be all right until Ellis comes up. I know you want to be with Bertram. Oh Mary, what will become of us all?"

Mary gave her a comforting peck on the cheek and squeezed her hand before she exited the room.

Everyone looked around uneasily when Penhurst reentered the drawing room. Mumbling a hasty apology, the vicar took his leave. Bertram and his mother looked at one another, then announced they would wait for Mary in the hall. Teel and Penhurst were left alone.

"I suppose I should commend you on your timing," Penhurst said sarcastically. "At least there will be no need for bigamy proceedings."

"Oh, I hardly think it would have come to that," Teel said smoothly. "Since I was presumed dead, it was an honest mistake. No court would have desired to prosecute."

"If you expect my heartfelt gratitude, you are mistaken. I can only surmise that since you arrived alone, Lea is actually dead?"

Teel nodded bleakly. "The storm swept up so fast . . . there was nothing we could do. Some fishermen dragged me half-dead from the water. Lea's body was never found."

"And it took you over a year to make your way back to England?" Penhurst's sarcasm was biting.

"I could not even move for months," Teel retorted. "Leg broken, three ribs cracked, and a sore head for weeks. I was stranded in some island fishing village, where no one even spoke English and I had no money. Some French visitors took pity on me and took me with them when they left."

Penhurst turned away and poured himself a large tumbler of

brandy. "So. You have returned. How do you propose to release Sophrina from your marriage so she and I can be wed?"

"I have no intention of ending my marriage to Sophrina." Teel spoke smoothly. "I fully intend to have her back at Charlton with me."

"Like hell you will," growled Penhurst. "You showed her what you thought of her when you chose my wife over your own. Don't try to cozen me into thinking you want her now."

"I know I caused her pain, but I want to make it up to her," Teel returned. "I want a family. A child to call my own. A *son*."

"You have Bertram to inherit. After playing viscount for a year and a half, he is rather good at it."

"Surely you can understand my position, else why would you be so eager to marry yourself? You, too, must desire a child of *your flesh.*"

Penhurst struggled to hold in the rage that boiled inside him. Here stood the bastard who had stolen his wife, who threatened to take back the only woman he had ever loved, and had the bloody nerve to taunt him about the child he raised as his own.

"There is no guarantee Sophrina can bear a child," Penhurst reminded him coldly. "Or were you too busy with Lea to pay much attention to that particular disappointment?"

Teel flushed. "Many women lose their first child."

"There are plenty of other ladies in England," Penhurst suggested icily. "Ones who would view the prospect of becoming a viscountess with delight. I do not doubt that with enough money we could work out a satisfactory arrangement in some court. Once your marriage is dissolved, you would be free to wed where you would."

"Why should I wish to go through all the inconvenience when I already have a wife?"

"She is not your wife." Penhurst's angry voice thundered in the room. "You relinquished your claim to her when you ran off with mine."

"In the eyes of the law we are still man and wife," Teel reminded him.

Penhurst was incredulous. "Give it up, Teel. You only want Sophrina out of spite. You're like a spoiled child who breaks one toy then demands another. You cast your wife aside without a second thought, but now that you've killed Lea, you want Sophrina back.''

Penhurst saw with malicious content that his barb had hit the mark.

"What you think is irrelevant," Teel sneered. "Sophrina is still legally my wife and I intend to enforce my rights.''

"You will have to deal with me first." Penhurst spat the words.

Shutting the drawing-room door behind her, the dowager neatly summed up the tense scene and let out a sigh of relief that she had entered in time.

"William, dear boy, give your mama your arm."

Penhurst was not fooled by her sudden display of infirmity, but he appreciated her attempt to diffuse the situation. In another minute, he would have planted Teel a facer.

"Sophrina is resting quietly," she said to Penhurst after settling on the sofa. "Now, William, I think I have had quite enough excitement for one day. You may escort me home and we can take up this matter again tomorrow. You and Bertram will have enough to discuss tonight.''

Teel nodded his acquiescence. He gave Penhurst a final challenging stare.

"Thank you, Lady Teel, for your help today," Penhurst said, walking with them into the hall. "You will understand if I do not see you out."

Penhurst bounded up the stairs, taking them two at a time. Racing down the hall in long, loping strides, he reached Sophrina's chamber. He knew not what he could say that would bring a measure of comfort to either of them, but he had to be with her. It was to have been their wedding day, before all their hopes and dreams were dealt this cruel blow. Hesitating, he knocked gently, then entered.

She had slipped out of her gown and crawled under the covers, and for a moment he feared she was asleep. But the form on the bed turned toward the door.

"Ellis?"

"I am here, darling." He sat down on the bed beside her.

She struggled to sit up, reaching for him as he pulled her into his arms. Sophrina clung to him in desperation, praying he would have a solution to this horrifying situation.

"Oh Ellis, what are we going to do?" Her voice broke with despair.

"I do not know," he said bleakly. "He says he fully intends to remain your husband. He wants heirs, he said."

"I will never go back to him."

"You will not have to," Penhurst soothed. "I will keep you safe, no matter what. It may take some time, but you will be my countess one day. Do not cry, love."

"I cannot help it," she sobbed, dampening his coat with her tears. "He will keep us apart forever, I know it."

"Hush now." He sought to calm her, stroking his hand over her back in long, sweeping motions. Dear God, what a coil they were in! Yet for her sake he must maintain an optimistic front. "I am certain we shall find a way out of this mess. I will send tomorrow for lawyers from London. They will surely find some ancient precedent in law and have you rid of Teel in a trice."

"Do you really think so?"

Her tear-blotched face was so filled with hope he almost felt guilty for inspiring such false optimism.

"I would be willing to wager you shall be my wife before the new year," he lied.

Sophrina lay back against him, feeling warm and secure in the hold of his arms.

He continued to comfort her with words and gestures, until she slipped into a light sleep. Carefully, he eased himself from her arms and left her to rest undisturbed.

Some perverse notion drew him back to the drawing room. The fire still burned in the grate. Someone had removed the glasses and champagne, thank God. But lying next to the sofa, unnoted in the confusion, lay Sophrina's bouquet. He reached over and picked it up. The flowers were bruised and crushed; at least one person had stepped upon them in the chaotic moments after Teel arrived.

Penhurst crumpled another blossom in his hand, watching the fragile petals disintegrate beneath his fingers. Ruined. Like all his plans and dreams for himself and Sophrina. Despite his words of encouragement to her upstairs, he was not nearly as confident as he made himself out to be. He prayed that the lawyers would be able to use Teel's adultery with Lea and his abandonment of Sophrina to free her from the unwanted marriage. The thought of life without Sophrina was unbearable. Somehow, he would win her free.

He felt like yelling, screaming against the malignant gods who had plotted their schemes against him. They had shown him hope, joy, and love, only to snatch it away before it was truly in his hands. He could imagine them now, with their mocking, jeering faces, laughing at how their latest joke had felled the arrogant Earl of Penhurst. First they had sent him a wife who betrayed him, now they dangled before him a woman he could not have. For the hundredth time, he wondered what he had done to deserve such a fate.

The room was in shadow when Sophrina awoke. For a moment she was confused; this was not her bed, or her room. Then all the memories came flooding back and she batted back the tears that sprang into her eyes. It was to have been her wedding day, the most marvelous day of her life. And it had turned into the worst nightmare possible. Nothing could compare to it. Not even that miserable day when she discovered Lea and William together. If she had tried for a hundred years, she could not have imagined a more horrifying situation.

Struggling to remain calm, she reminded herself that Ellis said they would find a solution. There were lawyers, he had said, lawyers who could find a way out of this mess. Ellis would take care of things and soon they would be together, just as they had planned. She and Ellis and Kate . . .

Slowly Sophrina crawled out from under the covers. She realized, sadly, that she must go home again. She could not stay with Ellis while they worked their way out of this mess. Appearances must be preserved at all costs.

With dismay she eyed the dress hanging in the wardrobe—the one she had planned to wear as she and Ellis left for their journey to the Continent. But she had no other garment but her wedding gown, and that she would not put on again until she was free to marry. With a sigh, she began to dress.

"Ellis?" Sophrina peered into the darkness of the drawing room, uncertain if he was there.

"Sophrina?"

She saw his shadowed form rise from a chair and come to her.

"What are you doing down here? You should be resting."

"I am fine," she said, waiting while he lit some candles. With a searching glance, she took in his pale and haggard face. He looked little better than she felt. She reached out and brushed back a lock of hair from his brow.

"Are you hungry? I was going to have a cold collation sent up." He sighed. "It sounds stupid to even think of eating right now, but I think we will both feel better for it." He nodded toward the glass near his chair. "I fear I could use some solid food."

She nodded. "I will eat a bit, I think, before I return home."

"Home?"

She nearly cried out at the hurt and pained look in his face. "I cannot stay here anymore, Ellis."

His shoulders slumped. "You are right, of course. But not tonight. My aunt is still here to act as chaperon. Please stay the night?" He drew her into his arms, hugging her fiercely. "Dear Sophrina, please tonight. I need you so very badly . . ."

She flung her arms around him and burst into the tears she had struggled against. "It is not fair," she sobbed against his chest. "I want you so much."

"Hush, hush, love," he said, stroking her hair and clasping her to him. His own vision blurred. "Everything will be all right. I promise."

She brought her mouth to his, kissing him desperately, clutching at his shoulders, holding Ellis against her in one mad bid to rid her mind of the disaster surrounding them. His lips tasted of brandy and salt from their mingled tears.

It was fear, not passion, that guided his hands over her lithe form. He could not lose her, he could not lose her. The litany burned in his brain as he stretched her out upon the sofa, stroking her into a fever pitch of arousal. He wanted her to need him as much as he needed her, wanted this physical assurance that she was still his, would still be his, in the long, bleak days to come. Murmuring soft endearments, he joined them together. He could not tear his eyes from hers, watching the play of emotion dancing across her face as he brought her to the edge, then pushed her over. And he knew there was pain as well as joy in the tears that filled her eyes.

Sophrina held him in her arms, his head nestled against her

breasts. She ignored his crushing weight, willing him to lay atop her forever. Sophrina clung to him, afraid to break the physical contact, needing the comforting reassurance of his body atop hers. She knew the doubt behind his earlier optimistic words, but clung to the hope like a drowning person. Without it, she was lost.

Chapter 14

Ellis slipped into her room at Talcott later that evening, making love to her again with a tenderness that left them both in tears. Throughout the long night they talked and clung to one another, promising that all would be well soon, although each knew the other spoke from optimism rather than conviction. As the cold light of dawn crept into the room, he reluctantly left her. Sophrina tried to sleep, but succeeded only fitfully between bouts of tears and despair. Finally bowing to the inevitable, she dragged herself from the bed and began to dress.

Staring at her wan face in the mirror, Sophrina grimaced at the blue shadows under her eyes. She looked a fright and it would only make the upcoming interview more awkward.

For she and Penhurst must sit down with Kate and attempt to explain to her why she would not be going to stay at Charlton with Susan again, and why Sophrina was not going to be coming to live at the house. Sophrina closed her eyes wearily. William's circle of pain was now extending to the next generation.

Penhurst greeted Sophrina with an encouraging smile outside the door to the nursery. She tried to summon up a smile of her own, but could not force her lips to move. He stood aside silently and followed her into the room.

Kate crawled onto Sophrina's lap and waited. Sophrina struggled for the words to tell Kate all that had happened, but how did one distill such a convoluted mess into words a four-year-old could understand? It was not fair to burden the girl with the problems of the adults in her life; she only needed to know the barest facts. Sophrina cast an apprehensive glance at Penhurst, then launched into her explanation.

"Your papa and I are not going to be married right away, Kate," she began haltingly. "We need to delay the wedding for a while. But we shall not be leaving on our trip, either, so this way you will be able to stay here at Talcott with your papa."

"Was it because of that man who was here yesterday?" Sophrina paled. "He is part of the reason, yes."

"Who is he?"

"He is Edward and Susan's uncle," Penhurst interjected.

"Will I still get to see you?" Kate's face looked troubled.

"Of course you will," Sophrina replied quickly. "You may come and visit me every day."

"I want you to come here!" Kate pouted.

"Sophrina will be able to visit occasionally," Penhurst explained gently, "but she will not be here as often as she had been—at least for a while."

"You will be here?" Kate looked doubtfully at Penhurst.

"I will be here, Kate." He gave her a reassuring smile. "We can battle with the soldiers on the drawing room carpet every day, if you like."

Kate looked up at Sophrina. "And I can visit you as well?" She nodded. "Anytime you wish, Kate."

"All right, then," Kate said, slipping from Sophrina's lap. She raced out of the room, in search of her kitten.

Penhurst saw the bleak look in Sophrina's eyes and hastened to her side. "It will be all right, love," he comforted, hating to see her pain. "After we are wed, this will seem naught but a bad dream."

She raised her hand to his cheek. "I love you so, Ellis," she whispered sadly. Then she found herself wrapped in his arms, crying against his coat as if her heart would break.

Sophrina spent the next four days in a daze. Removing to the cottage shortly after the talk with Kate, she went through the motions of her life without any real sense of what she was doing. Perhaps when the lawyers arrived and offered some concrete solutions, she would be able to concentrate once again. She could not bear the heartrending task of unpacking her trunks and restoring the cottage to order; Penhurst sent staff from

Talcott to assist Jenny while Sophrina spent the day playing with Kate.

A note arrived from William, but Sophrina threw it onto the fire unread. Elliston had told her all she needed to hear about William's plans for her. If she had been able to summon up any emotion, she would have been livid with anger that he could even begin to *think* she would ever go back to him after he had treated her so callously. But she did not have the strength of will to feel anything but a slow, creeping numbness.

Penhurst escorted her to Talcott on the morning set for the lawyer's arrival. They were both quiet on the journey. Sophrina found it achingly painful to be in the small, confined space of the carriage with him, knowing they would have to part again before the day was out. How different it was from their laughing, teasing return from London.

"The lawyers have arrived, my lord." Penhurst's butler brought the news to the study.

"Excellent. Send them up." Penhurst turned to Sophrina. "Now we will discover how to free you from Teel."

Sophrina gave him a reassuring smile, but inside she did not feel at all optimistic. All his encouraging words could not still the dread within her. She feared she would be bound to William until death.

It took some minutes for the three lawyers to unpack their papers and get settled. Sophrina sat quietly, staring at her hands folded in her lap. Penhurst's sapphire betrothal ring still graced her finger, mocking her with its glittering display. Everything else had gone so wrong; it seemed incongruous the diamonds and sapphires had not turned to ordinary stone at the same time. She could not bring herself to remove it; she needed some reminder that there had once been the promise of a future.

"Well now." The senior barrister, Simms, cleared his throat. "As I understand the problem, my lord, you wish to find a way to release Lady Teel from her marriage in such a way that she is free to wed you."

Penhurst nodded.

"Let me review the facts. Lady Teel wed the viscount in 1813. You state, Lady Teel, that in 1814 you discovered your husband was involved in an adulterous affair with the Countess Penhurst. In 1815, those two persons left England for the express purpose of pursuing their affair on the Continent. You, my lord, then procured an ecclesiastical divorce from your wife and lodged a Crim. Con. complaint against Lord Teel. You were granted damages, and a private divorce act was passed by Parliament."

"That is correct."

"Subsequently word arrived that both the countess and Lord Teel had drowned in a sailing accident. Lady Teel, believing herself to be a widow, then entered into an agreement to marry you. Lord Teel arrived during the wedding ceremony and is insisting that his wife return to him."

They all nodded.

The assistant, Barnett, turned to Sophrina. "Lady Teel, is there any hope of a reconciliation between yourself and your husband?"

"None," she replied firmly.

"Apart from the affair with the countess, do you know of any other unsavory actions engaged in by Lord Teel?"

Sophrina shook her head.

"Do you have any sisters, Lady Teel?"

She nodded.

"Did you ever notice your husband paying unusually close attention to them?"

"No." His question puzzled Sophrina.

"Lady Teel, I need to ask you some questions that you may find awkward. But it is important that you answer me honestly. During your marriage, did your husband ever strike you?"

"Never."

"Did he ever demonstrate any cruelty toward you? Imprison you in your chambers, or deny you sustenance?"

"No."

"During your marriage, did you have a normal wifely relationship with your husband?"

Sophrina's cheeks reddened. "Yes."

"At any time, Lady Teel, did your husband ever insist on any practice you found distasteful or unnatural?"

"What is the point?" Penhurst exploded, furious at the embarrassment the questions caused Sophrina.

"Unfortunately, my lord, mere adultery on the part of the husband is not enough to win a divorce case. If we could show cruelty, or unnatural practices, Lady Teel might have a valid complaint.''

"No," replied Sophrina, taking Penhurst's hand to calm him. "It was always very . . . normal."

"Hmmmm." Simms consulted a paper in front of him. "I am sorry to say, my lord, that there is very little likelihood that a divorce act could be passed on behalf of Lady Teel."

"That is incredible," Penhurst burst out. "The man committed flagrant adultery. He abandoned Sophrina for two years, forcing her to live on the sufferance of his relatives. And you say she cannot be free of him?"

The lawyer sighed. "There has been only one successful divorce suit brought by a woman in Parliament, my lord. It involved adultery, combined with an incestuous relationship with the woman's sister. Abandonment might have been a mitigating factor, but with Teel's return and apparent willingness to resume his role as husband . . . Lady Teel is now at fault for refusing to return to him."

"That is preposterous!" Penhurst's face grew dark with anger. "No woman in her right mind would go back to a scoundrel like Teel."

"Nevertheless, in opposing a reconciliation, Lady Teel has put herself into a position of wrong."

Penhurst shook his head in disgust. "What is the purpose of the law if it cannot help a woman in Sophrina's position?"

"The ecclesiastical courts would take into account past grievances," the third solicitor, Howe, interjected. "Lady Teel might very well win a permanent decree of separation."

"However, she would not be free to remarry," Barnett nodded.

"Unacceptable," said Penhurst.

The three lawyers looked at one another.

"Scotland, then, is your only hope," announced Simms. "However, even that option is no longer as promising as it was several years ago. There has been a great outpouring of objection here in England to the free and easy manner in which divorces are granted over the border. I must warn you at the outset, that any decree obtained in Scotland may subject Lady Teel to prosecution for bigamy should she remarry."

"The Duchess of Argyll obtained her divorce in Scotland," Penhurst pointed out. "I have not seen any charges brought against her."

"It was their divorce that prompted the outcry. It was so obviously a collusion between her and Lord Anglesey that many voices were raised in opposition."

"She certainly had just cause," said Sophrina.

"We are not discussing the merits of her complaint, my lady, but only the legal aspects. There is no question that the adultery evidence brought before the courts in Scotland was obtained with Lord Anglesey's cooperation. However, even those in Scotland who questioned the manner of that divorce have since ruled that adultery is adultery, whether it be manufactured for the court or not."

"Then all we need to do is charge Teel with adultery in Scotland and Sophrina will be free?" Hope leaped in Penhurst's eyes.

"Not exactly." Barnett hesitated. "There have been some cases where the adultery was committed outside Scotland and charges were successfully brought. But either the complaining party or the perpetrator must in some manner reside in Scotland. The case is heavily strengthened if the adultery takes place over the border."

"What you mean to say," noted Penhurst, "is that we need to convince Teel to remove to Scotland, bed some tavern wench in the presence of witnesses, then charge him in court."

"That would make matters much easier."

"William would never agree," Sophrina said with a despairing shake of her head.

"He might not be amenable at the moment," Barnett agreed. "However, if he sees, after time, that you are determined in your refusal to return to him, he may be more cooperative. If his purpose in wishing your marriage resumed is to acquire heirs, he must have a cooperative wife. In six months or a year, he may be quite willing to discuss the matter of a Scottish divorce."

Penhurst closed his mouth in a grim line.

A wave of despair washed over Sophrina. Six months? A year? William could walk away from her without a backward glance, yet she was still tied to him until he chose to release her. She gave Penhurst a disheartened look.

"Are there no other alternatives?" Penhurst asked. "Somewhere on the Continent, perhaps?"

Simms shook his head. "I am afraid not, my lord. One can obtain a divorce with more ease in several other countries, it is true, but any such decree would lay Lady Teel open to the charge of bigamy upon her remarriage. A Scottish divorce may be tolerated because of the union. But a foreign one would not."

A deep silence filled the room. Penhurst was filled with a deep sense of foreboding. An icy chill buffeted his body. Was he to be denied forever the woman he loved?

Simms rummaged through his papers again. "What I suggest, under the circumstances, is that I prepare a letter to Lord Teel, outlining your interest in obtaining a divorce for Lady Teel in Scotland and asking for his cooperation in the matter. Perhaps if the approach is made through lawyers, personal emotions will not be so easily aroused."

"I agree," said Penhurst. "I do not think it is a good idea for Teel and myself to speak, for I doubt I could keep my fist from his face."

"Ellis!"

"One other thing." Howe cleared his throat. "Is there any cause for Lord Teel to suspect he has grounds for a divorce suit of his own?"

Penhurst and Sophrina exchanged guilty glances.

"He does not have cause for such a suit," Penhurst lied smoothly.

"It is not always easy to keep such a thing quiet—servants will gossip. If there has been even a hint of impropriety in your conduct, Teel could very well use it against you."

"Lady Teel has always been properly chaperoned in any situation that might have been considered compromising," Penhurst reiterated. "We did spend several weeks together in London, but my aunt was in residence as well."

"I realize that it is not a pleasant alternative, but if Lord Teel were to charge his lady with adultery, it would solve your whole problem."

"I do not want Sophrina's name dragged through the courts,"

Penhurst said adamantly. "Under any humane judgment, she is the injured party and I do not want her labeled guilty. It is she who will bring charges against her husband."

"Frankly, Lord Penhurst, it is your best chance. I suggest you strongly consider the possibility."

"Never."

"Ellis . . ." Sophrina's voice was pleading. "Let us wait and see how William responds to the idea of a divorce in Scotland. Our fears may be premature."

Penhurst had no doubts regarding Teel's response, but he nodded. He did not want to cause Sophrina further upset. She had enough to worry about.

"What I would advise, my lord, is that you continue to observe the strictest proprieties in your dealings with Lady Teel. I would caution against inviting her to your home unless you have adequate chaperonage. And the same applies to any visits at her residence. You must not give Lord Teel any grounds for a complaint."

Penhurst nodded grimly, unwilling even to comprehend the implications of those suggestions. He stood, indicating the discussion was over.

Watching Sophrina as the solicitors filed out, he was filled again with an overwhelming sense of grief and loss. They had come so close to perfect happiness; now there was only uncertainty and worry—and guilt. He could not rid his mind of the lawyers' probing and questions. He and Sophrina *were* guilty of adultery. If their earlier transgression had been inadvertent, the last bittersweet night had been acted out with full knowledge that her husband lived. And he could answer with utter certainty how Teel would feel if he discovered the truth.

They would have to wait Teel out. They could only hope that when he realized Sophrina was firm in her decision not to return to him, he would grant his wife her freedom. But how long would it take? Months? Years? Teel would give in eventually, of that Penhurst was certain. But at what cost to Sophrina and himself?

Penhurst looked up from his musings and found Sophrina looking at him, a pensive expression upon her face. He gave a rueful smile. "Woolgathering, I fear."

"The news is not good, is it?"

He shook his head. "I cannot deny we are in a dreadful coil." He stepped closer and toook her hands in his. "But I am certain that I love you as much as is humanly possible, and I will wait as long as I must to make you my wife."

She desperately wanted to believe him. But the cold fear that had gripped her earlier was sinking its icy tentacles into her heart. Elliston wanted her now. But would he feel the same after months of agonized waiting? They had to find some way to force Teel's cooperation.

Penhurst looked down to their clasped hands before he lifted his gaze to hers. "I think we need to make some arrangements for Kate. It is obvious that your visits here will of a necessity be limited. I shall hire a governess to take care of her. You do not need the extra strain of managing Kate's lessons any longer."

"I think I would go mad if it weren't for my times with Kate," she protested. "It is the only thing that has not changed."

He slipped his arms around her and held her close. "I know this is a devilish situation. But there is a way out of it, somehow."

Standing like this, in the encirclement of his arms, Sophrina was almost tempted to hope. When she was with him, she felt safe and secure. But when they were apart, and most particularly at night as she lay alone in her bed, she was buffeted by stormy thoughts. So much could go wrong. William could keep her from Ellis forever, if he wished. They simply had to find a way out of the darkness, before it was too late for all of them.

Chapter 15

As the fall days drifted toward winter, Sophrina settled into an uneasy routine at her cottage. Penhurst had hired a governess for Kate, and although Sophrina bemoaned the loss of her prize pupil, she realized that it was best for the girl. With both herself and Penhurst constantly on edge, the detached calm of a governess was good for Kate. Ellis still brought her to the cottage every other day, after the morning lessons. Sometimes he would remain, but more often he would not. Sophrina missed his presence, but sensed that he, like herself, found the unbearable ache of not being able to wed weighing on them every moment they were together. If they were alone, they did not have to hide their sorrow. But in Kate's presence, they were forced to put up a brave front.

Poor Kate. It was so difficult for Sophrina to explain why she was not going to be Kate's mama, at least in the immediate future. Kate did not understand why the grown-ups in her life went about with sad looks on their faces, or why there were so many whispered conversations in corners, or abrupt ends to sentences when she walked into the room. All she knew was that Rina had moved back to her cottage and was no longer there to tuck her in at night. Bewildered, she retreated into silence. Kate's new quietness pained Sophrina, for she was helpless to right matters.

Even with Kate's visits, time hung heavily on Sophrina's hands. The mild autumn weather was long gone, and the blustery, rainy days of late fall did not encourage the tramping walks she so enjoyed. Restless and bored, she was forced to remain inside, sketching or sewing.

With candles supplementing the dim light of a late November morning, Sophrina worked the intricate smocking stitches into the garment's bodice. It was a frivolous use of her time to make an apron for Kate, when Penhurst could easily buy the same article in London. But the precision and concentration required by the work had a calming effect on Sophrina's nerves. It was difficult to think of other matters when one was counting stitches. Sighing, Sophrina snipped the end of a thread. She would soon have the girl decked out in every conceivable outfit of clothing. It was a small price to pay for sanity.

"The viscount is here, my lady." Jenny stood at the parlor door.

Sophrina glanced up from her sewing in surprise. Did she mean William? Here?

"I do not wish to see him, Jenny," Sophrina stated flatly. "You may tell him he is not to call here again."

"Now Sophrina, is that any way to treat your husband?" Teel

brushed past the maid and entered the room. In his arms was an enormous bouquet of deep red hothouse roses, which he held out to Sophrina. "I bought these for you."

Sophrina ignored his offering, glaring at him with ice in her eyes.

Teel stood for a long minute, the flowers in his outstretched arms, before he turned and shoved them into the hands of the maid. "Find a vase for these."

"Jenny, I wish you to send a message to Talcott," Sophrina ordered. "Tell Lord Penhurst that Lord Teel is here."

The maid hastily exited the room.

"Afraid of me?" Teel lifted a quizzing brow. "I did not think I was one to inspire that emotion in you."

"I have nothing to say to you, William." She tossed her head in a dismissive gesture. "You are here against my wishes and if you were a gentleman, you would leave."

"I hurt you very badly, didn't I, Sophrina?" Teel exhaled a long, drawn-out sigh. "I know there is nothing I can say or do that will remove that pain. All I can tell you is that I regret my actions. I was foolishly selfish. I would give anything to be able to go back and do things aright." Watching for her reaction, he sat down with deliberate slowness.

Sophrina eyed him with a stony glare.

Teel ran a nervous hand through his white blond hair, uttering a hesitant laugh. "Foolish of me to suppose you would be pleased to see me again." He flashed her an imploring look. "I thought of you often, you know."

"Not until you killed Lea, I am certain." Sophrina did not dampen the bitterness in her voice.

He winced. "Do not hold me responsible for that tragedy, Sophrina. It was a terrible accident. I realized running off with her was a stupid mistake long before that. Yet I discovered that too late, I am afraid. After Penhurst divorced her . . . well, I was responsible for her then. I had to remain with her. But I would have given anything to have been able to return home to you."

Sophrina abruptly stood, forcing Teel to scramble to his feet.

"What is the point?" she demanded angrily. "The damage was done, William. I can never look upon you in the same manner as I once did. I am no longer the sheltered innocent you married. For my sake, for all our sakes, admit defeat and let me go.''

"I cannot," he whispered, reaching out an imploring hand. ''I love you, Sophrina. Even when I was with Lea, I realized it was you I loved all along.''

"Spare me your lies.''

"It is true, I swear it.''

Sophrina turned her back to him, struggling to control her mounting rage. He was playing a devilish deep game. But for what purpose? She did not believe for a minute that he really wanted her. He was acting out of spite, angry because she wanted someone else.

"William, whatever affection I once felt for you is long gone. Dead by your own hand.'' She whirled to face him, anger in her eyes. ''Accept that and let me go. You can find another to love and wed and bear your children. Allow me to go to Penhurst.''

He stepped toward her, placing his hands lightly on her shoulders. ''Sophrina, I—''

"Do not touch me!'' She wrenched away from his hold.

All the hurt, humiliation, and anger she had endured at the hands of this man swept through her, yet she felt strangely calm now that she confronted her tormentor. Sophrina met his gaze without flinching, curious why he attempted to continue this charade they both knew was false.

He looked much like the William of old; the weeks at home had eliminated the gauntness from his face and frame. Even his deep tan was starting to fade. And just as he grew to look more and more like the man she remembered, so did his words sound familiar. Sophrina did not think for a minute he had truly changed, despite this new stance of abject apology. He was the same old William, concerned only with his selfish desire. He had cozened her into believing his words once, but she would never be taken in by him again.

He returned her gaze with an intensity she found frightening. A wave of dizziness, a sick apprehension, swept over her and she raised her hand involuntarily to her head.

In an instant William was at her side, full of solicitous concern. Taking her arm, he guided her to a chair, ringing for the housekeeper and barking out curt orders for a glass of water.

"You are not ill?" he asked.

"T'would be a miracle if I am not, under the circumstances," she snapped, before taking a sip of the proffered water. " 'Tis not every woman whose husband returns from the dead."

"I did not come here to cause you upset," he murmured softly. "I only wanted to talk to you." He sat across from her. "We have not had a chance to sit down and talk, face-to-face. We need to, Sophrina."

"That is my choice, William. I have nothing to say or discuss with you, except that I no longer wish to be your wife. Let us all go to Scotland and put an end to this farce of a marriage."

"I cannot let you go." He reached out his hand to her.

She stared coldly at his pleading gesture, until he self-consciously withdrew his arm.

"I should like you to leave, William. Now."

Teel opened his mouth as if to rebut her command, then firmly shut it again. "If that is what you wish."

"It is."

He bowed low. "I hope you will allow me to return."

"You are not welcome in this house." Her features did not soften at the sight of his pained expression.

"I shall send someone later to ensure you are feeling better," he said.

"You need not bother."

"I will not rest easy until I know you are all right."

What did it take to be rid of this man? Sophrina struggled to her feet. "I am fine, William. Just the thought of your imminent departure buoys my spirits. Must I show you to the door myself?"

He shook his head and quitted the parlor.

Sophrina sank back into her chair and buried her face in her hands. Dear Lord, how was this all to end? Would she never be free of him? When she had first seen him, that horrible afternoon at Talcott, the last thing she imagined was that he would actually want to resume their marriage. The idea would be laughable if it were not so terribly painful.

"Sophrina, love, is everything all right?" Penhurst burst into the room, agitation plainly written on his face.

Sophrina greeted him with a relieved smile. "I did not mean

to cause you alarm, Ellis. William barged in here so brazenly, it would have taken ten men to toss him out.''

Penhurst planted a hasty kiss on her forehead. ''What did he want?''

''Me.''

He gave her a startled look.

''It was very odd,'' she continued, taking his hand as he sat next to her on the sofa. ''He was profusely apologetic for all he had done, said he realized that running off with Lea was a mistake, and begged me to forgive him and take him back.''

Penhurst remained disturbingly silent.

''Ellis?''

''Well? Will you?''

''Take him back?'' Sophrina stared at him in surprise. ''Ellis, have you gone mad? Why ever should I want to do such a thing when I have you?''

''But you do not have me, do you?'' His voice was weary. ''Returning to him would certainly be the easiest thing for all of us.''

''How could you even suggest that?'' His words sent a cold chill of fear through Sophrina.

He reached out and pulled her close. ''I know, I must be mad. But it is killing me, love, to want you so badly and know I cannot have you as my wife.''

''Somehow it will all work out,'' she whispered soothingly, stroking his cheek with her fingers. ''It has to.''

''Unfortunately, this is not like the fairy tales where they all live happily ever after.'' His voice grew cold again. ''This is real life, Sophrina. Sometimes we cannot have everything as we wish it to be.''

Sophrina drew away from his arms. ''You sound like you want me to go back to William!''

''Of course I do not. But if it would be less painful for you . . .''

Sophrina suddenly sensed his need for reassurance. ''Ellis, darling, I cannot imagine living my life with anyone else but you. I will wait as long as I must until we can be together. I can bear anything, including the scandal of a divorce, as long as I know you will be there waiting.''

He crushed her to his chest, strewing kisses upon her face. "Oh God, Sophrina, I love you so much. I need you so."

"Love me, Ellis," she whispered softly. "Here. Now."

"In your parlor?" He drew back.

"Doors have locks," she hinted.

"Sophrina, I . . . we . . . we cannot. Now now, knowing William is alive. It would not be right."

She stared at him in disbelief. "I do not understand."

He looked down uneasily before meeting her troubled eyes. "Sophrina, it may have been precipitous of us to become lovers before our marriage, but there was nothing wrong with that at the time. We both thought we were free. But to take you to bed now, knowing you are still legally married to another . . . it would be deliberate adultery. We both needed each other that night at Talcott. But I do not want to compound our crime."

"What a horrible thought! How could you call our love such a thing?"

He paled at her words.

"If the thought is no different from that act, I am already guilty," she said fiercely. "I commit adultery in my mind every minute of the day, Elliston. I despise the man the law insists is my husband. Every wifely feeling, every desire, every need is directed at you. I do not care if that labels me an adultress."

Penhurst took her face in his hands. "Lord knows, I am as guilty as you, love, for I have the same thoughts and feelings. But we are rational beings, in control of ourselves. We cannot act on those feelings. It would be wrong."

"How can you say it would be wrong?" she cried, her voice rising in agony. She pulled away from his embrace. "Is it wrong for me to regret the fact that my husband is not dead? Is it wrong for me to love you? Is it wrong for me to want your body joined with mine, in order that we can forget for just a little while this horrible mess we are in?"

"Do not become upset, Sophrina, please" He smiled weakly. "William's visit has unsettled you. We can discuss this later, when you are feeling more the thing."

"I want to discuss this now!" Sophrina's mouth was set in a determined line. "Where are your wits, Ellis? First you accuse me of wanting to go back to William. Now you say we must live like pious monks and nuns until he deigns to set me free. I almost believe you want me to return to him.''

''No!'' His voice throbbed with pain.

''Then why are you making me feel like this? Making me feel it is wrong to love you, to want you, in every sense of the word? We loved with joy two weeks ago, why cannot we do the same today?''

He sighed. The hurt in her eyes pierced him like a knife. ''Sophrina, love, I will not willingly cuckold another man. You, of all people, should respect that decision. How can we continue to condemn Lea or William for what they did when we do the same? It would not be right.''

''I need you so,'' she said, her eyes brimming with tears.

Penhurst pulled her to him, holding her in his arms. Was he being a fool to insist on some stupid vestige of honor in this whole complicated mess? Would anyone care, in the end, if he took Sophrina to his bed, knowing she was the wife of another?

Only one person would. Himself. For his own peace of mind, he had to resist temptation, or he would never be able to live with himself. Whatever pain it caused her, it would not compare with the recriminations he would heap on his head if he weakened. He had to be strong for both their sakes.

''We should hear from the lawyers any day now,'' he consoled. ''If William agrees to proceedings in Scotland, we could have the whole business taken care of within a month. Surely we can wait until then.''

He felt the slight nod of her head against his chest and he hugged her tighter. ''I love you more than anything on his earth, Sophrina. And I want everything to be perfect for us. We can endure all the waiting, knowing what awaits us at the end.''

Sophrina prayed it would be so. And soon.

''The bastard.''

Penhurst angrily tossed the letter onto his desk. Teel refused to cooperate in obtaining a divorce in Scotland. ''His lordship does not wish to sever his connection with Lady Teel, firmly believing a reconciliation is possible.''

Damn. Penhurst's hands clenched in anger. If he was a more emotional man, he would be tempted to break something, anything, particularly Teel's neck. What in God's name were they going to do now?

How ironic. Only a few short months ago he held no more pressing concern than finding a new nurse for Kate. Then Sophrina had tumbled into his life and turned everything upside down with her presence. A slow smile spread across his face. How could he ever have thought her obstinate and interfering? She was so full of life, had shown him a gaiety and exuberance for living he had never known he was missing until he met her. All the old, buried dreams of childhood were possible once more. He could be a carefree eight-year-old again, be the boy he had been before the years of duty, obedience and obligation had worn away all the dreams of youth.

God, how he loved her. And now, as if by a cruel joke, he had been shown a glimpse of a future of unimaginable joy, only to have it snatched away from him before he could take it in his grasp. From the heights of exhilaration he was now in the depths of despair, and there seemed no escape from the nightmare.

It had all been too easy, he told himself ruefully. It was foolish of him to believe that he had finally found the peace and happiness he now realized he had been searching for. He did not know which perverse god he had offended during his life, but it must have been a powerful one, for he was certainly being punished with a vengeance. What had he done to deserve this fate?

"Papa?"

Kate's tentative voice broke into his despairing reverie. She stood before his desk, clutching her treasured doll in one arm.

"Are we going to visit Rina today?"

He smiled fondly at his daughter. For her sake, he and Sophrina must put up a cheerful front. Kate must never guess at their pain; her short life had already been filled with so much distress. "Is it that time already?" He pulled out his watch and carefully examined the hands while he strove to order his jumbled thoughts. "It certainly is. Are you all ready to go?"

She nodded.

He stood up and reached for her hand. "Let us call for the carriage then."

"Will you stay and play today?" Kate darted an imploring glance at him while they walked toward the stable.

Penhurst stifled a sigh. He had no desire to torture himself, pretending to be the family they could not become. But for Kate, he had to try. "I will stay today, Kate."

"Goody." She let go of his hand and skipped gaily ahead down the path.

Penhurst watched her with a pang. Life was so simple when one was a child. There were no tomorrows, only todays, with caring adults to shelter one from the worst of life's blows. He had a sudden desire to be four again himself. Sometimes it was too damn painful being an adult.

Chapter 16

Not wishing to spoil the visit for Kate or Sophrina, Penhurst held his tongue about the communication from Teel. Yet he knew he was doing a poor job of disguising his mingled anger and frustration, for he caught Sophrina eyeing him quizzically several times. Finally, unable to endure the delay, he cozened Kate into accompanying Jenny into the kitchen for a few minutes.

"I received a letter from Teel's solicitor today," he began, his eyes refusing to meet Sophrina's.

"And the news was not good," she finished.

He shook his head. "He absolutely refused to agree to a divorce in Scotland."

Sophrina sank back into her chair. She had thought he might lay out conditions, or stall, but she had not expected a flat-out refusal. She looked up bleakly at Penhurst.

"Oh Elliston," she moaned. "Whatever are we to do?"

He clenched his fists in frustration. For the first time in his life, he was powerless to do anything. His fate, the fate of the woman he loved, lay in the hands of another. Teel could make them dance like puppets on a string for years—forever, if he wished. Penhurst ached to take Sophrina in his arms, to comfort her, to ease the anguish from her face, but he could not move. There was simply nothing he could do to make it better for either of them.

"Did he offer any reason?" Sophrina asked softly.

Penhurst's expression was grim. "He is convinced there will be a reconciliation between the two of you."

Sophrina's eyes flashed in anger. "How can he be so obtuse? What does it take to convince him that I will never, ever go back to him?"

"I do not think that is the real reason," said Penhurst. "He is doing this because of me—because of what happened with Lea. I think he perceives my desire to marry you as revenge, pure and simple. He has the chance to keep you from me and he intends to use it."

"Is there any way . . . can we proceed in Scotland without William's cooperation?"

Penhurst shrugged. "I do not know. I will notify Simms and see what he advises. Although I suspect he will counsel patience."

"Patience!" Sophrina spat out the word derisively. "How can I be patient when I want so badly to be your wife?"

"Look what Jenny gave me!" Kate bounded into the room.

Penhurst flashed Sophrina a wan smile as he bent down to examine his daughter's treasure.

Kate came again the next day, without her father. Sophrina bundled both of them against the cold and set off on a walk across the meadow, enjoying the crunching sound of the frozen grass underfoot on the frosty December morning. The bracing air did much to clear her head of her gloomy thoughts. She watched fondly as Kate danced about, darting here and there to investigate some new wonder.

As a brisk gust of wind sent her cloak hem flapping, Sophrina realized it was time to return home, before Kate took a chill. She turned to call the girl, who was busy watching the wispy clouds of her steaming breath.

"Come, Kate," Sophrina urged. "The sooner we return home, the sooner we may have our chocolate."

Kate ran to catch up, reaching out with her mittened hand to clasp Sophrina's.

"I do so hope it snows this winter," Kate said brightly. "Papa says if it does he will take me sledding."

Sophrina smiled wistfully at the vision of Ellis whizzing down the long slope behind Talcott. There was still a trace of the little boy in him; if only it could emerge more often. He had been doing so well before the wedding. Now he daily grew more and more like his old stern, austere self. It frightened Sophrina to watch the change in him. Ever since William's rejection of a divorce in Scotland, Ellis had retreated ever deeper into somberness.

Kate nudged Sophrina. "Who is that?"

Sophrina looked up, only to recoil in dismay. William cantered toward them on his horse.

Sophrina knew Kate had not been in contact with her real father since the day of the aborted wedding. It had been an unspoken agreement among all the adults that Kate was to be left out of this conflict. Had William suddenly decided to change the rules? Anger and fear mingled in Sophrina's mind.

"Good morning, Sophrina," he greeted, vaulting out of the saddle in his usual easy manner.

"Good morning, William." Her grip on Kate's hand tightened protectively.

"May I have an introduction to your charming companion?" He looked expectantly at Kate.

Sophrina returned him a cold stare.

After waiting in vain, he turned to the girl. "Unless I am mistaken, you are Lady Katherine St. Clair." He bowed low. "I am Edward and Susan's Uncle William."

Kate stared at Teel for a moment, then looked to Sophrina as if for reassurance.

"You may say hello and curtsy to Lord Teel," Sophrina commanded.

Kate did as she was directed.

"I understand you often came to play with my niece and nephews this summer," he continued. "But you have not been to visit for some time. They all say they miss you."

"Stop it, William." Sophrina struggled to contain her anger.

"I was only expressing the children's sentiments," he said smoothly. "Surely you cannot fault me for wanting them to be happy?"

"It is too cold a morning to stand about talking," Sophrina announced firmly. "I do not want Kate to become chilled. Or your horse. Do not let us keep you from your ride any longer." With a firm grasp on Kate's arm, she dragged the girl away.

Kate followed obediently for a moment, then stopped. She looked back at Teel, who stood next to his horse, watching them.

"Is he the man who won't let you marry Papa?"

Sophrina groaned inwardly. Things were happening too fast. Kate knew so little and it was unfair to burden her with any more knowledge of the mess four adults had made of their lives. Nevertheless, she was affected by it all.

"Yes," Sophrina replied wearily.

Kate jerked suddenly from Sophrina's grasp and ran back toward Teel before Sophrina could grab her. Flinging herself at him, Kate began pummeling him with her fists.

"I hate you, I hate you!" she cried. "I want Sophrina to be my mama and you won't let her!"

Sophrina went rigid, horrified at the outburst, afraid yet curious as to William's reaction.

He gently took Kate's hands in his and squatted down so he could look into her eyes.

"You love Sophrina very much, don't you?"

Kate nodded, her face set in a petulant pout.

"Well, I love her, too." He was pensive for a moment, then brightened. "Sophrina can still be your mama, you know. You and Sophrina could come to live with me. Should you like that? You would have Edward and Susan—"

Sophrina struck him a glancing blow to the head.

"How dare you!" She jerked Kate from his hold, shoving the girl behind her. "I had thought you any manner of despicable creatures, William, but a worm could not stoop so low. I despise you."

Without a backward glance she pulled Kate with her, striking out for the cottage at a pace that forced the girl to run to keep up. Not until they were safely inside the house, with the door firmly shut, did Sophrina dare to stop shaking.

"Did he frighten you, love?" she asked Kate as she untied her bonnet ribbons.

"A little," Kate admitted. "Are you really going to go live with him?"

Sophrina shook her head. "I will stay right here until the day I move to Talcott with you and your papa," she reassured the girl, smiling at the look of relief in Kate's big blue eyes.

"But I want you there now!"

Sophrina pulled Kate into her arms. "I want that more than anything, too, Kate. It will happen, I am certain, but not just as soon as we would all like."

Sophrina wished she could erase the hurt and doubt she saw in Kate's eyes. She planted a soft kiss on the girl's brow.

"Let us see if Jenny has the chocolate ready."

"I will kill him." Penhurst's face was taut with anger as he paced across Sophrina's parlor.

"It would certainly solve our major problem," Sophrina said dryly, pouring the tea. "But I fear having a convicted murderer for a husband does not appeal to me."

"How can you treat this like a joke?" he raged. "It was bad enough when he was bothering you, but to drag Kate into the picture . . . it is unconscionable."

"Let us assume it was only a whim of the moment. He does not have any reason for further contact with Kate and so shall not be able to talk with her again. I only regret we ran into him yesterday."

"You will have to cease your walks, of course," Penhurst announced imperiously.

"For fear we will see him again? Do not be absurd."

"I cannot let him come close to either you or Kate. He cannot be trusted." Penhurst paced the room in his agitation.

"I am quite willing to do what I can to keep Kate from him, Ellis, but I have nothing to fear from him. He knows how I feel, for I made that abundantly clear."

"Still, I do not wish to take any chances." He stopped and gave her a long stare. "The weather is only bound to grow worse as winter deepens. You would not wish to be out in such conditions in any event."

"I am not a fragile hothouse plant," she protested. "I am quite accustomed to tramping about the countryside in all kinds of weather."

"I do not trust Teel and I do not want you to have any more 'accidental' meetings."

"What are you so afraid of?" Sophrina asked. "William would never do me harm."

Penhurst turned away, his shoulders rigid. "He is your lawful husband, Sophrina. It is well within his rights to snatch you up and carry you back to Charlton."

Sophrina laughed. "Like some ancient Viking warrior carrying off his captive? I can hardly picture William in that role."

"He wants you back," Penhurst reminded her.

The concern and anguish in his face startled Sophrina. "You are jealous!" she exclaimed. "Now I begin to think you are as obtuse as he."

"You are his wife," he said slowly, trying to keep his voice from betraying his real fear. "You cared for him once; you could learn to do so again."

"I will never go back to William!" she retorted. "If you are so concerned for my safety and my heart, accompany me on my walks."

"You know that is not always possible. I have meetings with the lawyers in London in two days."

"Where they will tell you, 'sorry, my lord, but we still have not found a way to rid Lady Teel of her husband.' Give it up, Ellis." She turned to him with a pleading look. "They have all said there is no hope. Let me talk with William. If I tell him about us, he is certain to divorce me."

"No! I will not have you brought before the divorce courts like a common strumpet."

"Like it or not, Ellis, we are guilty of adultery in the eyes of the law. If we admit it, I can be free."

"Teel would never agree," he said sullenly.

She laughed, but there was no mirth in the sound. "Do you think he would stand by quietly for even a moment if he knew we were lovers?"

"There will be no divorce unless it is your charge against Teel."

There was an implacable set to his jaw that sent a chill of apprehension up Sophrina's spine.

"What difference does it make who brings the divorce charges if I am free?"

"You know what life is like in society for a divorced woman," he said hastily. "You will be ostracized, cut off from all social contact . . ."

"What do I care? I have been cut off from social contact for years and I have not minded in the least."

"But I do," he blurted. "I want my wife to be respected and admired by society. Not ignored and slighted. I love you too much to see that happen." He ran his hand through his thick, dark hair.

"Then you shall have to find another to take to wife," she said stonily. "For unless William conveniently drops dead tomorrow, I shall have to be a divorced woman to marry you."

"If the divorce comes from *your* complaint, the blame cannot be assigned to you," he explained earnestly. "No one cuts the Duchess of Argyll."

Sophrina rose to her feet, struggling to control her anger. "I am tired of all this talk of blame, Elliston. We are all to blame. I was stupid to have married William in the first place, you were stupid to ignore Lea, they were stupid to have run off."

"And was it stupid for you to have fallen in love with me?"

Sophrina looked at him, tears misting in her eyes. He was angry and proud and scared and she did not know what to say to get through that wall of armor he had been so busily reerecting around his heart. A month ago, even two weeks ago, she could have reached him. But now . . . she was no longer certain she had the ability.

"I love you with all my heart, for all time," she said, softly. "But we are as guilty of adultery as were William and Lea. Let us admit it, take whatever punishment the world wishes to impose, and begin our lives together." She reached for his hand.

He turned away and in that instant she was afraid she had lost him. All due to his implacable stubbornness. Sympathy turned to anger in an instant.

"Is it too much for that vaunted Penhurst pride to admit to an error?" Her voice was bitter. "Can you not bear for the world to see that the mighty Elliston St. Clair was brought to the ground by simple lust? That you could not resist the temptation to cuckold the man who had done the same to you?''

He winced at the pain and hurt he knew was goading her words, but he could not bring himself to reply. She cut too close to the truth.

''Crimes that are hidden away only grow worse,'' she said, as she swept across the room to gather up her shawl. ''They grow and fester in the dark and turn into ugly things, Ellis. Far uglier than the original.'' She walked past his frozen form and fled up the stairs to the safety of her room.

He did not know how long he stood there alone, her scathing indictment ringing in his ears. How had it come to pass that they were fighting about something they both wanted? God, he would give anything to have her. Yet his actions were only pushing her away.

Penhurst felt as if he were in a runaway stagecoach, careening down a long, steep hill. He could see the sharp turn at the bottom, knew the coach would never negotiate it. Should he jump now or wait until the last minute, hoping for a miracle? He was no longer in control of his life; outside forces pushed him in conflicting directions. He pressed his face into his hands. He just wanted everything to stop, wanted things to go back to their old, neat, orderly ways. He could not bear this agonizing indecision for much longer.

Sophrina's taunting words echoed in his ears. '' . . . that vaunted Penhurst pride.'' He was guilty as charged. He *was* proud of his name, his long heritage, his position in society. From the earliest days his parents and tutors had drummed the twin notions of responsibility and pride into his head. He had to live up to the name. He must be honorable, trustworthy, above the common run of man to be a true Penhurst.

And now, here he was, pushed closer and closer to the admission that he was no better than all the others. To admit he lusted after—no, *had taken* another man's wife. He could still vividly remember the unsympathetic voices of his peers as they discussed the fall of the then Earl of Uxbridge, desperately needed in the struggle against Napoleon on the Peninsula, who had thrown it all alway in his lust for a woman.

They had all shaken their heads at the way Uxbridge turned his back on duty and obligation. The scandal had been on everyone's mind for the entire year preceding his marriage to Lea. Penhurst had sworn then it would be a mistake he would never make. Duty and honor were more important than personal desires.

And now fate was pushing him into a similar box. The Foreign Office wanted him back, was willing to give him nearly any post he wanted. Yet the smallest taint of scandal and that offer would be withdrawn instantly.

He was a good diplomat. He could say that without a trace of conceit. He enjoyed the complicated negotiations, deciphering the unsaid words, the opportunity to second-guess his opponents. It was a life that could go from deadly dull to intensely exciting in moments, and he missed it and wanted it back again. But he could never have it with a wife who had been labeled an adultress.

And Sophrina . . . Sophrina would be banned from all formal functions, ostracized by the other wives in the delegation. She would be miserable—and what kind of marriage would they have then? He could not ask that sacrifice of her.

Penhurst realized with growing despair that Sophrina would never be free from Teel without a scandalous divorce—and that course would be a disaster for all of them. Sophrina would forever be tainted by the scandal, his own diplimatic aspirations would be doomed and even Kate . . . Kate would suffer, with a stepmother who could not accompany her into society. It was more than any of them should be asked to endure. If they were unable to cozen Teel into a divorce in Scotland, Penhurst knew it would be impossible for Sophrina and him ever to wed. The price demanded would be too high.

Perhaps it would be for the best, in the end. Despite her vehement denials, Sophrina might decide that life with her husband was better than life with an arrogant, domineering earl. There would be no scandal. Teel was younger, handsomer, and infinitely more charming than himself. With Lea dead, perhaps they could make their marriage a success this time. He only wanted whatever course would make Sophrina happy.

The pain lancing through him belied his thoughts. He did not want that at all if it meant losing her. But what hope did he have of ever taking her to wife now? They only faced a future of pain and despair. If he withdrew, at least Sophrina would have a chance for happiness. He loved her enough to do what he could to make that happen.

Upstairs, in her room, Sophrina heard the crunch of carriage wheels on gravel that signaled Elliston's departure. Flicking the curtain aside, she caught a last glimpse of the coach before it disappeared behind the trees. She sank down onto her bed with a pained groan.

She was frightened. She could not believe his high-handed demand that she curb her walks to avoid Teel, even if the command was motivated by jealousy. Every day that this miserable little drama dragged on pushed Elliston back into his old ways. The laughing, caring Elliston whom she had agreed to wed would never have said such a thing to her.

Sophrina smiled at the bitter irony of it all. William claimed he had changed for the better; Elliston was changing for the worse. It was almost as if they both wished to drive her mad.

She rose and crossed the room to the cherry-wood dresser. Opening her jewel case, she drew out Elliston's engagement ring. In the dim winter light, even the diamonds seemed to have lost some of their fire. Like their love?

It could not possibly be too late. She knew all of Elliston's rantings were only the product of the strain he was under. If she endured it better, well, she had more years of experience than he in that area. Living with the knowledge for nearly a year that her husband had a lover had taught Sophrina much about not bowing to the pressures of life. If only she could show Elliston how to do the same.

She put the ring on her finger, deriving some small comfort from its weight upon her hand. A wistful smile flitted across her face as she remembered the evening Ellison gave it to her; the evening they had missed not only the first but the second act at Drury Lane. How carefree they had been during those weeks in London, the days filled with laughter, the nights with love. How she missed the comfort of his nearness, his touch, his whispered endearments in her ear.

She shook her head impatiently. It was partially Elliston's

foolish insistence on this ridiculous celibacy that caused so many problems. They both needed reassurance and sometimes actions spoke better than words. The physical longing was almost as bad as the mental wanting, and harder to extinguish. For a moment she let need wash over her, filling her, paining her. It was at least a poor reminder of what they had shared. If only she could hold him close, soothing away the doubt and tension with soft words and loving caresses. All would be wonderful— for a short time, anyway.

With a sigh, she took the ring from her finger and restored it to her jewel case. Someday, perhaps, she would be able to wear it again.

Chapter 17

Sophrina was surprised to find that Ellis had accompanied Kate to the cottage the next morning. She had thought, after their words the previous day, that he would stay away. With Kate present, there was no opportunity to discuss all they needed to say to one another. Had that been deliberate on his part?

"I want you to read, Rina," Kate announced as she bounced into the room. "Papa send to London for a new book and it arrived only yesterday and you can be the first person to read it!"

"I am honored, Kate," said Sophrina, pasting a cheery smile on her face. "Sit here beside me and we will begin."

Penhurst watched them wistfully from his chair. There were times, when Sophrina and Kate sat together, heads bent over a book, that he felt shut out from both their lives. Even though Kate was not her child, the two shared a strong mother-daughter bond. It was something he suspected no male would ever know or understand.

"My lady?" There was a strained note to Jenny's voice. "Lord and Lady Teel are here."

Sophrina knew that Bertram and Mary had returned to Charlton, and recoiled in stunned surprise when William and his mother entered instead. The four adults looked at one another in uncomfortable silence.

The dowager broke the awkward tension. "How do you do today, Lady Katherine?" She walked over to Kate and Sophrina.

Sophrina nudged Kate to her feet.

"Good day, Lady Teel," Kate said. "See my new book? Rina was reading it to me."

"*The Adventures of Tom Thumb,*" read the dowager. "I remember that story." She turned with an apologetic smile to Sophrina. "I am sorry for dropping in like this," she said in a low undertone, "but William insisted on coming and I thought you would feel more comfortable if I accompanied him."

"Thank you, Louisa," said Sophrina. She glanced at Penhurst, seeing the tight lines about his mouth that betrayed his anger at William's presence. "William, since you insist on barging in here without an invitation, the least you can do is pour the tea."

He gave her a startled look, then complied with the order.

Sophrina took a deep breath. The tension in the room was palpable; everyone's nerves were stretched taut. Yet for Kate's sake, Sophrina determined to maintain a veneer of civility.

"Perhaps you would like to show Lady Teel how well you can read, Kate," Sophrina suggested. By drawing attention to the girl, she hoped to remind the two angry men, staring balefully at each other, that they must not act precipitously in front of the child.

An uneasy silence fell upon the room, broken only by Kate's nervous stumbling over words she knew almost by heart. Sophrina sighed. It was foolish to think that Kate had not noticed the charged undercurrents in the room. Children quickly took their cues from the adults around them.

"That was very nice, Kate," the dowager encouraged. "You are doing well in your lessons. Do you like your new governess?"

Kate nodded. "She is nice. But I liked Rina better. She made it more fun."

Sophrina smiled fondly at the girl. Glancing up, she met

William's speculative gaze and the smile immediately left her face.

"Four-and-a-half seems a bit old to be just getting a governess," he said with a touch of malice. "When did Bertram and I start our studies, Mother? Were we not three?"

"I hardly think that is a matter we need discuss now," the dowager said quickly. She turned to Sophrina. "Have you heard the vicar is planning a Christmas tableau this year?"

"That will be nice to see," replied Sophrina, grateful for Louisa's help.

"Will it snow at Christmas?" Kate asked.

"That is one thing you never know for certain," said the dowager. "We can hope it will."

"I bet Kate wants to go sledding," said William, with an encouraging smile. "Is that right?"

She looked at him doubtfully. "My papa said he would take me if it snows," she offered with reluctance.

"Such a fatherly gesture," William responded, flashing Penhurst a mocking glance.

"If you wish to finish your tea, we can be going, William." The dowager looked pointedly at her son. "Sophrina has guests and we should not overstay our welcome."

William leaned back in his chair, cultivating a relaxed pose. "But it has been such a long time since we all had the opportunity to chat," he protested. He returned his attention to Kate. "Edward and Susan will be returning to Charlton for Christmas. I am certain they would like you to come for a visit then, Lady Katherine."

"Oh, will they be there?" Kate's eyes glowed. "I miss Susan."

"We will definitely plan on a visit," William assured her. "Perhaps you can bring Sophrina with you."

Kate looked uneasily at Sophrina. "She does not like you."

William eyed Sophrina with a smirking grin. "Of course she does. And one day—soon I hope—she will be coming to Charlton again to live."

Sophrina jumped to her feet. "That is quite enough, William," she said, her face flushing in anger.

"Is it?" He looked toward Penhurst. "How long do you think

he is willing to wait, my dear? A few months? A few years? He is past the age when most men set up their families . . ." Teel glanced pointedly at Kate. "He needs a son. One day there will be a lovely young chit who catches his eye, one who is immediately available, one who is younger . . ."

The room erupted in angry voices. Penhurst was on his feet, dragging William from his chair. The dowager was scolding her son in a loud, angry voice. Kate cowered against Sophrina, who was so astounded at William's malice that she could not respond.

Recovering her wits, Sophrina hastened Kate from the room and led her to the kitchen. Setting the girl firmly down on a chair, Sophrina took Kate's hands in hers.

"Sometimes," Sophrina began carefully, "adults behave in a very silly manner."

"My papa was very angry."

"Yes, he was."

"Why does Lord Teel want you to live with him?" Kate's eyes were round with innocent curiosity.

Sophrina took a deep breath. "I am married to him, Kate. Everyone thought he had been killed in an accident. But he was not, and that is why I cannot marry your papa."

"Ever?"

"Someday I will," Sophrina reassured her. "But it is very complicated trying to 'unmarry' someone."

"Will he take you away?" Kate's voice was anxious.

"No, of course not," Sophrina reassured her. "I will stay right here until I am able to marry your papa, then I will move to Talcott and be with you always."

Kate gave her a hug.

While Sophrina reassured Kate, the dowager looked scornfully at both men, who stood glowering at each other from opposite sides of the room.

"You are both acting like schoolboys squabbling over a toy. If I were Sophrina, I would wash my hands of both of you." She pierced William with an angry stare. "At this moment, I am ashamed even to admit you are my son."

"I am only attempting to get my wife back," Teel said petulantly. He cast an irritated glance at Penhurst. "Something the law says is my right."

"You gave up any claim to Sophrina years ago," Penhurst retorted. "I do not know what you are attempting to prove with this ridiculous show of fake contrition, but it won't wash, Teel. You are mad to think she would ever go back to you."

"Am I?" He lifted a quizzical brow, reaching for his mother's arm to escort her to the door. "Time will tell."

"Tell her you will cooperate with a divorce in Scotland," Penhurst shot back. "If you are so confident of her wishes, that action can pose no danger to you."

"I will never willingly part from her," Teel responded with a sneering smile. "I have found that a wife is too valuable a thing to cast aside on a whim."

Louisa quickly stepped between the two men, noting the ominous look in Penhurst's dark eyes.

"Say my farewells to Sophrina, Penhurst. Tell her I shall return at a more convenient time, when we ladies can chat without interruption."

An endless torrent of rain brought the cold, crisp days of early December to an end. The roads became quagmires; the footpaths were streams. Even dashing from the door to the carriage and back was enough to get one thoroughly wet. Sophrina thought it was all to the good; she could not have endured winterbright sunshine. The dreary rain perfectly suited her mood.

Ever since the blowup between Penhurst and William at the cottage, there had been a definite change in her relationship with Elliston. He was invariably polite, but more distant and aloof, much as he had been when they first met. If she did not do something drastic to turn him from his old ways, she feared she would lose him forever. How could she force him out of his shell?

Sophrina had spent the morning playing with Kate at Talcott but now, after lunch, while the girl took her nap, Sophrina went in search of Elliston. She simply could not go on any longer living this strange life, neither wife nor lover. For her sake, for his sake, something had to be done.

Penhurst's dark head was bent over the papers on his desk. Sophrina stood in the doorway, watching him with a fond smile on her face. He was such a conscientious landowner, undertaking all his responsibilities with a deep seriousness.

She made a slight noise and he looked up in surprise.

"I did not hear you enter," he said rising. "Has Kate gone to bed?"

Sophrina nodded. "I fear I wore her out with too many games of spillikins." She seated herself in the chair facing the desk.

He smiled faintly at her jest.

"It is good to see you smile," she said. "It seems you do it so seldom nowadays."

"There is little to smile about," he replied, his face solemn again.

"Elliston, I am going to speak to William," Sophrina announced. "This charade has gone on long enough. If I tell him we have been lovers, he will divorce me and I shall be free."

"No." Penhurst's voice was flat, emotionless.

"It is our only hope," she pleaded.

He looked at her sadly. "I don't want to see you hurt, Sophrina."

"I am hurting. Now. Nothing, absolutely nothing society can say or do can be worse than not being able to have you." Her eyes filled with tears. "It is tearing me up inside every day."

"Don't cry love, don't cry." He came around the end of the desk and drew her into his arms. "I am so sorry, Sophrina, so sorry. I could never have wished this upon you."

"Let me talk with William," she pleaded, her voice muffled against his shoulder. "He will free me, Ellis, I know he will."

"No. Under no circumstances will you confess anything to him." He looked down at her, his eyes glittering and hard. "You will abide by my wishes on this, Sophrina."

She could not hold his gaze. His dark eyes looked so harsh and demanding. Once again, she remembered the irate man who had accused her of kidnapping his daughter. That had been so long ago, and in the intervening time she thought he had changed so much . . . but had he? Would this cold, arrogant Penhurst always emerge when there was a crisis?

"Promise me, Sophrina."

She pulled away from his embrace. "I will promise you nothing when you demand it in such a way. I am not some retainer, to be ordered about."

"A divorce will be a disaster. Cannot you see that?"

"No, I cannot!" She glared up angrily into his eyes. "To me, the disaster is the way you are returning to your old domineering ways, Elliston. You want everyone to bow to your wishes. Well, let me inform you that I have a mind of my own and I am perfectly capable of making my own decisions. I do not need you to make them for me."

"We cannot do anything that will give William the advantage, Sophrina. If you confessed to him . . ."

"He will divorce me," she said bluntly. "Or is it that you do not truly want that, Elliston? Perhaps you no longer are so eager to make me your bride."

"Of course I am," he snapped, frustrated at her unwillingness to see how harmful her actions would be. "However, I do not want to force upon you the notoriety a divorce trial would cause."

"Why will you not understand?" she cried, breaking free of his arms and rising to her feet. "I do not care a fig for what society will say about me. You may ascribe that motive to your own reluctance, but do not tar me with the same brush."

She glowered at him, her eyes flashing with anger, but it took all her willpower to keep her lips from trembling. It was out in the open now, this widening rift between them, her growing doubts about his constancy.

He stepped toward her, placing his hands lightly on her shoulders as he looked down into her eyes. "We must give it more time, Sophrina. Let us at least wait until after the holidays. I do not want to make that time any worse for Kate than it already will be. We must try to put this out of our minds and put up a good front for her sake."

Sophrina compressed her lips in a tight line. *What about me?* she wanted to cry. She wanted to have a Christmas full of hope and love, not fear and despair. But by dangling Kate's happiness before her, he knew she would relent. Damn him and his arrogant manipulations.

"As you wish," she said coolly, turning away to stare out the window at the pouring rain.

The normally festive season did little to improve Sophrina's mood over the next week. Every time she forced a smile to her face, for Kate's sake, it only cut a deeper chunk out of her heart.

She knew she could not endure this agony much longer. Something had to be done.

She remembered last summer, when Ellis had been so reluctant for Kate to visit her cousins at Charlton. Sophrina had disobeyed his wishes then, and all had worked out well. It was time she rebelled again. Ellis was going to London at the beginning of January. She would talk to William then.

As Penhurst's appointed departure date loomed nearer, Sophrina grew more fearful. Was she doing the right thing? For herself, she had no doubts. Nothing society could do to her would be worse than this disaster of being tied to one man while loving another. No, it was not herself she doubted. But she was growing more and more uncertain of Ellis. Did he still really wish her as his bride?

He said he did, of course, but as his ardor grew cooler and cooler, she began to question his interest. Were his professions of fear that she would return to William really a veiled hint that she should? She knew Ellis abhorred the thought of the scandal a divorce would bring. Did he hate scandal enough to give her up in order to avoid it? It was a question she was half afraid to hear the answer to. But she had to know. And she knew that giving William cause to instigate a divorce for adultery would force Ellis to make a choice. At the worst, at the most horrible worst, he would abandon her to her fate. But at least she would be free of William. That one thought consoled her as she counted down the days until Ellis departed from town.

"Well, Sophrina, this is certainly a surprise." William led his guest to a chair in the study at Charlton. "Can I get you a cup of tea or a glass of wine?"

"Tea would be fine."

She chatted of inconsequential matters after William rang for the tray, knowing she would not wish to be interrupted when the servant arrived. Sophrina's nervousness grew with each minute. She much depended on what happened here today. She must use exactly the right words to convince William that what she desired was best for all of them. And if she failed . . .

She would not think on that now. If she did, her courage might falter.

"Well now, I am certain you did not come here today merely for a polite cup of tea." William looked at her with a curious anticipation.

"I have come to talk about a divorce, William."

"Now Sophrina, the solicitors have gone over all that already." He flashed her a patronizing smile. "I told them quite clearly I am not willing to stage some phony show in Scotland just to oblige Penhurst."

"I am not talking about Scotland, William. I mean here, in England."

He laughed. "Do you honestly think you could get a divorce act through Parliament? I admire your courage for even contemplating such a thing, Sophrina, but I fear you are doomed to failure. The consistory court might hear you out, but the Lords would laugh your petition out of the chamber."

"I think they would listen very intently—if you brought the charges."

Teel remained silent for a moment.

"You wish me to file for divorce?" he asked at last.

Sophrina nodded.

"On what grounds? Failure to cohabit?" He laughed harshly.

Sophrina took a deep breath. "Adultery."

She studied him carefully as he sipped his tea, apparently without concern. All hinged on his reaction.

"That is a rather serious charge, my dear," he said, setting his cup down with a smooth motion. "Are you certain you wish to be branded as an adulteress for the remainder of your life? Society can be very nasty to divorced women. Very nasty."

"I realize what it will mean to me, William. I still wish it."

"With whom is this supposed 'adultery' to have been committed."

"Use your head, William," she snapped.

"I find it difficult to imagine that frosty aristocrat summoning up enough passion for such a deed. Surely you have found a lover elsewhere?"

Sophrina ignored his remarks.

"Assuming I was interested—assuming, mind you—I presume you have 'evidence' to support your case?" There was a leering tone to his voice. "Servants who will testify to meetings, mussed clothing, the usual things?"

Sophrina flushed. He was going to make her squirm. "There would be reliable witnesses."

"Why," he said slowly, considering, "are you suddenly so eager for all this now? Why did you not simply ask for this months ago instead of insisting on that comic farce in Scotland?"

"Elliston preferred that you be named the guilty party."

"Yes, I am certain he would have. Although you would think one Crim. Con. trial would be enough for him." Teel sat back casually in his chair. "Be that as it may, why the sudden change, Sophrina? Surely Penhurst realizes how difficult it will be to marry you when all this is over. Divorced wives are such an awkward item in the diplomatic circles he travels in. Or has he decided to give that up and use his talents to grow corn?"

"William, do not torture us like this. No one is winning here. We are all unhappy with the situation as it is. Divorce me and let us all start over. You can find a wife who wants you and will bear your children. Ellis and I can wed and be happy."

He sat with a calculating expression on his face.

"Divorces are expensive."

"He will pay all the expenses."

"How magnanimous of him. Returning the money I paid him after my trial." He snorted derisively.

"William, let us not get caught up in past grudges. Will you agree to do this?"

He ignored her plea, calmly pouring himself another cup of tea with maddening slowness.

"Why not just take him as your lover?" His eyes were coldly mocking. "It would be so much neater, without destroying anyone's reputation. I must confess, I could hardly complain about such a liaison."

"I would still be your wife," Sophrina said bitterly. "And I do not wish to be."

"True, true, I suppose even Penhurst dreams about having an heir to carry on the blue blood. Still, he could easily find a complaisant chit who would not object to a mistress."

"One could say the same of you, William. You know you want an heir. Married to me, you would never have one."

He eyed her carefully. "You think you could hold out forever?"

"William, it is over. You know that. You only insist on this fantasy of a reconciliation to soothe your conscience. Lea may have wanted you, but I do not.''

''You certainly have a winning way with words, Sophrina.'' Teel sighed. ''All right, supposing I agree. What, exactly, is Penhurst prepared to offer in the way of financial remuneration?''

''He will pay all the legal costs for the trials and, of course, whatever civil damages are ordered.'' She thought that a reasonable offer.

He shook his head slowly. ''Not enough, I am afraid. Surely I am entitled to some compensation for the loss of my beloved wife.''

''You are outrageous,'' she hissed. ''You left me of your own free will two years ago. Don't talk to me of loss.''

''Nevertheless, I think I deserve something.''

''I am sure you will get an adequate amount from the civil damages. Do not be too greedy, William.''

''I can be as 'greedy' as I wish, Sophrina. I am the only one who can give you what you want. I would say that I hold the winning hand, wouldn't you? And I mean to see that your precious 'Ellis' dances to my tune if he wants you so badly.''

''Why do you insist on punishing him like this?'' she cried. ''He has done nothing to harm you. You are the one who owes him a debt, running off with his wife, saddling him with your child . . .''

''Ah, yes, little Kate. So noble of Penhurst to raise her as his own.'' He smiled slyly. ''But certainly, if he gets both my wife and my child, I should receive some recompense?''

''Have your lawyer prepare an agreement,'' she said wearily. ''Unless you demand something totally outrageous, I am certain it will be satisfactory. You can file the case at the next term.''

''Why such haste? These delicate negotiations could take some time.''

''I want a honeymoon in Paris. In the spring,'' she replied acidly.

''How romantic. I can just picture you and your ice-encrusted husband strolling through the Tuileries . . .'' He gave her a searching look. ''Do not forget, my dear, that I am well-versed in Penhurst's failings as a husband. Lea could recite his faults for hours.''

"And I could do the same of you."

William flashed her an angry look.

Sophrina gritted her teeth to control her tongue. Anger would accomplish nothing, she reminded herself. She was desperate for William's cooperation. She must not do anything to upset him.

"Have your lawyers draw up the papers," she repeated, rising to her feet. She must get away from here before she ruined everything.

"I am certain we can reach a satisfactory arrangement." William stood and escorted her to the door. As she reached for the handle, he lay a staying hand on her arm. "I only caution you, Sophrina, to be very certain this is what you want. Once the process begins, I will not change my mind and take you back."

"I understand that very well, William. You can be very certain that this is what I want."

Sophrina felt an enormous sense of relief as she left Charlton. The deed was done. Now she could only pray that the results would be what she had intended. She prayed that Ellis would not be so furious as to cast her off. But it was something she had to do, in order to keep her sanity. Even if it destroyed whatever was left of the love between her and Ellis, she had to be free from Teel.

Chapter 18

"You—did—what?"

Sophrina nervously twisted her fingers as she looked down at the fire blazing in the grate.

"Ellis, there is no other alternative. Either William divorces me, or I will be chained to him for life. You have heard and read everything the lawyers told us. *There is no other way.*"

He turned to stare into the flickering flames. God, she had done it again. Refused to listen to him, refused to accede to his wishes. Why couldn't she accept his wisdom on this matter? Why did she always have to do things her own way?

"I cannot comprehend," he said at last, "why you felt it was necessary to go behind my back on this."

"You know as well as I you would never have agreed, Ellis. We would have waited on William until we were old and gray. This way, we have a chance for happiness."

She did not tell him her worry—that the longer they waited, the more likely their marriage would never happen. It would be too easy to put off the confrontation, to avoid the infamy, until the memories of their love dimmed to the point where it did not seem so important anywhere. She had to do everything in her power to snatch back the joy before that happened.

He shook his head, smoldering anger building inside him. How dare she take it upon herself to decide what course was right for them? She did not understand the issues involved; she did not know the irreparable damage she may have caused with her rash action. The scandal would follow them for the rest of their days.

"Is it always going to be like this, Sophrina? Will you never heed my words?"

"Not when I think they are wrong or misguided," she retorted. "We are not grand nations, Ellis, with each interaction to be carefully analyzed and calculated by a roomful of diplomats. We are dealing with people's lives here—yours, mine, and Kate's. I will do what I feel I must to see that we have a chance for happiness."

"If you were Kate, I would turn you over my knee and thrash you soundly!" he thundered. "I cannot believe you capable of such a foolish action. You may have ruined everything."

"Nothing could be worse than the living hell we are enduring now," she said, her eyes flashing in anger. "I cannot endure it another day."

"Perhaps if Simms contacts Teel's man, we can stop the process before it gets too far."

"Stop it?" Sophrina turned toward him, aghast. "Whatever for?"

Penhurst continued as if she had not spoken. "He may be willing to listen to reason. If we explain you were overwrought, not feeling yourself, we may be able to smooth it over."

A deep foreboding filled Sophrina. She had known her action would force Ellis to make a choice between her and scandal. It grew apparent that he would avoid scandal, at whatever the cost.

"I will not allow you to stop the divorce," she said slowly. "It is what I wish and I will do anything I must to see that it comes about."

"I see."

The coolness of his tone tore at Sophrina's heart. Had it come to this, already, the death throes of the love she once thought would last forever? Had it burnt itself out with its intensity, like the shooting stars that streamed across the night skies? She stood up quickly.

"I am tired and I would like to rest," she announced. "You can see yourself out."

"Sophrina?"

She paused at the door and looked back at him. There was still anger in his face, but it mingled with sadness and confusion. It took every ounce of strength she possessed to refrain from flinging herself into the comfort of his arms. But it would only be a temporary respite from the pain.

"Ellis, I had to do it. For all of us. It is our only chance. If you cannot accept that, so be it." She shut the door firmly behind her.

Penhurst sank down onto the sofa. God, what was going wrong? Suddenly everything in his world was spinning madly out of control. He no longer knew anything with a certainty, and it frightened him. How could Sophrina say she loved him and yet go against his wishes so openly? She was closing all the doors, forcing them down the pathway of *her* choosing. Why was she so blind to her folly? What in the hell was he going to do?

Fury threatened to overwhelm him. Sophrina had deliberately disobeyed him to bring the matter to a head. She had told her husband the truth, and as a result Penhurst could find himself held up to ridicule and scorn. All those lectures from his youth flooded back into his mind. "A gentleman never does anything to draw attention to himself." "A gentleman behaves properly at all times." "A gentleman never acts in a manner that incites gossip or scandal." He had hated the notoriety that the Crim.

Con. trial against Teel had brought, and now Sophrina was attempting to pitchfork him into a scene a thousand times worse.

And for what purpose? To guarantee she would spend the rest of her life in disgrace? She could not possibly have thought out all the ramifications of her actions, and now her rash confession was pushing them pell-mell into disaster.

With an angry scowl, he stood up again. Grabbing his hat off the table, he clamped it firmly onto his head. He would be damned if he allowed Sophrina to ruin everything. By working quickly, he might be able to salvage the situation. If Teel could be placated, the present state of affairs might be maintained until they found some less torturous solution to their problem.

And if not . . . There was no question he must marry Sophrina then; honor demanded such a course. A trace of panic arose within him. What a damnable state of events! He was neatly trapped into a situation that would be a disaster for both of them, with only a slim hope of escape. All because of her impetuous disobedience.

Sophrina heard the crunching of gravel as Penhurst's carriage left the cottage. It was overly dramatic to think she would never see him again, but she knew their relationship would never be the same. She now had the answer she had sought—Penhurst wanted to avoid scandal at any cost. And in the process, she had angered Ellis to the point where she would be lucky if he ever looked upon her with regard again. Guilt washed over her. She had done what she thought was right for both of them. But if Ellis did not see it that way, her motives mattered little.

With a groan she rolled over and buried her face in her pillow. Surprisingly, the tears did not come. There was only a burning ache in her throat and chest. She had thought, had hoped, he loved her enough to overlook all else. How foolish of her to allow her dreams to overshadow reality. She should have learned her lesson with William, but she had deluded herself into thinking that this time it would be different. Was she to be forever barred from finding happiness wth the man she loved?

"Fifty thousand pounds? How could he?" Sophrina slammed her hand on the tabletop. "Surely he is joking."

"Do you think he is?" Penhurst eyed her shrewdly.

Sophrina sat down in the wing chair flanking the fireplace.

"No," she said woefully. "I am fully certain he intends to extract his pound of flesh."

Penhurst leaned against the far side of the mantel, frowning. "We do not have much choice, do we?"

"You can still change your mind," she said, knowing deep inside herself that he wanted to. He should have the opportunity to extricate himself from the mess she had created. "The trial could be stopped and you would not need to give him the money. And you would not be saddled with a disgraced divorcée for a wife."

He sighed deeply. "It is too late for that consideration now," he said with a touch of bitterness. "The papers have been filed; I have been charged with the crime of being your adulterous lover. Even if Teel withdraws his suit, the news is out. What would people say if I abandoned you now?"

"What does it matter what other people say?" Sophrina exploded. "What is it that *you* want, Ellis?"

"We will wed when the divorce is final," he said impassively.

"It makes me feel as if . . . as if I am being purchased."

"You are," Penhurst replied in a curt tone. "Teel knows he has a valued commodity and he can charge what he will."

Sophrina wearily closed her eyes. "Do you have that kind of money?"

He nodded. "Oh, it will put a damper on things for a while. But the harvest was decent last year, and the consols have not gone down. I think I can manage."

She gave him a wan smile. Guilt ripped through her. She had gone against his wishes in confessing to William and now Ellis must pay dearly for her action. She was forcing him into a marriage he clearly did not want. If only she could be assured that all would be well once they wed. But that was no longer a certainty. In fact, their marriage could turn out to be a dreadful mistake. Yet now their hands were tied; they had to play through this scene until the bitter end now. She had guaranteed that.

"Well, I do not think we should bow to his first demand," Sophrina regained some of her spirit. "Certainly, we must negotiate a bit."

"Trying to devalue your worth?" He arched a brow. "My solicitors know what to do. They will bluff him along, in hopes he blinks at an amount I find more reasonable."

"How long will the entire process take, do you think?"

Penhurst shrugged. "It is up to Teel. I see no point in contesting the ecclesiastical hearing, or the Crim. Con. charges—"

"Oh!" she said in a startled gasp. "I had forgotten about the trial damages. He could drive you into the poor house."

"That is why we are having Simms plead our case. I will not contest the charge, but I will fight a damage claim."

Sophrina raised her eyes reluctantly to his. "How much were you awarded for Lea?"

"Twenty-five thousand pounds."

"My God, if he gets that, it will total seventy-five thousand!" Sophrina said with dismay. "I cannot ask you to make that kind of sacrifice."

"If matters grow too bad, we can break the entail, sell Talcott, and move into your cottage."

"Ellis! Do not joke about such a thing. I feel terrible enough as it is."

Penhurst's smile was distant. "I would not worry overmuch. In the first place, I do not think Teel will receive a very large damage award. He can hardly claim his relationship with you was harmed, since he abandoned you three years ago. And he very well may come down with this initial demand. I do not think it will total forty or fifty thousand overall and that I can live with."

Sophrina sighed. "It all seems so dreadfully unfair."

Penhurst nodded. "It is. I wish he had the honor to accede to a divorce in Scotland. But if he wishes to be stubborn and play this out, we have no other alternative."

"I am sorry, Ellis."

"So am I," he said, drawing her into his arms. "I promise I shall do my best to make you happy when all this comes to an end."

She laid her head against his chest. How she longed to believe his words. But words, after all, were only words, and she did not think they were enough to offer her hope. Too much had occurred for her to think they could ever regain that delirious happiness of last fall.

Tilting her chin up, Penhurst brushed her lips with his. "We can only pray that matters move smoothly. A quick resolution is the best for everyone.''

After Sophrina returned to her cottage, Penhurst restlessly paced his study. He had tried to suppress his doubts about allowing the divorce proceedings to commence. But he had not been able to totally still those whispering voices. A divorce would cast Sophrina outside the pale of society, no matter how quickly he married her. The title of countess would offer no protection. It would be years—and in some cases forever—until she was accepted into the drawing rooms again.

He fought even harder to still his own concerns about being able to return to the Foreign Office. It seemed selfish in the extreme to worry about his own desires, when Sophrina would sacrifice so much more. Yet he could not stifle that tiny twinge of resentment. Marriage to a divorced woman would forever bar him from taking a foreign post.

Shrugging, Penhurst sat down at his desk. It would not be a bad existence, really. Without the menace and intrigue of the conflict with France, life in an embassy post would be decidedly flat. They would settle down here at Talcott instead. He would manage the estate; Sophrina would raise their children. It was an existence that many would envy. No one ever received everything they wanted out of life. He should count himself lucky to have Sophrina and Kate.

He glanced again at the demanding letter from Teel's solicitor. Penhurst did not mind the amount of money; that was not the issue here. Yet it was galling in the extreme to be forced to pay Teel for Sophrina's freedom. Pure and simple, it was a tit-for-tat revenge for Teel's Crim. Con. conviction three years ago. If Sophrina had wished to marry any man other than himself, Penhurst suspected Teel would have been magnanimous and agreed to a divorce in Scotland. But with the present cast of players . . . Teel held all the cards and he knew it. He would play them out slowly, one by one, to satisfy his own warped sense of justice. Penhurst suspected Teel would not capitulate fully until he had deemed Penhurst had suffered enough. Sophrina was caught in the middle once again.

He gave a long, lingering sigh. At this point there was little he could do to alter the situation. He would simply have to go along with Teel's plans, unless they grew too outrageous to bear. He had spoken the truth to Sophrina—it was the best for everyone if this whole mess could be resolved quickly. Teel would have to be humored until the divorce decree was final.

One thing Penhurst refused to do, however, was to sit idly by while the wheels of justice churned their slow, laborious way in London. Distrustful of Teel, Penhurst wanted to be in a position to respond immediately to any change in tactic. He would have to go to London. He disliked the idea of leaving Sophrina here when her emotions were rubbed as raw as his, but it had to be done. He would tell her tomorrow of his plans.

If London was not hell, it must be the closest thing to it. Penhurst groaned, staring bleakly out the front window to the damp streets below. On his last visit, all his time had been filled with Sophrina and their happiness and plans for their marriage. But now the town was beginning to fill in anticipation of the upcoming Season. And the leading topic of conversation in the drawing rooms, the halls of government, and the clubs was the lawsuit filed by Viscount Teel in Sheriff's Court for Criminal Conversation against the Earl of Penhurst. Not even the Roseberry/Mildmay divorce of 1815 had generated so much interest.

Penhurst tried to keep to himself as much as possible, but he was unavoidably forced out into society on occasion. He could not help but notice how conversation came to an abrupt halt when he entered a room. Lord, he hated gossip in the first place, and knowing he was the premier topic of every discussion in the capital did nothing to improve his disposition.

He wished he could have reamined at Talcott, where he could remain blissfully ignorant of the stir the trial had caused, but he wanted to be on hand while the lawyers engaged in their courtroom battles. Thank God there was no reason for him to appear at court; even his challenge to Teel's damage claim was to be handled with briefs from the trial over Lea. The ecclesiastical proceedings had been mercifully short; Teel and Sophrina were already divorced in the eyes of the church. But neither could remarry until the Parliamentary divorce bill passed. And that process awaited the resolution of the Crim. Con. proceedings.

Penhurst had not gathered up enough nerve to talk to the Foreign Office. It was one reason he avoided the social scene; there was less chance of coming face-to-face with Castlereagh. Penhurst did not want to face his old superior's look of disapproval and disappointment. When Penhurst ventured out at all, it was only to intimate dinner parties or to one of the smaller clubs with Seb Cole, who had come to town to offer what assistance and encouragement he could. Penhurst was grateful for his concern.

Yet even his friend's support was not enough to soothe Penhurst's ragged emotions when Teel's solicitor informed him that the petition to Parliament was being "temporarily" withheld.

"The bastard." Penhurst stalked to the far end of the drawing room, his frame rigid with fury. "How dare he pull this stunt at the last moment?"

Simms cleared his throat. "If I may offer a suggestion, my lord . . . ?"

Penhurst whirled about, fixing the solicitor with an icy stare. "What?" he demanded harshly.

"Lord Teel may be reacting to the—ah—size of the penalty award," the lawyer pointed out.

Penhurst bit off a sarcastic laugh. "You think he may have taken offense at the jury's decision? I cannot understand why. Certainly if I had asked for twenty-five thousand pounds and only been awarded *one pound* I would not feel the slightest bit of irritation."

"Perhaps if you offered the sum originally requested, he might be amenable to bringing the petition before the Lords," Seb suggested. "It might speed the process."

"And what if he wants fifty or seventy-five thousand pounds?" Penhurst asked bitterly. "Am I to bankrupt my estates and sacrifice my children's inheritance to feed the greed of that loathsome toad? I already gave him twenty-five thousand when he agreed to file charges. How much more does he want?"

"Unfortunately, Elliston, Teel is calling the tune right now and you are not in a position to wait for him to change his mind." Seb's voice was cautious. "He is under no obligation to apply to Parliament for a divorce. He can keep you and Sophrina apart for as long as he pleases."

Penhurst clenched his fists in frustration. "There must be some way to force him to present that petition."

"A disinterested third party could approach him . . ." Seb's voice trailed off.

"Thank you for the offer, Seb, but I do not think it will be of any use." Penhurst uttered a long, drawn-out sigh. "Perhaps a carefully worded letter, Simms, sounding out his lordship on the matter of additional payments *when* he presents the petition to the Lords."

Simms nodded in agreement, gathering up his papers to withdraw.

Penhurst turned to Seb with a weak smile. "How like this whole bloody mess! I should be overjoyed the jury thought Teel had no case, and yet their insight is going to cost me." He shook his head wearily. "If only provides more fodder for the gossip mills. It will be years before I dare show my face in London again."

"Has the Foreign Office said anything yet?"

"No. Privately it has been explained that no decision can be made until the matter is 'resolved.' I assume they mean to see if I marry Sophrina once Teel divorces her."

"Is that not a certainty?"

"Of course it is." Penhurst spoke bitterly. "Her life will be difficult enough as it is. I could no more abandon her than Kate. I only pray that I can bring her some happiness."

"I do not think you need fear that," Seb consoled. "The woman I saw in November was madly in love with you."

"We cannot seem to talk anymore," Penhurst scowled. "We tiptoe around the major issues. She knows how adamantly I opposed this divorce, yet she deliberately forced it upon us. That is the basis for a successful marraige?" He uttered a bitter laugh.

"You must have both hoped for a happy marriage once, else she would not have agreed to wed you," Seb pointed out.

"I think that was a lifetime ago," Penhurst said wearily. They had said far too much to each other to ever go back to that golden time. Yet every attempt at conversation between Sophrina himself ended in accusations and recriminations. Silence had become the safer course.

* * *

Sophrina grimaced at Elliston's scrawled letter. She knew he hated the notoriety the Crim. Con. trial had brought him. The sweet justice of the jury's failure to award William damages pleased her. How like him to be vindictive and threaten to withhold the divorce petition. Well, she hoped he was writhing with humiliation at having her disdain for him exposed to all the *ton*. If he even felt one-tenth of the mortification she had felt when he ran off with Lea, it would be enough for her.

The thought of Ellis having to pay more money to Teel infuriated her and increased her sense of guilt at having forced Ellis into this situation. She knew how angry he was. She had pitchforked the man she loved, an intensely private man who hated being the center of attention, into the middle of the juiciest scandal to hit London in years. It would be a miracle if he did not hate her.

An agonizing pain gripped her. Sophrina wished he was here, so she could cast herself at his feet and beg his forgiveness. She feared it would be a futile gesture; words were inadequate to atone for her ill-advised action. She had only wanted to bring them happiness, yet they were both more miserable than ever now. All because of her selfish impetuosity.

Chapter 19

Penhurst was glad he had decided to return to Talcott while awaiting Teel's action on the divorce petition. It was a relief to escape from the intense scrutiny of all the curious eyes in London. Here, at home, he could pretend all was well. He could spend needed time with Sophrina and hope that Kate's childish exuberance would restore his spirits. So even on this cold winter's morning, a carriage drive with the two women in his life promised to be a pleasant occupation.

"You do not think the weather too cold for a drive?" Sophrina glanced anxiously out the window at the leaden sky. "It looks as if to snow."

Penhurst shrugged. "We can always return early. Kate has been pestering me constantly about this drive. I do not think I could endure it another day if we postponed our plans. I shall toss in some extra rugs; we shall be warm enough."

Sophrina stifled her misgivings. The recent spate of cold weather had left everyone edgy and she had the beginnings of a headache dancing around her temples. But Elliston was right; Kate had been disappointed in so many things. It would not be fair to delay this outing only for the convenience of the grown-ups. Sophrina donned her heavy pelisse and bonnet and followed Penhurst out to the carriage for the return journey to Talcott.

Kate was bright with enthusiasm as Penhurst helped her into the curricle, a large smile wreathing her face as she perched beside Sophrina.

"Won't this be fun?" Kate laughed, clapping her tiny gloved hands with glee.

"That it will," agreed Sophrina, balancing herself as Penhurst climbed in beside Kate. She tucked the carriage robe firmly around the girl. "Now you must be sure to tell us if you grow cold," she cautioned.

Kate snuggled against the two adults. "I will be as warm as can be."

Despite their best intentions, neither Penhurst nor Sophrina were able to conjure up the carefree attitudes they tried to cultivate in Kate's presence. Kate, in turn, grew more voluble as the adults quieted until her chatter became incessant.

"That is enough, Kate!" Penhurst roared after one lengthy monologue. "One cannot even think with your constant jabbering."

Sophrina spoke soothingly. "It is fun to sit and watch the world rush past from our elevated perch, is it not? And when you sit quietly, you can hear all sorts of noises you hear nowhere else."

"Like what?" Kate demanded sullenly.

"Oh, there is the jingle of the harness, and the clip-clop of the horses hooves. Even the carriage makes its own creaking noises. Hush now and listen."

Penhurst flashed Sophrina a grateful look. She had such a knack with the child. He had once thought he was doing better with Kate, but with the strain of the last months, his temper had shortened and his toleration for four-year-old antics had lessened.

Sophrina shut her eyes and tried to focus her attention on the sounds she had just described to Kate. The mild headache she had felt earlier had blown itself into a sharp, throbbing ache behind both her eyes. Fed by the cold air, every jounce of the carriage sent a shooting pain through her head. Unconsciously she rubbed her fingers across her forehead.

"Are you all right?" Penhurst asked with concern.

She gave a woeful smile. "I have a bit of a headache," she confessed.

Penhurst reined in the horses. "We will return home. There is no point in you being out here if you are not comfortable."

"I don't want to take Rina home," Kate pouted. "You promised we would take a long drive today."

"Sophrina is not feeling well, Kate," Penhurst tried to explain in an even-tempered voice. "You do not want her to be uncomfortable, do you?"

"There will be other days to drive," Sophrina reassured her. "I own I do have a dreadful headache, Kate, and the bouncing carriage is not the best thing for it."

Kate set her mouth in a sharp line, but she said no more as Penhurst carefully turned the carriage around in the narrow lane.

"I am cold," Kate said when they were half the distance back to the cottage.

Sophrina reached down and tucked the carriage robe more firmly around her.

"Is that better?" she asked.

"No," said Kate sullenly. "My feet are cold."

"Try to wiggle your toes in your boots," Sophrina suggested. "That is a trick my mama taught me when I was little."

"I can't," Kate protested in a grating whine. "My boots are too tight and my toes won't move."

"Then stamp your feet lightly on the floor of the carriage," Penhurst said. "We will have you home soon enough."

Kate complied with his suggestion, but stamped so hard as to bounce the carriage.

"I said *gently*, Kate," Penhurst admonished. "Besides jolting the carriage about, you are making a deuce of a racket. I am certain it is not doing much to improve Sophrina's headache.''

"But I am cold!" Kate wailed, twisting like a hooked fish on the seat between them.

"Sit still!" Penhurst commanded.

Sophrina shut her eyes wearily. More than anything she wanted a hot cup of tea in front of a roaring fire, and the serene silence that marked her cottage.

Penhurst looked apologetically at Sophrina. "I think it best we take Kate home first," he said. "Will you be able to endure a few minutes' delay?"

She nodded without opening her eyes.

Perhurst brought the curricle to a stop at the front steps of Talcott. Handing the reins to the instantly appearing groom, he climbed from the seat and reached back to help Kate down.

"I want to stay with Rina," she said, leaning away from his outstretched hand.

"Sophrina does not want you when you are acting like a misbehaved brat," he said in a cold, stern voice. "Now come over here now and climb down from that carriage."

"No!"

"Kate," said Sophrina warningly. "Please do as your papa asks."

Kate flashed Sophrina a petulant look, then inched her way across the seat. She allowed Penhurst to help her down, but the moment her feet touched the round, she raced off across the lawn instead of heading toward the house.

"Damn that girl." Penhurst took off after her with long, loping strides.

Sophrina sat silently on the carriage seat, her eyes closed against the pain that even the dim gray winter light whipped into a white-hot stab of heat. Shivering against the cold, she closed her mind to all but the thought of that hot cup of tea.

Kate led Penhurst on a spirited chase across the front lawn before his stamina won out over her willful determination. With a final lunge, he grabbed her arm and jerked her to him, causing her bonnet to fall to the ground. Penhurst had only a tenuous grip and when Kate tried to pull away, she fell down with a thump, landing upon her hat. Penhurst stood over her glowering.

"Stand up!" he commanded hoarsely.

When she scrambled to her feet, she noted the ruined bonnet.

"My bonnet!" she wailed.

"Stop that crying this instant, Katherine! You have only yourself to blame for ruining your hat."

"It was your fault!" Kate screamed. "You pushed me! You pushed me!"

"Not another word, Katherine. You march into that house at once."

"No!"

Sophrina's eyes flew open at the sound of a resounding slap.

"You will go straight to your room, where you are to remain for the rest of this week!" Penhurst roared to be heard over Kate's hysterical screams. "Now move!"

Kate ran straight toward the carriage. "I want Rina!" she shrieked.

Penhurst caught her about the waist before she reached the vehicle and lifted her kicking and screaming form off the ground. His face white with fury, he strode with determination toward the house.

Sophrina, frozen with horror at the scene, willed her body to move. She scrambled from the curricle and raced across the lawn behind him.

"Ellis!"

He ignored her call and continued his march to the front door. He had to devote all his concentration on Kate, who struggled to wriggle out of his arms.

Reaching the top of the steps, he saw with relief that both Mrs. Gooch and the governess were waiting at the front steps.

"Kate is to go straight to her room and be put immediately to bed," he ordered furiously. "And she is not to have one bite to eat until I have been consulted." He glared angrily at the governess. "I shall speak with you later today about this incident."

He dumped the squirming girl unceremoniously onto the step and turned to confront Sophrina, who stood at the bottom of the stairs, her face white with shock and anger.

"How dare you strike her!"

"Leave off, Sophrina," he said wearily, slowly coming down the steps. "Come, I will drive you home."

"That will not be necessary," she said with marked stiffness.
"I prefer to walk."

"Don't be a fool," he muttered, taking her arm. He was well
aware that interested observers still filled the yard. "Let us get
away from this curious crowd." He turned and faced the
gathered servants. "Do none of you have any work to do?"
In the face of the earl's anger, the yard emptied.

Sophrina wrenched her arm free and turned to face Penhurst.

"I do not want to see you ever, ever strike Kate again," she
said, her voice icy with rage. "What a brutish thing to do!"

"She well deserved it," Penhurst retorted. "The girl is sadly
lacking in discipline. You and the women of this household have
spoiled her shamefully. She needs to be taught she cannot put
on these abominable displays of temper without facing punishment."

"Ellis, she is only four-and-a-half! You cannot hold her to
adult standards of behavior. *She is a child.* Children can and
will lose their tempers and behave abominably at times.
Particularly when the adults around her set such a glowing
example."

"How in the hell am I supposed to react when she acts like
an ill-mannered brat?" he exploded. "Say 'please, Kate?' She
is my daughter and the sooner she learns that my word is to
be obeyed, the better it will be for all of us."

Sophrina took several deep breaths to calm her racing pulse.
It had been building for weeks, this feeling of impending doom,
and now it was upon her and she was beset with panic and fear.
All the concerns she had pushed to the back of her mind rolled
forward, gnawing at her insides. The words rolled inside her
head like a gong. "He will never change, he will never change."

"Ellis, I do not think this is the best time to discuss this. We
are both upset. Tomorrow, when tempers have cooled . . ."

"No," he said adamantly. "We have been tiptoeing around
this for weeks, Sophrina, and you know as well as I that we
have to talk. I am not going to allow you to always take sides
with Kate against me. Your attempts to coddle her have only
restored her willfulness. I will not permit your softness to rule
her life. There are certain rules of behavior that we all must
conform to, and Kate must learn that."

"So she can be as coldhearted as her father when she grows up?" Sophrina said bitingly. "Yes, it would be a more placid household if you beat her into submission, but at what price, Ellis? At what price?"

"At least there would be one female in my life who would obey me," he snapped.

"Tyranny breeds disobedience," Sophrina retorted.

"You wanted me so badly you confessed to adultery before your husband so you would be free to marry," he said. "Well, madam, you are very close to getting your wish, so I suggest you reconcile yourself to adopting some wifely obedience."

They faced each other, eyes locked in a furious silent battle. It was Sophrina who looked away first, shivering at the rage and intensity in his gaze.

"You are cold," he said finally. "Allow me to take you home."

"No, I prefer to walk."

"If you will not drive with me, at least permit my groom to drive you," he said in exasperation. "There is no point in you taking ill out of sheer stubbornness."

"I shall walk," she announced and immediately struck out for the cottage.

Penhurst stood there watching her rapidly shrinking figure until she disappeared from view.

He was losing her, he knew. It seemed if they were on a mad pell-mell dash into disaster that neither one of them knew how to stop. He fought a mad impulse to run after her, to draw her into his arms, to kiss away the angry words and the hurt. Yet that would only make things right for a little while. In a day, a week, there would be another scene, more angry words.

He would never become the man she wanted him to be. Penhurst smiled sadly. He had tried to change. But it had not been enough. He simply could not live up to her standards. He would always fail her in the end.

Just as he had failed Lea. Admittedly he had not even tried with her. But for Sophrina, he had tried so hard, yet failed just as dismally. He raised his face toward the sky. Why could he not find happiness? Why was he doomed to despair and hurt?

With a muffled groan he thought of the divorce petition

lumbering its way through Parliament. Would it be possible to stop the proceedings at this late date? Would Teel still be willing to take Sophrina back after the humiliation of the Crim. Con. trial? Teel would be a poor husband for her, but Penhurst knew he was not any better. At least with Teel she would have the protection of his name. As a divorced woman on her own, she would have nothing. Sophrina deserved worthier men, yet she was now doomed to choose between two men she despised.

Penhurst did not want her to marry him out of desperation. And that was precisely what she would be forced to do if this divorce went through. Damn her! If it had not been for her willfulness in confessing to Teel, they would not be backed into this corner. He was honor bound to marry her—even if she no longer wanted him. He could not allow her to go on alone. She would need his name, his protection, in the stormy years to come as they tried to rebuild her shattered reputation.

And when she looked at him, in those years, would it be with love or revulsion in her eyes? He was very certain she would no longer wish to wed him if she had a choice. She could find another who would suit her better, who was a more patient, tolerant father. A man who was not subject to fits of anger, or who provoked her into acts of independence with his autocratic demands. There must be hundreds of men who were better suited than he. And she would be forced to settle for him.

The walk home did nothing to dampen Sophrina's anger. She could have struck Ellis a blow herself after that scene with Kate. How could he lose control like that? His wretched temper had spoiled everything.

She was shaking with cold and anger and fear when she finally reached the haven of her parlor and sank down into a chair. She buried her face in her hands. Dear God, what had she done to them? She had been so determined to direct the path their lives would take and had gone to William, secure in the knowledge that she was doing the right thing. But her action had only precipitated disaster. Elliston was still furious with her, and she no longer had any doubts about his unwillingness to marry her. In a short while she would be divorced, and alone, with only fading memories to remind her of what might have been.

She had demanded too much of him. She had tried to mold Elliston to her ideas of what a father and husband should be. She had not been willing to accept him for what he was. Dissatisfied with each change she wrought, she had asked for more until he snapped. And now she had turned him against her forever.

She could not even cry. She had shed so many tears these last months she thought they had finally dried up. There was not even that horridly familiar aching sensation in her throat and chest. She only felt cold and hollow inside. As if a part of her had died.

Sophrina was suddenly very frightened. It would only be a short time until her divorce from William passed through Parliament. She would be a divorced woman, and despite Elliston's views to the contrary, she knew how difficult a situation that would be. She had always thought that with him by her side, she could endure anything. But without his protection . . .

She knew Elliston was equally well aware of that. And no matter how unpleasant he found the thought, he would marry her, because duty demanded it. And she would hate that most of all. She did not want a marriage of obligation. It would be the most horrible thing imaginable.

Despite the foaring fire, she shivered with a chill that no heat could warm. She had made a royal mess of not only her life, but Elliston's and Kate's. And the way to make amends was to let them both go. It was the only way to ensure the happiness of the two people she loved the most.

Chapter 20

Four long days had passed since that awful scene at Talcott, and still Sophrina shrank from what she feared would be the final confrontation with Elliston. She had sent him a polite note, apologizing for her outbursts and asking him to forgive her. He returned a curt reply, stating the matter was all but forgotten.

But he did not call on her. When Kate arrived at the cottage today, accompanied only by one of the grooms, Sophrina's heart sank.

"Papa left for London this morning," Kate announced brightly as she danced into the parlor.

Sophrina drew in a sharp breath. "Did he say how long he would be gone?"

Kate shook her head. "But he promised to bring me a present. Do you think it will be another doll?"

"Is that what you want?" Sophrina tried to still her racing pulse. Why had Elliston gone to London? And why had he not told her? Was it somehow connected with the divorce? Had he gone to talk to William? If Teel withdrew his petition from the Lords, there would be no divorce. Penhurst would not be forced into an unwanted marriage with her.

"I think so," said Kate. "What else would he bring me?"

Sophrina smiled fondly at the girl. "They do have some marvelous things in London, Kate. And when you are a little older, you will not even be able to choose among them all. Although I think right now that a doll is the very nicest thing you would want to have."

"What other things are there?"

"Well," began Sophrina, with a pang of remembrance, "when I was shopping in London I bought gloves, lace handkerchiefs, bonnets, ribbons, and all manner of odds and ends."

"You are right," said Kate. "I think I would rather have a doll."

Sophrina gave her a swift hug. "I cannot wait to see the day when you are a grown-up young lady and the thought of ribbons and laces entices you more than dolls."

"Will you be my mama then?" Kate looked at her with child-like innocence.

"I hope so," said Sophrina. She could not bear to tell Kate now, with Penhurst gone.

"I hope you get to be my mama soon," Kate rattled on. "Papa has promised to take me to the seashore this summer and it would be ever so much fun if you came with us. He says the water goes on and on forever and it is full of salt and there are shells and pretty rocks."

"And did he tell you about the crabs that pinch your bare

toes if you are not careful?'' Sophrina teased, fighting the urge to laugh as Kate's eyes grew wider.

''Really?''

Sophrina nodded solemnly. ''But if you are very careful, you can pick them up and hold them in just such a way that they cannot bite.''

Kate wrinkled up her nose. ''I do not think I will like crabs,'' she said.

Sophrina laughed. ''You will enjoy yourself immensely.'' The thought filled her with a pang of longing. It was very likely she would *not* accompany Kate and her father on this trip. A creeping sadness stole over her. How different things were turning out from what she had planned.

''Why do you look so sad, Rina?'' Kate asked. ''Papa looks sad all the time.''

Sophrina grabbed Kate into a crushing hug. ''Sometimes even adults are unhappy.'' She struggled against her tears, wiping her eyes surreptitiously. ''But it is silly of me to be sad when I have such a delightful guest at my cottage. Now, there is a huge plate of biscuits on the table that I cannot possibly eat by myself. Can you help?''

Penhurst stared out the window of his study at the dismal sky. His only consolation was that the gray drizzle outside matched his mood.

His trip to London had been a failure. He had wanted to buy some time for Sophrina, time in which she could look deep into her heart and be certain that she still wished to go through with this irrevocable step. He had swallowed his pride and gone to Teel, hat-in-hand, asking him to at least temporarily withdraw the divorce petition from Parliament. All had begun amicably enough, with polite chitchat and glasses of brandy in hand.

''Would you consider withdrawing your petition from the Lords?'' Penhurst asked at last.

''Having second thoughts, are you?'' Teel sneered.

''No,'' said Penhurst calmly. ''But I fear Sophrina is. And I do not want her forced into an untenable position by events.''

''She sounded quite adamant last time I spoke with her.'' Teel smiled knowingly.

"Would you take her back, if that was her wish?" Penhurst's questioning gaze raked the viscount.

Teel abruptly rose from his chair and sauntered across the room to the sideboard, where he refilled his brandy glass.

"What would I want with an adulteress for a wife?"

Penhurst struggled to retain his temper. "Give it over, Teel. You were considered dead. And in any case, you are not one to quibble about other's sleeping habits."

Teel's eyes narrowed. "Lea still rankles, eh?"

Penhurst's voice was icily calm. "I do not give a damn about what transpired between you and Lea. What I do care about is Sophrina's happiness. I am no longer convinced that rests with me and I am attempting to ensure that she will have someone to look after her."

Teel leaned back against the table edge, crossing his arms in front of him.

"It would be laughable if it involved anyone else," he said bitingly. " 'Tis only a pity Lea is no longer here—we could spend the remainder of our paltry lives trading wives around."

Penhurst was on his feet in an instant, the contents of his glass dripping down Teel's shirt front.

"Do not ever put Sophrina and Lea in the same sentence," he said with cold deliberateness. "My wife was a whore. Sophrina is a lady. 'Tis a pity you do not know the difference."

Teel calmly mopped his wet shirt with his handkerchief. He gave Penhurst a smirking smile. "The Bill passed to the Commons this afternoon, *my lord*. Your precious Sophrina should be free in less than a fortnight."

"I should have put a ball through you four years ago," Penhurst enunciated as he strode from the room. Teel's biting laughter followed him down the hall.

Penhurst closed his eyes wearily at the remembered scene. His only consolation was that his words and actions had not furthered the damage—it was already done. There was no stopping the divorce now; Sophrina's ties with Teel would be severed forever, and she would soon be in Penhurst's care.

He hoped she would not grow to hate him. He would do all he could to avoid that prospect. He would not interfere with her handling of Kate. He was well aware that was often the major bone of contention between them. He was willing to give up his responsibility for her, and any other children they might have, if it would keep the peace between them. That was the area where he had disappointed her the most. If he removed himself from that domain, perhaps she would gain back some of her respect for him. He could not bear the thought of life with a woman who despised him.

Dinner with Seb at their club and an evening of far-too-steady drinking did little to improve his mood.

"The irony of the situation," Penhurst enunciated his words with the precision of one who had drunk too much, "is that *she* is the one who precipitated the whole trial."

Seb eyed him quizzically.

"Tried to get Teel to agree to a divorce in Scotland," Penhurst slurred, reaching an unsteady hand toward the brandy decanter. "He refused. Kept insisting Sophrina wanted to come back to him." He gave a short laugh. "Man's a fool for thinking that. She will never go back to him. Never!"

Seb glanced uneasily at his companion. Elliston was never one to drink overmuch; then again, how many other men had endured two Crim. Con. trials in their lives? The first trial over Lea had been difficult for his friend. The role of cuckolded husband had not sat easily upon him. But the role of adulterer fit worse.

"It would have come to this eventually," Seb said. "Can't say I would wish to be in your shoes, with the notoriety of the trial and all, but you have a lady who is worth all the trouble."

"Have I?" Penhurst questioned morosely. "I am no longer certain Sophrina wants to have me. I never can seem to live up to her expectations." He leaned forward toward Seb. "She wanted to go to Teel and ask him to divorce her. I said no. So she went ahead and talked to him anyway." He sat back in his chair. "Can you imagine the utter humiliation she must have felt, having to do that on her own? God, I should have been the one to go to Teel. But I thought—" he hiccuped, "that a divorce would be a disaster for Sophrina."

"It is an unusual situation, Ellis," said Seb hesitatingly, "But you have heard how sympathetic most people have been. Only the strictest homes will be closed to her."

"It is not just the divorce," Penhurst protested, waving a weaving finger in the air. "Take Kate, for example. Sophrina is always taking me to task for the way I deal with the girl. I don't talk to her enough. I talk to her too sternly. I expect too much from her." He ran a hand through his hair. "Lord knows, I am attempting to be a good father. But Sophrina expects perfection and I fall so very short . . ."

Seb grew increasingly alarmed. This seemed more than a matter of trial-induced nerves.

"Certainly you are both overset from all that has transpired," he offered encouragingly. "Do not let anything said or done at this time hold much weight. She is in a precarious position, and is likely just as worried about you. Sophrina may be starting to realize exactly how difficult her situation is going to be in the future."

"The worst of it," Penhurst went on, as if not hearing his friend, "is that I no longer know how she feels." He tipped his head back, draining his glass. "I have this terrible fear that when this is all over, Seb, she is going to regret she threw over her respectability for me. That her love will turn to hate."

Penhurst buried his face in his hands. "God, Seb, what am I going to do?"

Seb shook his head sadly. How could two people, who had beamed with happiness that last time he saw them, he brought so low in such a short time? Love could be a damnable coil. He was glad he had never fallen into its snares. He settled back into his chair, prepared to listen to more of his friend's maudlin ramblings. And when Penhurst was talked out, he would help him to his bed. There was little else he could do.

Sophrina stared at William's letter with growing horror, hardly daring to believe what she read. Penhurst had actually begged him to call off the divorce. She had been right—he no longer wanted her at all. The letter fluttered to the floor.

At least, she thought dully, William's letter had given her some warning. She would have time to prepare before Penhurst's return.

Staying in the neighborhood was out of the question. William's presence would not bother her, but she could not bear to live so near to Penhurst and Kate. She would go far away, where no one knew her, where she could live a quiet life. The divorce settlement would leave her with a modest income, enough for a small cottage and household help. She could visit Mary and Bertram—and Louisa would remain in touch. But to lose Kate . . . It was almost more than she could bear.

She could not even think about a life without Ellis. There would be weeks, months, years to torment herself with that. It would take every bit of strength left in her to endure the next few weeks. There would be the tasks of finding a new home, making arrangements with the bankers, packing her belongings. She did not have the strength to think beyond that. She must keep her mind focused on each day as it came.

Sophrina's hand trembled ever so slightly as she picked up the fallen letter and scanned the rest of its contents. Such an undramatic denouement to the agony of the last months. It directed her to the bank where her funds would be deposited and informed her she was under no pressure to leave her present home. It was a short, concise letter. She was free of William forever.

What was Elliston thinking now? Or what had he been thinking for the last two days, since he would have heard the news in London? He would be relieved in a way; at least the worst of it was over for him and he could go about picking up the pieces of his life. Sophrina did not even wish to speculate as to why he had not written to tell her the news himself. She was glad, for it would give her the time to plan what she would say to him when he finally came to her.

Sophrina did not know how to interpret the ominous silence from Ellis that stretched on and on. She was under no illusion that he still wanted to marry her; she knew these last weeks had destroyed whatever tender feelings he had once held for her. She almost hoped his absence from Talcott was his subtle way of telling her that; his way of asking her to free him from his commitments to her. For as an honorable man, he could never voice those sentiments. Honor demanded that he take her for his wife, no matter how reluctant he was to take that step.

Despite the warmth of the fire-warmed room, Sophrina shivered. She knew, in her heart, what she had to do. It would cause her considerable pain, but she could not allow Ellis to marry her. It would be a life of unbearable torture, knowing he had married her out of obligation and not out of desire. Without her, he would be free to resume his diplomatic duties, as he so wanted. He would be able to find a wife who could grace his side at embassy balls, host his parties, and entertain his guests. One who would bring joy and gladness to his life, instead of bitterness and resentment.

They would never be able to find happiness together now. Marriage would force Penhurst to give up too much. Sophrina truly did not care if society ostracized her, but she realized, belatedly, just how much society's opinion mattered to Penhurst—and Kate. The divorce would reflect upon them both. She could not allow Penhurst to make any more sacrifices for her. An audible moan escaped her lips. He had paid dearly for her freedom, in money and public humiliation. She would never be able to repay either. However, if she refused to marry him, it would at least be a small way to atone for her reckless behavior. She would need every ounce of strength she possessed to go through with her plan. But it was the best course for all of them.

Penhurst put off his return to Talcott as long as he dared, but after a week he knew he had to return home and play out the final scene of this drama. He had attempted, a thousand times, to write Sophrina. She must have heard the news by now—Teel would have made certain of *that*. Penhurst frowned sourly. He did not even dare to think how Sophrina had taken his silence on the matter. Yet he found he simply could not put his thoughts on paper when they were still in such turmoil.

He was so confused. A part of him wanted Sophrina as much as ever. Despite everything, she had brought joy and pleasure into his life and shown him a glimpse of future happiness that he had not deemed possible. Yet, uncertain about her present feelings for him, cornered by honor and obligation into a marriage he was no longer convinced she wanted, he could not suppress a twinge of desperation.

It would be a miracle if they could ever achieve the semblance of a happy marriage. Where once he had hoped for a union blessed with joy and ecstasy, he would now be grateful for a life filled with amiability and toleration. What a hell on earth that would be. To never see the love shining in her eyes, forced to hide his own feelingss for her lest she realize just how much he loved her. The last thing he wanted was her pity, or sympathy. Yet under the circumstances, he was doubtful he could hope for more. Too much had happened to damage their feelings toward one another; the trust, love, and respect they had once shared had been trampled underfoot. If ever they achieved a tolerable companionship, they would be lucky. It was all he deserve after the way he had acted.

But not all he wanted. Sophrina had showed him the path toward happiness, showed him the joys of loving and caring. And he had turned on her, with his anger, his failures, and his doubts, rejecting all she had offered. He had denied happiness for himself, but in his selfishness, he also denied it for her. Would she ever forgive him for that? Would she sit across the table from him at dinner, bemoaning the fate that irrevocably bound her to him? Would she lie in her bed at night, longing for a lover with compassion and tenderness? He had failed her so miserably. She deserved so much better. And she was forced by circumstances to accept him.

He wished with all his heart that it could have turned out differently for them. That the delirious happiness of those long-ago days of November could have remained with them forever. Now, at best, they could look forward to a lifetime of . . . of what-might-have-beens. Oh, they would make the best of things, he was certain. They would achieve an amiable comfortable-ness. He would have the estate and land to manage; Sophrina would have children—if they were lucky—to coddle and fuss over. It would be no worse than most other marriages, and better than some. But not what he had once thought to have with her.

With a sigh he rose wearily from his chair. He had avoided matters long enough; he could no longer postpone his return to Talcott. There were new marriage arrangements to be made, settlements to be reworked, a honeymoon trip to plan. The last thought brought forward a harsh laugh. Perhaps that event was best ignored.

Sophrina gripped the arms of her chair so tightly her knuckles grew white with the effort. Elliston would be at the cottage any moment. Since his note arrived yesterday, she had steeled herself for the interview. She only needed to keep her turbulent emotions under control for a short while longer, and then it would all be over.

Over. The word held such a ringing finality.

Her ears caught the sounds of the approaching carriage. Taking a deep breath, she closed her eyes and calmly began counting down the seconds.

All her resolve wavered and trembled when he entered the parlor. She had not seen him for nearly a month and in that first instant all her old longings swelled up inside, threatening to spill over and ruin everything. He looked tired, she saw with a pang, the creases in his face looking more pronounced. Stripped of both arrogance and happiness, he threw off a boyish vulnerability that caused her chest to tighten. Rising swiftly to her feet, Sophrina stepped forward and held out her hand in welcome. It must be done this way, she reminded herself.

Penhurst raised her hand briefly to his lips, then divested himself on his hat and driving coat. There was a palpable tension in the room, exacerbated by the silence.

"Well," he said finally, turning to her, forcing brightness to his voice, "it is over at last."

"Yes," she replied.

He looked down in embarrassment. "I know I should have written, but I just could not put words to paper, Sophrina. I wanted to wait until we were together before I said all I need to." He took her hands in his. "Has it been unpleasant for you since . . . ?"

She shook her head. "Louisa has been over several times. And I have heard nothing from William, which is certainly a blessing."

"I spoke with the vicar yesterday. The special license is still valid. He can perform the ceremony this week if you wish."

Sophrina gently disentangled her hands and turned away.

"I do not think there is any reason for haste," she said slowly. Now that the time had come, she was hard-pressed to force the words from her mouth.

Her obvious reluctance hit Penhurst like a blow. He had tried to cozen himself into thinking that somehow, it would all work out, that a hasty marriage would be easiest. There would be time and enough later to work out exactly what kind of marriage they would have.

"I do not want to heap any additional fuel on the fires of gossip," he explained. "You were not in London; you have no inkling of what it was like. Once we are wed, there will be nothing left to say and some new story still catch their attention."

Sophrina turned reluctantly to face him, although she directed her gaze to his left shoulder.

"I do not think we should wed merely to still the gossip, Elliston. As long as we are in the country, they will have no news of us anyway."

"Still, I feel it is best if we take care of things quickly. It will be the best for all of us. Particularly Kate."

Her head came up with a jerk and she at last found the nerve to meet his eyes.

"I think, particularly because of Kate, it would be prudent for us to wait." She lowered her gaze again. "We both need time to think, Elliston. I thought I would take a cottage somewhere; perhaps at summer's end we could . . ."

"Summer?" he asked weakly, a sick feeling growing in the pit of his stomach. "Sophrina, that is months away. What purpose will it serve?"

"I made a serious mistake with my first marriage. I do not wish to do the same with my next one." There. She had said it.

"I see." Penhurst's voice failed to betray the pain that shot through him. Her words confirmed his worst fears; she no longer wanted him. He wanted to grab her and shake her until she retracted her statement; shake her until she agreed to marry him that very afternoon if necessary. But he stood as if rooted to the floor, unable to move a muscle.

In the ensuing silence the ticking of the mantel clock dominated the room. Penhurst felt at a loss for words. What could he possibly say to convince her that she should marry him, when he half believed himself it was the wrong thing for her? He could not say, with absolute certainty, that he would ever be the type of husband she wanted. Did he have the right to force her into a marriage not of her choosing? She could very well end up hating him, and that was one thing he could not bear. Rejection was infinitely more pleasant than hatred.

He shifted slightly and for an instant her gaze met his again.

"I agree that we both need time to consider the matter," he said, choosing his words with caution. He did not want to make any irrevocable remarks now. He mustered up all his diplomatic tact. "Do not feel it is necessary for you to move from the neighborhood. I will not seek to importune or persuade you, if that is your wish." He flashed her a wan smile. "And I will not blackmail you with Kate. Although it will be difficult to keep her away."

"Perhaps it would be best if you did take her away for a while. She would love London." Sophrina instantly rued her words, recalling Elliston's account of their notoriety there. "Or one of the coastal towns. She said you were planning to take her to the seashore this summer. She is very excited about that."

"I will think upon it," Penhurst said.

"Thank you," said Sophrina.

He feared to leave Sophrina here by herself. It would be too easy for her to dismiss himself and Kate from her mind if they were gone from the neighborhood. Even if they never saw one another, their sheer proximity at Talcott would always be at the back of Sophrina's mind. As long as she thought of him, perhaps there was hope . . .

"Sophrina, I . . . "

She turned and faced him again, meeting his eyes, knowing she visibly trembled.

He reached out and caressed her cheek with his hand.

"I am sorry," he said. "For everything that has happened. Please believe that I wish you to be happy. If we wed, I will do everything in my power to make that happen."

She nodded, not trusting herself to speak. Tears misted in her eyes. All her well-planned intentions faded. She shut her eyes to fight back the love and desire that threatened to overwhelm her.

Penhurst kissed her gently.

"If you need me, you need only to send to Talcott," he whispered. Quickly he took his coat and hat and exited the parlor.

Sophrina stood there in the middle of the room, unable to move, her eyes tightly shut. She could still feel his hand gently stroking her cheek, felt the warm softness of his mouth on hers. She would hold on to this moment for as long as she could, knowing it would be her final memory.

Chapter 21

Penhurst shook his head bitterly. He could not imagine a worse hell than this last week. Since his dismissal at Sophrina's hands, he had done little but berate himself for his own folly at alienating the only woman he had ever loved. Worse, he had been faced with the unenviable task of gradually introducing Kate to the knowledge that Sophrina would not be coming to live with them—ever. He had no illusion about Sophrina's request for more time. She no longer wanted him.

The first few days, it had been easy to fob Kate off with the excuse that Sophrina was busy, or unwell. But after several unsuccessful pleas to visit her friend, Kate grew more demanding.

"I want to see Rina," she said, pouting at her father.

"Today is not a good day to visit Sophrina," he said quietly. "I shall take you for a drive in the carriage if you like."

"You can take me to Rina's!"

"No, Kate, I cannot do that."

"Then bring Rina here."

He took a steadying breath. "I do not think Sophrina will be coming to visit anymore, Kate."

She looked at him in stunned silence, her brow puckered in confusion. He beckoned for her to climb onto his lap. When she was settled against his arm, he haltingly tried to explain.

"Sometimes, Kate, grown-ups decide that they do not get along as well as they once thought. And when that happens, they do not see each other as often."

"But Rina is my friend."

"I know that, Kate. However, Sophrina is unhappy with me

right now, and we both feel it is best if we do not see each other for a while.''

"She is not unhappy with me?"

"No, Kate, Sophrina loves you very much. Sometimes when grown-ups are unhappy with each other, other people get drawn into their quarrel. It would not be right for Sophrina to see you as often, if she is not going to be visiting Talcott again.''

"But she will be here after you marry her.''

Penhurst winced. "I do not think Sophrina and I are going to be married, Kate.''

"You promised!'' she wailed. "You said Sophrina was going to be my mama.''

He hugged her tightly. "When I said that, I believed it to be true. That is no longer the case.''

Kate glowered at him. "Then I will go live with Rina.''

He shook his head. "That is not possible, Kate. Your place is here with me.''

She scrambled off his lap. "This is your fault,'' she cried heatedly. "Rina wanted to be my mama. You won't let her.''

"I wish with all my heart that Sophrina would become your mama. But I cannot force her to do something she does not want to do.''

"Will I ever get to see her again?'' Kate's eyes brimmed with tears.

"Of course you will,'' he reassured her. "It is only that right now everyone is a little sad that our plans did not work out. When Sophrina is happier, I know she will want to see you again.''

"I want Rina!'' Kate cried, racing from the room.

Penhurst watched her flee, his own heart aching for Kate's pain as well as his own. She was still young, though, and he knew that the natural resiliency of childhood would eventually heal her hurts. He envied Kate for that, knowing his future held no such promise.

He felt little better the next afternoon as he tried to sort out the chaos on his desk. He had partaken too heavily from the brandy decanter the night before, for he found it increasingly necessary to coat his mind with the soothing numbness if he expected to sleep.

"My lord?"

Penhurst looked up with irritation. It was not that he was enmeshed in the estate books, for he was well aware that he had been staring at the same page of the ledger for over an hour. But he did not want human company of any kind at this moment. Sophrina no longer wanted him; Kate had not spoken to him since he had talked with her yesterday. He only wanted to be left alone.

"What?" he rapped out angrily at Mrs. Gooch.

"Is . . . is Lady Kate with you, my lord?"

"No, she is not. Is there a problem?"

Mrs. Gooch fumbled with her apron. "It has been quite some time since anyone has seen her."

Penhurst instantly sat up. "How long?"

"Since breakfast."

"Breakfast!" he exploded. "Am I not paying a qualified governess to educate and supervise the girl? Where is the woman?"

"She is up in the attics, looking for Lady Kate," Mrs. Gooch explained nervously. "Apparently Lady Kate told her that there would be no school today, at your request."

"Damn that girl," thundered Penhurst, jumping from his chair. "She is going to have her bottom warmed for this escapade. Organize the household staff and search the house. I will alert the stables."

An hour later, Penhurst's anger had transformed itself into deep concern. There was no sign of Kate anywhere inside or outside the house. They searched and re-searched the rooms and alcoves, yet there was no trace of the girl.

The governess, at whom he had initially thundered, proved efficient as she organized the staff. And it was she who had discovered the key evidence—Kate's boots and cloak were gone. And more important, she had taken her doll. That knowledge set a tingle of alarm down Penhurst's spine. The doll was Kate's favorite possession.

In a burst of realization, he knew she had gone to Sophrina. Dashing down the front steps, Penhurst cried orders to the staff as he raced around the edge of the house toward the stables. Waiting for his horse to be saddled, he gulped in air, willing his racing pulse to quiet. Kate knew the way well enough, having walked it innumerable times. But it was damnably rude of Sophrina not to have sent word that the girl was there. She knew Kate was not permitted to leave the house on her own.

Despite his certainty that he would find Kate at the cottage, he dispatched the Talcott grooms to search the far reaches of the estate for the missing girl. He wanted nothing left to chance. Climbing into the saddle, he headed his horse down the drive.

After several minutes of frenzied pounding on the cottage door, Penhurst realized with a pang that Sophrina was not at home. Where could she have gone? Was Kate with her?

He could easily have missed them if Sophrina had decided to take the runaway back home, for they would have taken the short path across the meadow. Remounting, Penhurst whipped his horse across the lane. He would probably arrive at Talcott to find them both ensconced in the front drawing room, in front of a roaring fire.

Sophrina walked briskly to ward off the damp chill. She had enjoyed the visit with Louisa; the dowager listened with patience as Sophrina poured out her tale of woe. The viscountess only counseled caution, warning Sophrina not to do anything rash until she was certain of her own heart—and Penhurst's.

They were wise words, but they did not lighten Sophrina's gloom. She had no doubt of Ellis's mind. She only needed to remain firm in her own resolve. If she refused him long enough, he could finally take his departure with his honor preserved—and hers as well.

Sophrina had barely removed her bonnet and cloak when Penhurst burst into the parlor. His eyes frantically scanned the room.

"Please say that Kate is here with you!"

Panic seized Sophrina. "Elliston, she is not. What is wrong?"

"No one has seen her since this morning," he said, is face ashen pale.

"Dear God," groaned Sophrina. "Did you search the entire house?"

"From the attic to the cellar. We looked under every bush in the garden . . ." His voice broke with emotion.

"She ran away once, Ellis, do you think she has done it again? Things have been so unsettled recently . . . Children understand more than we give them credit for."

"I was hoping she had run to you." His eyes met hers in a bleak appeal.

Sophrina was filled with worry for Kate, but her heart ached for Elliston. He looked so lost and distraught, his face a white mask of agony . . . How could she ever have thought him an uncaring father? She rose and walked toward him, her only thought to offer him comfort and hope.

"I have been at the dowager's all morning, so if Kate came here, she would not have found me." Sophrina forced a smile of encouragement. "She has probably discovered a marvelous new hiding place. Where else have you looked?"

"I have the stable hands looking between Talcott and here, thinking she might have tarried along the way or taken a meandering route. I crisscrossed the meadow, but there was no sign of her. I will head toward the village next."

Sophrina glanced out the window and shivered. "It is so cold out. Did she take anything with her?"

He nodded. "Her coat and boots are gone, thank goodness, so she is somewhat protected. And her doll."

The doll. Kate's most prized possession. That knowledge alone brought tears to Sophrina's eyes. If Kate had taken her doll, she really did plan to leave.

"Since she is not here, I must be gone again," he said. "I think we will run ever-widening circles around the neighborhood, hoping someone has seen her. I will send you word as quickly as I know."

"You will find her soon, I am certain," Sophrina said, as if the words could make it true. "If she turns up here, I will send news to Talcott."

Penhurst looked down at her for a moment, seeing the concern in her eyes. Pulling her into his arms, he drew a small measure of comfort from her nearness. Lord, he had missed her, missed holding her close against him. For an instant he wanted only to stay with her, seeking the warm shelter of her arms which he irrationally thought could shield him from all harm. Nothing was going right without her, and nothing would go right again until they had reconciled, he knew that. But there was no time now.

"I love you," he whispered softly, then kissed her with a passion he had not allowed himself to feel for an age.

Sophrina stared in bemusement as the parlor door banged shut behind him. Touching her fingers to her lips, she heard those words over and over in her brain. Was there still a chance for them? Pray God, let it be true.

She attempted to distract her mind with sewing, but after a futile attempt at concentration, Sophrina tossed her handwork aside in discouragement. Glancing out the window, she noted the weather looked as cold and damp as ever. Where had that wretched child gone? Sophrina desperately wanted to be of some use in the search, but knew there was little she could do to help. Penhurst and his men would be most thorough. She should be at home in any event, in case Kate did appear.

What if Kate had been here earlier, when Sophrina was at the Dower House? She groaned audibly at the thought. Why had she decided to visit Louisa today? What would Kate have thought, coming here and finding Sophrina gone? Where else would she go?

Sophrina fought down the panic rising within her. Kate would be all right, she told herself over and over again. Elliston will find her and everything will be fine.

Shivering despite her warm woolen dress, Sophrina trudged up the stairs to retrieve her heavy shawl. She would build up the fire in the parlor, and by then Jenny would have returned from the village. Sophrina could walk to Talcott and ask if there had been any news. It was foolish, she knew, for Ellis would send a message, but Sophrina felt she had to do something.

She stopped with a start in the doorway to her room. There, curled up on the bed with her doll clutched at her side, lay Kate, sound asleep.

Sophrina did not know whether to laugh or cry. How long had she been there? She must have slipped in while the cottage was empty—and had been sleeping here peacefully while Elliston was so worried downstairs.

"Kate, how could you do this?" Sophrina chided as she shook the child awake.

"Rina?"

"Yes it is Rina. Whatever are you doing here? Your poor father is frantic."

"I wanted to be with you," Kate cried, wrapping her arms around Sophrina's neck.

Sophrina gently disengaged Kate's hands. "You did not ask if you could come here, did you?" she said in a stern voice.

Kate shook her head.

"You have been very naughty," Sophrina scolded. "Not only your poor father, but the whole staff at Talcott has been racing about the countryside looking for you. What were you thinking of to do such a thing?"

Kate looked at Sophrina with a bewildered expression, then burst into tears.

"Papa said you were not going to be my mama ever," she sobbed.

Sophrina drew Kate into her arms, rocking her softly back and forth.

"Poor Kate," she whispered. "We grown-ups have made a mull of things for you, haven't we? I am sorry."

"Why won't you come live with us?" Kate asked with a sniff. "I would be very good, I promise."

"I am certain you would be," Sophrina said with a smile. "But it is not that simple, Kate. It is something that your father and I must decide. Right now, the most important thing is to let him know you are safe."

"He will be angry with me for running away."

"Yes he will, and rightly so! I have half a mind to turn you over my knee and paddle you myself." Sophrina fixed her face into a stern expression and set Kate back on the bed. "Now, let us wash your face and then I will take you back to Talcott."

"Are you mad at me, too, Rina?"

"Yes I am, Rina. And very disappointed. You are far too old to pull a prank like this."

"I'm sorry," Kate whispered.

As the darkening sky heralded the coming of the night, Penhurst pounded his fist against the saddle in frustration. Where had the foolish child gone? He and his men had looked everywhere, it seemed; all the land between Talcott and Sophrina's had been gone over with a fine-toothed comb. There was no trace of her on the path to the village, and no one there had seen a small child wandering unaccompanied. The vicar had not seen her, nor had she wandered in the direction of Lady Groves. He could think of no other place in the neighborhood where she could have gone. Charlton was the closest estate, but with Bertram and Mary gone, the children were no longer there. What attraction could it have?

It was probably a foolish whim, Penhurst thought, as he headed his horse toward Charlton. But there was still someone at Charlton known to Kate. Could she have gone to her father?

The butler looked at Penhurst oddly as he stood on the front steps in all his dirt and disarray. But he offered no objection when Penhurst demanded to see Lord Teel. Penhurst felt a petty sense of satisfaction at dragging his muddied boots over the carpets.

"Penhurst." Teel's voice betrayed a hint of emotion. "This is a surprise. What business brings you to Charlton?"

"Is my daughter here?"

"*Your* daughter?"

Penhurst glared angrily at Teel. "There is more to fatherhood than the mere spilling of seed," he said sarcastically. "Is she here?"

"Have you misplaced her? Tsk Tsk. Rather careless of you. Most men take better care of their possessions. But then, you were always rather careless with your women."

Penhurst exploded with rage. Hurtling himself across the room, he grabbed Teel by the lapels and jerked him to his feet. "*Is Kate here?*"

Teel paled and shook his head.

Penhurst released him slowly. He saw with a grim sense of satisfaction that his violent outburst had shaken Teel.

"She has not been seen since this morning," Penhurst explained. "We have been searching for her all afternoon . . ." His voice trailed off as he turned toward the door.

"Penhurst?"

He stopped, his hand still on the latch.

"You can be certain I will escort her home if she makes an appearance here."

Penhurst gave Teel a long, deliberate stare.

"Thank you," he said at last and exited the room.

Penhurst was cold, tired, and hungry when he reached Talcott. But there was still another hour of daylight left. With fresh horses they would be able to trace and retrace their paths one more time. Penhurst wolfed down the sandwiches laid out on the kitchen table at Talcott, motioning for the grooms to help themselves as well. They could all use a few minutes' rest.

They would find her eventually, he told himself, forcing his mind to remain calm. She had probably been leading them in a merry circle all day and would make her appearance as night neared. He could not even bear to think of what would happen if she was not found by dark. It was far too cold to even contemplate a small girl outside alone during the long hours of darkness.

"My lord!" Mrs. Gooch hastened down the kitchen stairs. "It's Lady Kate. She is back!"

Penhurst knocked down his chair in his hurry to reach the steps.

"She's in the drawing room," Mrs. Gooch gasped as Penhurst brushed past her. "Lady—um—Miss Sophrina is with her."

Penhurst stopped to take a deep breath before he flung open the drawing room door. Lord, let me keep my temper, he offered up in hasty prayer. He had to show Sophrina he could maintain control, under even the most grievous provocation.

Both Kate and Sophrina turned away from the fire as he strode into the room.

"She was at the cottage all the time," Sophrina explained. "She slipped in while I was at the Dower House, then fell asleep on the bed. I feel dreadful for not discovering it sooner; I know how worried you were."

Penhurst nodded briefly, then knelt before an apprehensive Kate.

"You have caused a good deal of trouble, young lady. You know you are not allowed to leave the house without telling anyone."

Kate hung her head. "I wanted Rina," she said with a small voice.

Penhurst glanced quickly at Sophrina. She met his gaze for

a moment, then turned away, but not before he caught a glimpse of—longing?—in her eyes.

"And did running away accomplish that?"

Kate shook her head. "Rina said I was bad and brought me home."

"As she should have."

"Are you going to spank me?" Kate spoke in a whisper.

"No, I am not," Penhurst replied. "Because I think you realize just how naughty you have been. You promised me once you would never run away again, and you have broken your promise."

Kate nodded slowly.

"You are to go upstairs and remain in your room until I come to talk with you. I need to escort Sophrina home first."

Kate's eyes filled with tears again. "I don't want Rina to go home."

"We shall go and visit her tomorrow, you and I." Penhurst looked anxiously at Sophrina, who nodded her assent.

"Promise?" Kate raised her tear-streaked face.

"Promise," Penhurst replied, surprised when Kate flung herself at him. He gave her a fierce hug. Thank God she was safe.

Sophrina moved to follow Kate out the door, but Penhurst laid a forestalling hand on her arm.

"It will take some minutes for the carriage to be readied," he said.

"It is still light outside," she countered. "I can easily walk home."

"Let me escort you," he said, a note of pleading in his voice.

She nodded. While Penhurst went to order the carriage brought around, Sophrina wandered aimlessly about the drawing room. She could never be in this room without the memories of that disastrous wedding day flooding back. But today, instead of remembering the shock of William's reappearance, she remembered all that had come before—her anticipation and hope. She had been nearly bursting with joy that day. There had been so much sorrow since; could it ever be possible to recapture that feeling again?

"The carriage will be ready in a few moments," Penhurst said, reentering quietly.

"You were rather lenient with her, you know," she said with a faint smile.

"I know," he said, running his hand through his hair. "I was so blasted glad to have her safe that I could have forgiven her almost anything."

Can you say the same of me? She almost voiced the question, but uncertainty kept her silent. Sophrina did not know if she had the strength to risk his final rejection.

They both sat silently during the short carriage ride to the cottage. Sophrina was glad of the growing darkness, so Ellis could not see her face clearly inside the dim coach. She had been so overjoyed to see him this afternoon, realizing how desperately she missed him. She hoped, she prayed, that he was experiencing the same sensation of loss. He had not recoiled from her embrace; he had kissed her with great feeling. But he had been distraught over Kate's disappearance. Tomorrow, with Kate safely home and peace restored, he might not be so emotionally susceptible. Tomorrow, he might very well retreat behind his wall of polite aloofness again. She did not know if she could bear that any longer.

Selfishly she longed to accept his renewed offer of marriage. She had been deluding herself into thinking that her feelings for him had changed. The kiss this afternoon had left her weak and dizzy with desire. She wanted him with an all-consuming ache. Yet could she ever be certain that he felt the same? Could she endure a life of wondering whether he had married her only out of obligation?

He had said he loved her. It had been ages since she had heard those words from his lips. Did he truly mean them? Or were they only a gesture of politeness? She half wished to fling herself into his arms and do her best to undo the hurt and pain she had caused him over these last months. Would an apology be enough to right what she had done? Could he ever forgive her and come to love her again as he had in the fall? Dear Lord, she loved him so. She did not think she had the strength to let him go. Even mere affection would be enough for her, if they could be together. She had enough love for both of them.

Penhurst stared out onto the darkened landscape. There were so many things he wished to say to Sophrina, but where was he to start? Kate's disappearance had frightened him nearly out of his wits. She might not be his flesh and blood, but he knew he could love no natural daughter more. Even though he had done little to deserve it, she had accepted him as her father, looking to him with love and respect because he held that exalted position. Today, when he feared he had lost Kate, he had been nearly brought to his knees. He could not imagine a life without her anymore. He relished the idea of watching her grow and learn.

Kate was his family, the only thing he had in the world beside his titles and estates. And family was much more precious than those. He had been deluding himself these last months, denying how much he wanted to become a dull, settled husband and father. He desired that more than anything else in the world.

Sophrina had shown him just how wonderful that sort of placid existence could be. Shown him that there were sometimes things more important than great diplomatic events or the social whirl of the European capitals: a little girl's smile on a summer afternoon, the look of love in a beautiful lady's eyes. Dear God, he could not allow it all to be thrown away.

He could not bear the thought of life without Sophrina. She had felt so wonderful in his arms this afternoon, even though he had been frantic with worry over Kate. He would do anything to win her regard again, would go down on his knees before her and beg for another chance. He had to convince her that he would be a worthy husband and father, that he could make her happy.

He needed her. More than he needed a diplomatic post, his standing in society, or even his pride. Her absence had left an aching void in his life that begged to be filled. There was only a deep emptiness without her.

What could he say to convince Sophrina to marry him? Even his first proposal had not been a masterpiece of language; now, when he needed every advantage to win her over, his mind was blank. He could talk of Kate. About how he had grown to cherish the girl. About how she needed a mother who adored her.

He could tell Sophrina how much he admired her spirit and bravery. She had humbled herself before her husband and confessed her adultery, when more rightly it was Penhurst who should have gone. He grimaced at how he had resented her action then. Yet had she not done so, they would be no closer to marriage now than ever. She had given them the opportunity to grab their happiness; he was the one who had dampened their chances with his arrogance. Could she ever forgive his misplaced anger?

He could tell her how much he needed her. He could speak of those lonely nights, lying in bed, wishing she were nestled close in his arms again. It was more than just the physical relations that were missing; it was the closeness afterward, the drowsily whispered endearments, the joy of waking up beside one's lover that burned in his memory. He wanted to regain that intimacy with Sophrina, wanted to savor and relish it for the rest of their days.

Tomorrow. He could start tomorrow, when he and Kate visited. He would beg, plead, cajole . . . anything to get her to change her mind and agree to wed him. He could make her happy, he could make her love him again, he knew it of a certainty. He only had to convince her of that.

The carriage ground to a halt.

Sophrina closed her eyes and took a deep breath.

"Should you like to come inside for a moment?"

The invitation surprised Penhurst. This could be the opportunity he needed. He could confess his sins of pride and stupidity, and beg her forgiveness. Beg her to be his wife, again, no matter what the cost. Would she listen and believe him? Or had he irretrievably destroyed their chance for happiness?

"Yes, I would," he replied slowly.

Feeling like an awkward schoolboy, he followed her into the parlor. He watched while she undid her cloak, his whole body aching at the sight of her. It had been so dreadfully long.

"I feel I should take some of the blame for Kate's actions today," she said, motioning for him to sit. "I know she is very confused with all that has been going on. Perhaps if I talk with her, she will be less perplexed."

Penhurst reached out and took Sophrina's hand. "I did not come in to discuss Kate."

"Why did you come?" Her hazel eyes assessed him calmly.

"I want to tell you I . . . I would like you to reconsider my offer of marraige. I do not want to wait until summer's end. I would like you to become my wife now.'' His gaze caught hers and a leap of hope surged through him. She did not look dismayed.

"I know I have disappointed you many times over these last months. I . . . I am not a perfect man, Sophrina, nor shall I ever be. But I will do all that is in my power to make you happy.''

He caressed her cheek. "I love you, Sophrina, even if I sometimes have a strange way of showing it. I've hurt you terribly with my stubbornness, I know. Today . . . when I feared Kate was lost, I realized just how very foolish my actions have been.''

He stood up abruptly.

"It does not matter one whit to me whether I ever work for the Foreign Office again, or if certain narrow-minded idiots label us sinners for falling in love. What you and I, and Kate, can have together is much more important than any of that. I feel like a fool for taking so long to realize it. I only pray you can find it in yourself to forgive me and give me the chance to try again.''

"Oh Ellis,'' she whispered, her eyes brimming with tears. "You have endured my selfishness for far too long. I can never forgive myself for forcing the divorce upon you.''

"If you had not, you would still be wed to Teel,'' he whispered softly, sitting at her side again, taking her hand in his. "You are free now, to wed where you will.''

She averted her eyes from his penetrating gaze. "I do not want you to marry me out of obligation.''

His heart lightened at her words. Was her reluctance merely a matter of misplaced honor?

"You think I wish to marry you only out of obligation?'' She nodded.

He laughed with relief, watching the hope steal over her face.

"I *am* obligated, you know,'' he said lightly. "For I could not live with myself otherwise. I would wither away and die without you.'' He took her hands in his. "I need you, Sophrina. To brighten my days with your presence. I never really understood how one person could need another so until I met you—

and until I realized how much in danger I was of losing you."

He pulled her out of her chair, onto his lap, into his arms.

"I love you, Sophrina. More than I ever thought possible. And I want to spend the rest of my days showing you." His kisses, at first tentative, grew in intensity and passion, until they both breathed in ragged gasps. His hands, gently stroking, found their way past the layers of clothing until he caressed her satiny skin.

"Oh, how I have missed you," he whispered against her hair before he claimed her mouth again, teasing, thrusting with his tongue until he elicited soft moans from her.

"Oh Ellis, stop," she pleaded. "Do not torture me like this."

"You call my lovemaking torture?" A teasing smile lit his face.

"No, but—"

He smothered her reply with a kiss. "Marry me, Sophrina. The license is still valid; the vicar can have us man and wife in an hour."

"Are you certain?"

"So very certain," he whispered before touching his lips to hers again.

"I will," she agreed, when he allowed her to speak again. She laughed softly as he trailed kisses down her neck.

"We will wed within the week?" he demanded.

"Yes," she whispered, the brush of his lips sending chills down her spine.

"We will be happy, love, I swear it."

"I know." She settled back in contentment within the encirclement of his arms.

Epilogue

May, 1821

In the early morning mists, the gulls swooped and dived above the ancient harbor, their raucous cries piercing the air. An affective method to roust prospective travelers from their beds, thought Seb Cole, as he stood upon the dock where the Dover packet was preparing to sail.

"They are so noisy!" Kate clasped her hands to her ears.

Sophrina smiled fondly, hugging the blanket-wrapped bundle in her arms more closely to ward off the morning chill.

"Where is Papa?" Kate asked. "I want to get on the boat."

"He will be back shortly," Sophrina said, yet she, too, glanced down the dock for a glimpse of Penhurst.

"You are in no danger of missing the sailing," Seb reminded her. "And even if you were, I think they might hold the boat for the next assistant ambassador to Paris."

Sophrina lifted a questioning brow. "I did not think he was quite *that* exalted a personage."

Seb grinned as he saw the tall figure at the end of the dock. "I shall be certain to tell your husband your high opinion of him."

Sophrina also caught sight of Elliston, and she watched lovingly as he came slowly down the dock, his characteristic long strides shortened to match the slow gait of the chubby-legged youngster next to him.

As two-year-old Frederick St. Clair caught a glimpse of his mother, his face broke into a grin of delight. "Mama, Mama," he called, frantically waving with both hands.

Penhurst reached down and snatched up the boy, eager himself to rejoin his family and have his last few words with Seb before their departure.

"Did you have a nice walk with Papa?" Sophrina asked, turning her cheek to allow Frederick to plant a noisy kiss upon it.

He nodded. "Birds!" He pointed up to the sky.

"Very noisy birds, Freddy," said Kate, taking her brother's hand and turning his attention to the harbor. "Did you see our ship? It is that one there."

"Is Louisa still asleep?" Penhurst looked dubiously at the lumpy bundle in his wife's arms.

Sophrina nodded. "Amazing, is it not? Perhaps she has decided that screaming at the top of her lungs is not as much fun as it first appeared to be."

"Or perhaps she has no more screams left." Penhurst shuddered at the memory of their miserable carriage journey from Talcott. Watching Sophrina, his eyes filled with concern. "Would you like me to hold her? I do not want you to become overtired. You remember what the doctor said."

"Elliston, the doctor said that a *month* ago. I am fine now. I do not need to be wrapped in cotton wool forever."

An increase in the bustle around them indicated that the packet was at last ready to accept their passengers.

"The winds look good," Seb noted. "You should have a short crossing."

"I hope so. It is my fondest wish to get to Paris as quickly as possible and restore some order to my household. Never agree to travel anywhere with small children, Seb."

"I will remember your advice—if I ever need it. But since you already snapped up the fairest lady in the kingdom . . ."

Penhurst smiled at Seb's jocular teasing. "I know how hard you have been trying to make comparisons."

"Maybe I shall accompany you." Seb debated. "My sister-in-law is growing increasingly tiresome in her insistence that I wed." He smiled at Sophrina. "I keep telling her I am only waiting for Louisa to grow up, for I know she will be as lovely as her mother."

"I hate to discourage you, *Mr.* Cole, but I will simply not allow my daughter to marry the doddering old man you will be by the time she is old enough to wed."

Seb looked crestfallen at the news. "Alas, you wound me again, my lady."

"Rina," Kate cried plaintively. "It is time to get on the boat."

"That it is," said Penhurst. He turned to his friend. "Thank you for all your help, Seb. I know it couldn't have been easy persuading the Foreign Office to test the waters. I . . . I thank you.''

"This way I shall have a guaranteed place to stay when I travel to Paris," Seb said with a laugh.

"Ellis . . ." Sophrina's voice sounded an impatient note.

Penhurst took Seb's hand. "Visit soon. And often."

"I shall."

He watched as Penhurst picked up his son and followed Sophrina onto the boat. Throwing ostentatious kisses to Kate and Sophrina, Seb watched as the mooring lines were released, raising his hand in a farewell wave as the boat pulled away from the dock.

"I hope he does visit often," said Sophrina as they watched the shore recede.

"Afraid you will grow tired of my company?"

"That I could never do." A dazzling smile lit her face.

Penhurst looked deeply into his wife's eyes, the world around him disappearing for a moment as he wrapped himself in her love.

"Papa. Papa!" Frederick's voice was insistent.

Sighing, Penhurst gave his wife a regretful glance and bent down to his son.